THE IMPOVERISHED DOWRY

The De Petras Saga, Book 2

Emily E K Murdoch

ARE YOU SIGNED UP FOR DRAGONBLADE'S BLOG?

You'll get the latest news and information on exclusive giveaways, exclusive excerpts, coming releases, sales, free books, cover reveals and more.

Check out our complete list of authors, too!

No spam, no junk. That's a promise!

Sign Up Here

www.dragonbladepublishing.com

Dearest Reader;

Thank you for your support of a small press. At Dragonblade Publishing, we strive to bring you the highest quality Historical Romance from some of the best authors in the business. Without your support, there is no 'us', so we sincerely hope you adore these stories and find some new favorite authors along the way.

Happy Reading!

CEO, Dragonblade Publishing

Additional Dragonblade books by Author Emily E K Murdoch

The De Petras Saga
The Misplaced Husband (Book 1)
The Impoverished Dowry (Book 2)
The Contrary Debutante (Book 3)
The Determined Mistress (Book 4)
The Convenient Engagement (Book 5)

The Governess Bureau Series
A Governess of Great Talents (Book 1)
A Governess of Discretion (Book 2)
A Governess of Many Languages (Book 3)
A Governess of Prodigious Skill (Book 4)
A Governess of Unusual Experience (Book 5)
A Governess of Wise Years (Book 6)

Never The Bride Series
Always the Bridesmaid (Book 1)
Always the Chaperone (Book 2)
Always the Courtesan (Book 3)
Always the Best Friend (Book 4)
Always the Wallflower (Book 5)
Always the Bluestocking (Book 6)
Always the Rival (Book 7)
Always the Matchmaker (Book 8)
Always the Widow (Book 9)
Always the Rebel (Book 10)
Always the Mistress (Book 11)
Always the Second Choice (Book 12)

The Lyon's Den Connected World
Always the Lyon Tamer

CHAPTER ONE

November 14, 1809

IF ONE MORE person asked her when she was going to marry, Coral de Petras was going to scream. Hideous, irritating people!

Such a pity they were her own family.

"But you are five and twenty years old!" Emerald said, a frown creasing her forehead as she gazed at her sister, standing by the looking glass. "Five and twenty! You cannot keep waiting for a love match, you'll be waiting forever!"

Coral sighed as she placed the necklace of coral and pearls around her neck. "And this is concerning?"

She knew what her younger sister was going to say, of course. Only three years between them, Emerald had been her shadow for goodness knows how long. Forever, it felt like. At least they did not share a bedchamber anymore.

The de Petras house rang with excitement and expectation as the ladies put the final touches on their apparel. It was almost time. They were very nearly late.

"Mama was four years younger when she married Papa," Emerald insisted, sitting on Coral's bed and twisting her gloves between her fingers. "Many of our acquaintances are married, some are even—"

"Emerald, I do not want to hear it," said the eldest de Petras child stiffly, not looking around.

Coral did not need to, after all. She could see her younger sibling quite clearly in the looking glass, and besides, she'd had enough of this conversation. There was nothing to it, no depth, no real meaning.

As the eldest, everyone had expected Coral to marry almost as soon as she entered Society. The *ton* had been rather surprised that Opal de Petras, their mother, had prevented Coral from doing so until she was three and twenty. Old enough to have a little sense, as Mama had put it.

But the truth could not be denied or avoided; she was entering her third year in Society with plenty of proposals, but no wedding bells.

"If you do not accept someone soon," said Emerald quietly, the worried look on her face growing, "why, you may never receive another offer of—"

"Oh, of course, she will—you worry too much, Em!"

Coral smiled gently as she carefully placed on her pearl ear-bobs. That last sentence could only be from the youngest de Petras.

Sapphire de Petras, bold and brash at fourteen years of age, had stormed into her oldest sister's bedchamber and thrown herself theatrically into a chair. There was a wicked glint in her eyes that was nothing like the concern in Emerald's.

"What was his name—the Earl of Chester?" Sapphire giggled. "He was so certain you would accept him, Coral, I almost died laughing when Mama had to send him away with his tail between his legs!"

"I did not mean to offend him," said Coral quickly, her stomach twisting painfully at the memory.

Not her finest moment. She had not intended to be rude, but apparently, that did not matter when it came to affairs of the heart.

But really, the man had chosen to propose by telling her he

had taken pity on her at the end of the 1808 Season and thought it most unfair she was not wed, and he would rescue her from such a terrible fate.

Rescue her! Her, Coral de Petras! The cheek of it!

"Did not mean to offend him?" Emerald repeated with wide eyes as Sapphire collapsed once again into giggles. "Coral, you told him his eyes were too close together and his mortgage repayments too far apart!"

Coral tried not to smile. It was a challenge. "Well, he was rude in the first place!"

It had been a rather trying time for them all, even she had to admit. With Micah being…Micah, there was no other description for it, and Emerald hating company so much she could barely be forced to attend anything, Coral had borne the weight of the de Petras name in good Society.

It was rather a wonder they still secured their Almack's vouchers for this Season…

Sapphire sighed dramatically as she picked up a coral brooch from the dressing table. "I wish I could come with you."

Coral and Emerald exchanged knowing glances. That was the trouble with having a sister so much younger. The baby of the family may be approaching the age to come out, but she had not lost her wild ways—and besides, until Coral or Emerald married…

"I think you should accept the very next proposal you receive," said Sapphire, her eyes dancing. "Then I can attend your wedding, dance with every single gentleman there, and break at least ten hearts."

"And that," Coral said dryly, plucking the coral brooch from her sister's mischievous hands and placing it back on the dressing table, "is precisely why Mama has not permitted you to come out yet."

"Oh, the scandal if all three of us were out together!" Emerald shivered as though she could not imagine a worse fate than the eyes of all focused upon the three of them. "No, Sapphy, better you stay here and—"

"Have you seen Micah?"

The three looked over to the door, where their mother stood.

Opal de Petras was a magnificent woman, slight but elegantly beautiful, having lost none of her looks as she had grown older. She had been a real beauty in her day, thought Coral with a wry smile, though Papa kept saying her day was not yet over, and at any moment, she may decide to cast him aside and find a better husband.

There was something in that jest. Something that made both her parents laugh, yes, but there was a twisting painful truthfulness in it Coral had never liked.

She could well remember the absence of her father. For seven long years, Jasper de Petras had gone missing and the whole family had believed him deceased. Then he had stridden back into their lives, causing all sorts of upset…

And now, like father, like son.

"Micah is not in his bedchamber?" Emerald asked anxiously.

Coral glanced at her sister. The last thing they needed was to make Emerald more anxious before they had even departed for Almack's—and they were definitely going to be late if they could not find her wayward brother.

Opal shook her head. "Nor can I find him downstairs—I admit, I had hoped he was in here with you."

It really was too bad of Micah. He was getting completely out of control, and though most men of that age were a lit-tle…unruly…Micah was starting to give them all a bad name.

What a relief it was, in a way, to know he would never be the head of the family.

A sparking tension shot across Coral's shoulders, and she stood more upright. No, that was her burden. The strangeness of the de Petras family meant it was the eldest daughter, not the son, who inherited the money, the power, and the responsibility.

She would have little jocularity keeping this unruly brood in line, so she was waiting for a love match. After deciding against it in her youth, after being determined to look for wealth rather than character, she had finally allowed herself to be brought around to her family's point of view—though she would never reject wealth and love together.

"Do you think he's gone out gambling?" asked Sapphire eagerly.

Coral tried to shoot her a glance that told her in no uncertain terms to hold her tongue, but Sapphy either did not see it or completely ignored it.

Their mother bit her lip. "Do you think?"

"Perhaps he has already left for Almack's with some of his friends," said Coral hastily. She hated to see worry creasing her mother's face. Opal had borne much of the family's scandal when Jasper had appeared as though from the grave, and it had taken…well, not all this time, but much of it to restore the de Petras family in the eyes of the *ton*. "Do not worry yourself, Mama."

Opal caught her gaze and saw the lie. Coral was sure.

Micah was not here, but he was certainly not on his way to Almack's.

"Well, we shall have to hope to see him there," said Opal quietly. "A few more minutes, girls, then we'll be off. Your father is staying here with you, Sapphire."

Sapphire pulled a face. "You are sure I cannot—"

"No, Sapphy," said Coral, Emerald, and Opal altogether.

Sapphire frowned as Coral laughed, despite herself. "See, Sapphire, we are all united against you, so there is no point in attempting to get around us. You are staying here, until—"

"Until you get married," snapped Sapphire, two red dots appearing on her cheeks now as genuine upset overtook her. "Which will never happen, because you refuse to consider anyone!"

"Not so," Coral disagreed, turning back to her looking glass to ensure the ribbons of her gown were straight. "Not until I meet someone who can truly tame my heart."

"You were just a baby, Sapphire, when Coral made her determination," came the quiet words of Emerald from the bed. "A determination which did not last long, did it, Coral?"

Coral felt the back of her neck flush but refused to look around. That was the trouble with being a redhead, of course. The curls were a bit of a nuisance, but at least they prevented her from needing to wear papers overnight; her hair simply curled naturally.

No, it was the color that was the trouble. A brilliant, fiery red, her mother called it—a scalding red, her father called it.

Coral merely knew she was far too quick to flush and far too quick to lose her temper.

Something she was in great danger of doing now if her sisters did not cease their teasing...

"Tell the story again, Em, I never tire of it," said Sapphire eagerly.

It appeared, from what Coral could see in the looking glass, that the youngest de Petras had completely forgotten her bad temper in her eagerness to hear the story the family trotted out at the beginning of every Season. Why, it was almost a tradition now.

Emerald warmed to her tale, looking far more comfortable now the true focus of the room was on Coral once more. "You had just been born, a scrawny, tiny little thing—"

"Crying most of the time," interjected Coral with a smile.

Anything to put off the completion of the tale for just a little longer—but Emerald's smile told Coral her sister had seen straight through that.

Damn. It was a word Coral had rarely said aloud. Her father had told her rather sternly—perhaps one of the few times she could remember him ever telling her off—that ladies did not swear.

Still, it felt good to think. *Damn, damn, damn, damn—*

"And Coral was holding you," continued Emerald, "and we were discussing...oh goodness, it was so long ago now, I can barely remember what we were talking about."

"Then best not to tell the tale, if you cannot be sure whether you tell it accurately," said Coral swiftly.

The tension in her shoulders was most irritatingly starting to creep up her neck. If she was not careful, it would soon develop into a headache, one that would surely dog her the entire evening.

There was nothing so bad as a headache at Almack's.

"Well, whatever it was," Emerald said, waving a hand as though brushing aside Coral's concern, "the topic meandered to money, and Coral said—"

"We all know what I said," said Coral, heat searing her cheeks as she turned around.

It really was most infuriating. She had not thought her words particularly radical, indeed, she thought them sensible. What any considerate and thinking young lady would think, given the dramatic twists and turns of family fortune they had suffered in the short years Coral had lived through at that time.

The way her family told the story, it had been a ridiculous thing to say!

"Coral said that she would only marry for money," Emerald said triumphantly.

Sapphire descended into peals of giggles, and Coral smiled weakly. "Well, there you go, the same old story—and yes, I changed my mind. That is something that happens when one gets older."

"Not wiser, then," said Sapphire slyly.

Coral glared.

Her youngest sister did her the courtesy of looking a little shamefaced. "Sorry, Coral."

Coral drew herself up, pulling at the lace sleeves of her gown to make sure they were even. "You were not even born, Sapphy, and Emerald, you were born on the day Papa left. You cannot know...you cannot remember and will never understand what it was like to grow up in a house where one's father was misplaced, his fate unknown. Seeing Mama and Papa, the way they loved each other…is it not a surprise that I changed my mind?"

She swallowed, the memories of those childhood years rushing back. Oh, the pain of seeing her mama in that state—hardly knowing whether she was coming or going, seeking her husband, desperate to find him, certain that misplaced could not mean dead, could not…

And the strangeness of his return; the way the de Petras family became the gossip of the whole of London for what felt like months, if not years. The way people stared when she had first come out into Society; the desperate attempts Coral had made in her first, and now she came to think of it, her second Season to try to restore the de Petras name to some sort of respectability.

Coral held her head high. "I make no apology for seeking a rich husband. I just…well. I want love now." She was grateful her mother had gently changed her mind about marrying for money.

Emerald sighed wistfully. "Love."

"Love?" Sapphire snorted in much the way her mother did when bills turned up at the house with Micah's name upon them. "Love can grow—or not, as the case may be. How do you tell when you are in love? What does love feel like, what does it—"

"Girls!" Opal's voice rang out from downstairs, and all three turned to the door. "The carriage is ready!"

Sapphire groaned as her two elder sisters rose. "You could sneak me into the carriage. Mama would never need to know!"

Coral had to laugh as she grabbed her pelisse and reticule. "Sapphire, you may be the baby of the family, but you are not so small that we could hide you in the carriage!"

"Just be grateful that you are able to stay at home," Emerald muttered, rising from the bed and smoothing her skirts. "I'd eagerly give up my place."

Sapphire's eyes widened. "Would Mama permit us to switch—"

"No," said Coral firmly. *Goodness, it was like herding cats, trying to get everyone out of the house in time for Almack's.* She could see why her mother was starting to gain a few gray hairs. "Sapphy, go and sit with Papa. He'll be bored out of his mind without you. Come on, Emerald."

Both her sisters looked remarkably miserable as they descended the staircase to find their mother in the hall.

"Oh, such long faces," said Opal with a wry smile. "Never fear, Almack's will be over before we know it."

Coral sighed but said nothing. *Almack's.* The same place her mother had danced when she was their age. It did not seem to have changed in any meaningful way, as far as she could tell. The company would be dull, the food inadequate, and the punch absolutely disgusting.

She would be forced to meet with a number of gentlemen, most of whom would not tempt her, then they would return to hear Sapphire's whining that she had not been permitted to go.

Surely the Season was supposed to be far more interesting than this?

Sapphire flounced away, slamming the door to the parlor behind her.

Opal sighed. "We really must think about some way to distract her, you know, Coral."

Coral nodded but said nothing as Mrs. Clarkson, the housekeeper, opened the door to reveal the waiting carriage in the street.

She knew why her mother spoke that way to her, of course. It was not purely that she would be the head of the de Petras household once her mother…but she would not think of that. Her mother would live forever.

No, it was because the entire family knew it was Coral's lack of a wedding that kept Sapphire indoors on nights like this. If only she were to marry, Sapphire could enter Society and thoroughly ruin her reputation for herself.

"We should be back before midnight," her mother was saying to Sapphire sternly. "And if I do not find you abed—"

"Opal!"

The ladies of the de Petras family turned around, Coral pulling on her gloves as she looked up to see her father stagger out of his study.

She blinked. He had staggered, which was most unusual. Jasper de Petras was not a man particularly light on his feet, but he rarely touched any strong liquor, and it was not late enough for tiredness to overwhelm him.

Her stomach lurched at the sight of her father's face. Pale complexion, wide, disbelieving eyes, a sense that the world had ended.

What on earth was going on?

"Jasper?" Opal stepped forward to take her husband's hand, which held a crumpled letter. "Jasper, what is it?"

Coral did not think; she did not need to, her instincts led her forward. Taking her father's other hand, she helped her mother move the unspeaking gentleman from the hall to the drawing room. Emerald followed them, silent as ever, and so did Sapphire, managing to hold her tongue.

There was a strange pall across the house, and Coral's heart was beating painfully as she slowly lowered her father into an armchair.

She had never seen him like this. Unflappable, calm, usually cheerful, Jasper was not a man to be easily overwhelmed.

Something had happened. Something dreadful.

"Jasper, dear?" Opal whispered, sitting opposite her husband. "What is it?"

Coral swallowed as she sat beside her mother. For a fraction of a second, Jasper's eyes had flickered to her, pain within them so dark she half thought she had imagined it.

But his expression slowly darkened. "News. The very worst kind."

It was all Coral could do to keep her voice calm. "Not—not Micah—"

"Oh, no," he said hurriedly, glancing at his wife.

Coral looked at her mother, too. She was pale, but her brow softened as it was confirmed that the only son of the family was not involved in whatever dreadful thing had occurred.

"I…I do not know how to…the news is very…"

Instinct once again took over. Well, she was the heir, wasn't she? She was involved in all her parents' financial affairs, had met the tenants of their Bath properties, was sometimes included in conversations about their investments.

Why should she not know what is happening?

Coral took the paper out of her father's hand, ignoring Emerald's gasps that she had been so bold, and unfolded it. the letter was scrawled, rather than written, as though it had been penned in great haste by a man ill-used to ink.

Sir—

All ships lost, repeat, all ships lost. Cargo gone, hands presumed dead. Will send further details when I have them.

Burnham

Coral blinked. The words swam in and out of her vision, making no sense, though each word was just about legible.

All ships lost? All cargo gone—hands presumed dead?

Her father's shipping business had only increased in strength in the last few years, a third ship joining the fleet only six months ago. It was a pride to her father that he had built it up from nothing—it was her mother who had inherited wealth.

And now it was all…gone?

She lifted her eyes to her father's and saw the truth within them. "No."

"Yes," he said heavily. "It's all gone. It's over, the business is at an end."

"The shipping business?" Opal looked between her daughter and her husband with wild eyes. "No!"

"Is your man certain that no lives were saved?" asked Coral urgently. The thought of all those people, alone at sea, unable to find a safe haven…

Jasper said nothing, and Coral felt an incredible need to be sick. Here she was, seated on a comfortable sofa in a warm house in London, dressed to impress for an appearance at Almack's she was sure she would no longer make—and out there had been men desperate for dry land under their feet.

"If the shipping business is gone," asked Emerald's quiet voice, "what does that mean for us?"

Coral looked instinctively at the head of the household.

Opal sighed. "I would need to look over the accounts, talk with your father, talk with Burnham, once he returns to London…but I would imagine there will only be one change."

She exchanged a look with her husband, and a strange sense of foreboding swept across Coral's heart.

"There will be enough from my inheritance to keep us afloat, with very little changes to our lifestyle, I believe," said Opal slowly, "but the capital…it will be the dowries. That will be the problem."

An icy blade stabbed Coral's throat, slipping through her gullet into her heart. Dowries?

"These last few years," she said as quietly and as calmly as she could manage, "you have encouraged me to marry for love, to seek a love match. I have turned down many a gentleman for just such a reason—"

"And you still can," said Opal softly. "It's just…well. We should be able to scrape together enough for two dowries, possibly even three."

Coral stared, horrified. "But not four."

And that was the trouble, wasn't it? with Coral as the heir, they had decided long ago—she and her parents—that Micah would be given a dowry in exchange for his loss in the typical birth order.

That meant a family with three daughters needed four dowries.

"We should be able to scrape together enough for two dowries, possibly even three."

There was nothing else for it. Coral could feel the rightness within her, knew what had to be done. She had been preparing for this, in a way, she thought darkly, her entire life. She was the heir; she held the burdens and responsibilities of the family. She would have to make the hard decision, sacrifice herself whenever necessary.

If that was what it took to keep the rest of the family happy.

"We will have to keep this quiet," her mother was saying. "Until we have the time to understand precisely what—well, what we're going to do. We must keep this between us."

"Can I tell Maltravers?" piped up Sapphire.

Coral rolled her eyes.

"No," said Opal firmly. "That young man may be a family friend, but he is a terrible gossip, Sapphy, you know that."

"But what are we going to do?" That was Emerald, her voice quavering. "Without dowries for all of us…"

Coral's mind was racing. Yes, that was the only way it would work. It would be painful, yes, but she would make do with the situation as it was. She would find a husband in a different way.

"I will go without a dowry," she said clearly.

The effect was immediate. Sapphire gasped, Emerald looked rapidly between her and their mother, and Jasper dropped his head in his hands.

"You wanted to marry for love," Opal said gently.

"If I do not, then my siblings can," Coral said, hardly aware what she was saying, her heart twisting most painfully. "And besides, love is not the only thing."

"It is rather important," Emerald murmured.

"But not more important than you," pointed out Coral. "Or Sapphy or Micah. No, I…I will marry for different reasons."

CHAPTER TWO

November 16, 1809

Edward Barlow, Duke of Glaenarm, came to the Dulverton Club for a good meal—not that his cook was lacking, but it was a different kind of fare—and then a lazy afternoon seated in an armchair in the sunshine, with the gentle snoring of other members to lull him to sleep.

Edward smiled ruefully, eyes closed, as he shifted in the chair, newspaper unfolded on his lap. He was hardly a lazy man, far from it; his responsibilities were varied and wide, often consuming his waking hours for days at a time.

And that was why every now and again, and it really was getting most irregular, he could not recall the last time he had been here, he treated himself to a day of…nothing.

He should be at home by now, that was the trouble.

Edward did not need to open his eyes to know it was late in the afternoon. The gong had gone for four o'clock, when members could invite others if they wished, and he had that damned ball to attend later.

Almack's.

He shivered. The place where mamas paraded their young things in the hope of securing someone precisely like him. A duke. A wealthy man.

Why, before they even bothered to be introduced to him, they had already decided that he was the perfect match for their daughters.

Edward snorted, knowing that no one at Dulverton would mind the sudden noise. Really! These ladies, they had no idea what they really wanted from a match. It was ridiculous. It was outrageous!

It was enough to make a man snooze in his club longer and longer, putting off the inevitable—

"Glaenarm!"

Edward slowly opened one eye, rather unwillingly. Being dragged into reality would mean having to talk with…

Face brightening, he sat up and grinned at the gentleman who was striding across the room toward him, a newspaper in his hand and a look of mischief on his face.

"Maltravers!" Edward said in welcome, indicating that the younger man should be seated beside him. "I have not seen you here these few months!"

"And neither would you, as you are hardly ever here yourself," James Gresley, the Earl of Maltravers pointed out as he dropped happily into the armchair. "Too busy on far more important matters, I'll be bound."

Edward rolled his eyes. "If you mean adjudicating arguments between my butler and my steward, then yes."

The two men chuckled, then Maltravers nodded at the newspaper on Edward's lap. "You've read it, then?"

Edward dropped his gaze to the newspaper. In truth, he had not read a single line. He always found it the perfect protection, a shield almost, to unwanted conversation at the club. When he just wanted an hour or so to himself, without any of the responsibilities of his title, without a man asking delicately—on the advice of his wife, undoubtedly—whether the duke was in the market for a bride…

The newspaper made it far easier to avoid such nonsense.

"I have not," he said smoothly, "yet, at any rate. Was there something, in particular, I should have done?"

"It's all about town, I would have thought you had seen it," said Maltravers eagerly. "Which edition do you have? This morning's?"

Edward shrugged, entirely nonplussed. What on earth could have got into his friend to be so exuberant about a paper? Was it possible, and the thought rather revolted him, that either of them was mentioned in it?

People like them, entitled and ennobled, rather wished to be out of the papers rather than in them.

"I seek no scandal and have no wish to see such things," Edward said with a heavy sigh. "You can keep your gossip to—"

"It's not gossip," said Maltravers impatiently, opening up the newspaper in his own hands and rifling through it as swiftly as he could manage, almost tearing the pages. "At least, it wasn't originally, but I'd bet my hat it will be in a few hours."

Edward sat up a little straighter. What could have got into the man? There must be something entirely outrageous printed in there for Maltravers to be so eagerly seeking it.

A death, perhaps? An unusual marriage?

Maybe the announcement of a sale of a business or land. Perhaps Prinny was back in town. Perhaps Lady Romeril had...

Edward snorted as Maltravers continued to search in the paper for whatever it was. Chance would be a fine thing.

"Maltravers, honestly man, I have little interest in—"

"You have to see it, it is the best jest I have ever seen," said his friend firmly. "There. There!"

With great reluctance and more than a little feeling that he would have been better off not coming to the club this afternoon, Edward took the newspaper from Maltravers.

It was folded tightly to expose just half of one page, right in the middle.

Edward looked down with a heavy sigh. "If this is just the results of the races, I have already—"

"Damnit man, read it!"

There did not appear to be anything else to be done. Wondering what could have got his friend into such a state, and hoping to goodness it was something Edward could brush over—he did not seek scandal—he looked down at the page once more and started to read.

A GENTLEMAN IS SOUGHT

A gentleman is sought for matrimony, swiftly and securely to a lady of good name, respectable breeding, beauty, and wit.

Her requirements are as follows, and any gentleman not matching this list should consider themselves unworthy and unsuitable.

The gentleman in question must be handsome and charming. Those are the most basic requirements. Dark hair is a must; all blonde-haired gentlemen need not apply.

Edward broke off his reading to look up at Maltravers, his mind whirling.

It had to be a jest; it had to be! No self-respecting lady would ever permit anything of the sort to be printed in a newspaper. It was brazen!

"This is a joke," he said weakly.

"There is no possibility that you have read the entire thing, you cad, now read it!" said Maltravers, leaning back with a grin in his armchair. "I promise you, it only improves with each line!"

Edward's head was spinning. A lady seeks a gentleman? This was not how it was done; not that he had much experience in the matter, naturally, but he had been born and raised a gentleman.

Ladies did not…this was not the way of things!

"Should she not approach Miss Ashbrooke, if she wishes for a matchmaker to—"

"Read it!"

With great reluctance, yet a growing curiosity, Edward returned to the newspaper.

The gentleman in question must be handsome and charm-

ing. Those are the most basic requirements. Dark hair is a must; all blonde-haired gentlemen need not apply.

His income will be at least five thousand a year, and proof must be supplied of a dearth of debts, loans, or mortgages on property. On the subject of property, the gentleman must have a house in the country and one in the right part of London.

"Right part of London," Edward found himself saying aloud under his breath.

The right part of London? House in the country—no mortgages?

He snorted. Well, the woman, whoever she was, was swiftly reducing her pool of potential candidates down, and no mistake. Why, he had to be one of the few gentlemen left in London who had not been forced to mortgage, just a little.

The gentleman's family is important: he must have a sister, be content with a large family, and have never been engaged to be married before.

"Never been engaged to be married?" Edward said, glancing up at Maltravers. "What on earth—"

"Do you not see why I required you to read it?" Maltravers said, his eyes dancing with glee. "Continue on, continue on, the best is the ending."

The ending? Edward could hardly imagine what such an ending could entail.

But most importantly of all, the gentleman's character must be utterly spotless. No hint of scandal must be attached to his name, he must sing beautifully and have a distinct love of Mozart. He is a great reader, has been to Italy, and any additional positive features will be taken under advisement.

Gentlemen interested should supply a card to the editor of this newspaper under the instruction of it being shared with CP.

Good luck.

"Good luck?" Edward said in astonishment.

Maltravers shook his head with a wide smile. "Have you ever seen such a thing?"

Edward stared, hardly able to believe what he was seeing; but no matter how many times he blinked, the dratted advertisement remained in black and white.

> *Gentlemen interested should supply a card to the editor of this newspaper under the instruction of it being shared with CP. Good luck.*

"She is brazen," he found himself saying. "Brazen, to think it appropriate to do such a thing!"

Edward's eyes flickered over the long section again, attempting to take it all in. charming, handsome, Mozart, a sister…what an extremely odd list. It was almost as though it had been written as a jest, for it was perhaps the sort of thing a lady concocted with her sisters or mother…but surely no one would ever take such a thing seriously?

"It is a jape, surely," he said, dropping the folded newspaper into his lap and looking up at Maltravers. "Surely no one would—"

"Ah," said Maltravers with a grin. "But let us be honest with ourselves, does not every lady, even in the secret quiet of her heart, have such a list?"

Edward snorted. "Yes, but—"

"And does not every gentleman?" persisted Maltravers, as though he had given the matter much thought. "Do we all not have a picture of what our future bride will look like, act like, what family she comes from, her interests?"

Now there was a thought. Edward had never given much thought to marriage. He would have to eventually, of course, the line of Glaenarm could not end with him.

But as to the woman's character, her merits…whether she had been to Italy or not?

"It cannot be serious," Edward said, his voice half vague as he glanced back down in the newspaper. "I mean to say…the woman will only marry a gentleman who has a sister?"

"The later edition has been amended," revealed Maltravers with a grin. "Here, look at this."

Pulling out a page torn from a newspaper from his waistcoat pocket, he handed it to Edward who took it wordlessly, hardly able to take in why his friend was so interested in all this.

Was it possible…but the man had no sister. It did not appear that he was suitable, according to this harpy's list!

He unfolded the page, his eyes scanning down until he saw the difference Maltravers had mentioned.

The gentleman's family is important: he must have a sister, be content with a large family, and have never been engaged to be married before. NB: the requirement of a sister is simple; I wish to receive a recommendation on his behalf from a lady.

"Recommendation on his behalf—Maltravers, this woman is a monster!" Edward exclaimed with a laugh. "No, it cannot be serious."

"Oh, it is," said Maltravers mysteriously, taking back both page and paper. "More serious than you can imagine."

Now that did prick up Edward's curiosity. There was a reason, after all, that Maltravers had bothered to find him and show him the damned thing. There must be a purpose to this conversation…

And only then did it strike him that there may be a very obvious purpose. A purpose Edward should have guessed at the moment he started reading the thing.

"You're not thinking of pursuing this CP yourself?"

For some reason, Maltravers's cheeks reddened. "Pursue Coral? Never fear!"

Edward sat up, something prickling his stomach most unusually. "Coral?"

Gentlemen interested should supply a card to the editor of this newspaper under the instruction of it being shared with CP.

Good luck.

Coral P?

"Coral de Petras," Maltravers said triumphantly. "The woman who wrote the list!"

"You know her?" Edward asked, amazed.

He had known the Earl of Maltravers—goodness, almost three years now. The man was young, hot-headed, but essentially good-natured.

He would never have put him down as a gentleman with that sort of woman in his acquaintance!

"I know the family," said his companion airily. "A rather strange lot, I will say, though there's plenty of good in them. Unusual."

Edward stared. Unusual was putting it mildly. Placing an advertisement like that in a newspaper—paying so much attention to it that she would update it for a later edition—was something so unheard of, he was still not entirely certain whether Maltravers was jesting with him.

What sort of woman would write such a thing?

His mind thought wildly about the list this Coral had written. Handsome, charming, well, was it not human nature to wish for a spouse with such characteristics?

Love of Mozart… Edward almost laughed. Mozart was perhaps the dullest composer he had ever heard.

The sister was strange, but then the whole thing was strange. What kind of lady would consider this the best way to find a husband? Would she not be inundated with offers of matrimony from the most unsuitable of men?

"She must be very beautiful," said Edward slowly. "To write such a thing, I mean, with the assumption that this perfect suitor she writes of would wish to marry her."

"She…well, I suppose so," Maltravers said with a shrug.

Edward narrowed his eyes. "You suppose so?"

There was that reddening of his cheeks again. Had Maltravers tried for her, perhaps, and been unsuccessful?

"I know no ill of her, and many call her beautiful," his friend said a little stiffly. "Yes, I suppose she is beautiful. To those that like redheads."

Now that was interesting. What an intriguing woman indeed—sure of herself, certain of what she wants, and unafraid to demand it. And a redhead.

"You'll have to introduce me."

Edward blinked. Only then did he realize it had been his own voice that had spoken.

Maltravers's laugh filled the whole room, disturbing a few of the other gentlemen who were happily snoozing. "Introduce you?"

"Yes," said Edward. Well, he had said it now, he may as well continue with the whole charade. And it would be interesting, would it not, to meet such a brazen woman?

Not that he had any interest beyond that.

"But—but you don't match her requirements!"

Edward snorted. "You think I would wish to marry such a—such a harpy? No, I want to see precisely what the prize at the end of this strange competition is. Who is this Coral de Petras, that she can demand such a man!"

He had attempted to keep his voice light, neutral, but for some irritating reason, there was a hint of genuine interest.

Well, Society could become rather dull after a while…every card party the same, every promenade in Hyde Park unchanged, the same fluttery-eyed ladies with heavy bosoms and nothing between their ears.

It would be a change, to meet a woman who was so…so odd.

There was, unfortunately, a rather knowing grin on his friend's face.

"Well, do not say I did not warn you," said Maltravers with a laugh. "I think she will surprise you."

CHAPTER THREE

"I STILL CANNOT believe you did it," said Opal.

Coral tried not to smile as she sat lazily on the sofa in the drawing room as they waited for Emerald to be ready.

Her sister was taking longer and longer to get ready these days, further proof, as though they needed any more, Coral thought dryly, that Emerald really had no taste for social occasions.

It would not be long before they would be dragging her kicking and screaming to balls or card parties or afternoon teas.

"I told you that I would be willing to sacrifice a love match," Coral said lightly, "but that does not mean all my standards have been left by the wayside."

"All your—you printed it in a newspaper!"

Coral could not help but grin. So she had. Well, she had a little pin money left over after selecting her gowns for the Season, and really, she had little else to spend it on.

Why not consider it…an investment?

Though she had been rather surprised at the response her words had garnered.

"Thirty cards have been left, and it has only been two days," Opal pointed out, a smile tugging at the corner of her lips. "What on earth will you do if you receive the cards of every gentleman in London?"

"And further afield," said Jasper mildly from his seat near the fire, his face mostly hidden by his newspaper. "I can see here, there is a letter from a gentleman attempting a similar thing."

Coral perked up. "Truly?"

"Indeed, though I do not believe his list as impressive as yours," teased her father. "He wishes for good childbearing hips and a better-than-ugly face."

Laughter sounded from across the room, Sapphire giggling in her seat by the window. "You are ever so brave, Coral," she said admiringly. "Perhaps that is what I should do when I finally enter Society, put out a list and—"

"The day I let you enter Society, my girl, will be when you have managed to curb your wild ways!" Opal said with a laugh. "I am not sure Society is ready for you!"

The door opened, and Emerald slipped in. It truly was incredible, thought Coral, how her sister was able to do it. Why, Em lived here, she was a lady of the house—at least, one of its daughters—yet she still had the ability to sidle into a room almost unnoticed, unless one was making a true effort.

"What are we talking about?" she asked quietly.

Coral opened her mouth, but Sapphire got there first.

"Whether any gentleman in the world will ever live up to Coral's list!" she said triumphantly, grinning. "Truly, have you ever met such a gentleman?"

"I've barely met any," said Emerald quietly. "And—"

"There you are then," interrupted Sapphire, as though that proved her point equivocally. "You'll end up an old maid, Coral!"

"No, she won't," Opal said firmly with a glint of mischief in her eye. "I think Coral has done perhaps the cleverest thing I could have imagined."

Coral turned to look at her mother. Cleverest?

None of her family had been informed about the list going to the newspapers—she had not even conferred with them about the list itself.

But then, why should she? She was the one who was going to

end up living with the man who met all her criteria; it was her choice, after all.

She had expected a little…disgruntlement, to put it mildly. She had expected her mother to roll her eyes, her father to snort a laugh, then pretend it was a cough, for Emerald to be mortified, Sapphire to find it hilarious, and for Micah to have no opinion at all.

But a clever idea? She would not have predicted her mother to term it that.

"Clever?" Coral repeated.

Opal raised an eyebrow. "Well, you have no dowry now, Coral. You are pretty, yes, but we have no title, no other way to mark you out. but now…"

Her voice trailed away delicately, and Coral flushed. So her mother thought she had done it to impress others, to make herself stand out from the crowd of ladies hunting husbands this Season?

Had they not bothered to read it?

"Everything on that list is essential in a partner," Coral said firmly. "Anyone who does not meet it—"

"You truly think there is a gentleman out there who meets all your requirements?" Sapphire's eyes were wide. "Coral, how many handsome, dark-haired-readers have a sister and a house in the right part of London?"

"And you did not specify what the right part of London is, you know," Emerald pointed out.

Coral sniffed. "The right gentleman will know."

And was that not the point? She did not wish to spend half the Season speaking with gentlemen who were unsuitable; really, one needed to establish some sort of interview system to ensure they were fit for her hand.

Was this not the easiest way to do such a thing? Was it not far simpler than having that awkward conversation with a stranger where one attempted to ascertain their fitness without directly asking?

Why not establish it right from the beginning?

"I think you may find that some gentlemen rather dislike being marked on a checklist," Jasper said dryly from behind his newspaper.

Coral swallowed. "Perhaps. But then he is not the gentleman for me."

Did they not understand? Could they not see how simple this was? The list was a precursor to meeting any gentlemen. It would protect her from potentially losing her heart to someone entirely unsuitable.

"That reminds me, what was that letter about?" Jasper asked his wife.

To Coral's great surprise, her mother flushed. "It does not matter."

"But I thought it—"

"I will tell you later," Opal said under her breath.

Well, it was impossible not to ask. How was Coral supposed to merely let that go, without inquiring further? Besides, she was her mother's heir. If it was important to the family...

"—arrive soon?" her father had said in an undertone.

"Who is coming?" asked Coral swiftly. "A visitor? Someone we know?"

Her mother fixed her with a stern look. "When it is time for you to know who is coming to visit, if I decide to extend an invitation after such a bold letter—you leave it to me, Coral. You need to focus on this list, and whether anyone will ever meet it!"

"But you could end up unmarried," Sapphire said with wide eyes. "An old maid—and I will never go out into Society!"

"You will if Emerald marries," Coral said without thinking.

Oh, if only she could take those words back. A hot flush was rushing across her sister's face, Emerald's gaze dropping to her hands immediately, but saying nothing.

"I did not mean—what I meant was—"

"I do not think you should have added that a gentleman must sing beautifully," said Opal, staving off the awkward conversation that Coral was slipping into. "What if he plays the piano?"

"What if he plays the harp?" said Sapphire, a mischievous grin on her face.

"What if he loves Mozart but cannot sing?" Opal added.

Coral sighed. This was precisely why she had not shared the list with her family before she had carefully enclosed it in letters to the three most popular newspapers in London.

Who could endure such a critique?

She had lost her dowry, and through no fault of her own—no fault of anyone's, really. But her sacrifice meant she would not compromise in other areas. She would not.

"And what about dogs?"

Coral blinked. Her father had emerged from his newspaper and had a teasing air in his expression.

"I beg your pardon?"

"Dogs," repeated Jasper. "We really should consider getting another dog at some point. Admiral—"

"No dog can replace Admiral," said Sapphire fiercely.

Coral shot her youngest sister a look. No dog could, though she would not have guessed that Sapphire had felt the loss of their dog the hardest.

"I was not saying that," said their father mildly. "I just meant, what if your future intended does not like dogs?"

Every eye turned to Coral. She smiled. "I shall have to add that requirement to the list."

"This list of yours!"

Coral started. The voice which had just boomed around the room did not belong to a single member of her family, but she did recognize it.

Oh, yes. There was only one person who spoke like that.

Lady Romeril swept into the room, her skirts, thick velvet, and feathers plumping from her ornately pinned hair. There was a sharp look in her eyes that told Coral she was about to be reduced to cinders in the fiery red-hot temper of her mother's closest friend.

She steeled herself. She would not allow herself to be—

"Outrageous!" Lady Romeril said impressively as she sat down without invitation right opposite Coral. "To think that a young lady of my acquaintance would do such a thing—"

"Please, do sit down, Lady Romeril," Coral said sweetly.

"Coral, that is not helping—"

But Coral ignored her mother's words. Lady Romeril may have helped her mother out of a scrape years ago, but that did not mean she could march in here—their home!—and chastise her for something that was absolutely none of her business.

"I have high expectations for my future husband, Lady Romeril, and I see no reason to beat about the bush," Coral said firmly, calmly meeting the eye of the formidable woman before her. "And if I choose to advertise for said gentleman in a newspaper—"

"How could you have been so foolish?" Lady Romeril cut in, shaking her head impressively. "You know what sort of reputation you will attract now, of course?"

Coral straightened her back a little and continued to not look away. "One of impeccable taste, I would imagine."

Lady Romeril's splutters were left uninterrupted, and Coral found quite to her chagrin that her heart was beating rather fast.

Well, she had known that there would be people in Society who would think her method...a little unorthodox, to put it mildly. She knew it would attract attention, both of the right and the wrong kind. She knew it would make her a little...not notorious. Whatever was less exhausting than notorious.

But to hear these words from Lady Romeril's own mouth, a woman of flawless and unimpeachable honor; a woman, no less, who in many ways dictated the reputations of many of the young ladies and gentlemen in Society...

A wrong word from Lady Romeril and Coral would have no reputation.

She glanced at her mother and could see that Opal was thinking precisely the same thing.

Just for a moment, a flicker of doubt managed to find its way into Coral's heart. Had she been rash, publishing her list in the newspapers? Should she have perhaps kept it to herself, used it as a private ruler to measure the gentlemen she became acquainted with?

"—and how you allowed her to do something so foolish, I do not know," Lady Romeril was now speaking to her parents.

Coral saw with a smile that her father had retreated behind his newspaper—a perfectly natural response against the wave of opinion that was Lady Romeril—while her mother calmly met her friend's gaze with a vague smile.

"I do not understand, Lady Romeril," said Opal. "What did you expect me to do about the notice once it had been published?"

Coral almost laughed aloud but managed to halt herself from doing such a thing. There was no point in further antagonizing the old battle ax...

Lady Romeril swelled. "Well! I should have thought you would be preventing the printing in the first place! No daughter of mine—"

"Once Coral has made up her mind, no one can change it," said Opal, and Coral was surprised to hear just a little more firmness in her tone. "I have never attempted something so foolish, and I would advise you not to do the same."

There was an awkward moment of silence in the drawing room. Coral glanced at her sisters, intrigued to see what they thought of the whole thing.

Sapphire was watching the exchange agog, eyes wide. Of course, Coral should have expected that. Little Sapphy was so rarely in company, not being out like the rest of her siblings, that she was lapping up the scandalous conversation eagerly.

Emerald, on the other hand—where was Emerald?

"Well," said Opal brightly, as though no cross words had been exchanged, "I believe it is time to leave. Almack's will not wait forever."

Coral rose, her skirts rustling as she smoothed them down, and almost missed the whispered astonishment of their guest.

"You…you are taking her to Almack's?"

"Why not?" Coral asked Lady Romeril, eyebrow raised. "I have not lost my voucher."

"But…but…" Lady Romeril looked beside herself. "The whole of Society read that list of yours—at least five thousand a year, never engaged before!"

"And a dog lover," said Coral seriously, trying not to permit her lips to break into a smile. "I forgot that one, most injudicious of me. I shall have to ask each gentleman I meet now, which is a real bother."

"Better to start off with their income, why not!" Lady Romeril said, her voice reaching a fever pitch. "Far easier to filter out the bad 'uns!"

"An excellent piece of advice, Lady Romeril, I thank you," said Coral, still maintaining her serious expression, though certain she would burst out into giggles at any moment. "And if I ever need further advice in securing a husband—"

"Coral de Petras!"

"—and I will do as I damned please," continued Coral, glorying in using the word that was so often forbidden, "for my damn marriage—"

"Thank you, Coral," interrupted her mother with a glare. "Lady Romeril, let me help you to your carriage—and then we are all leaving, do you understand, Coral?"

Coral sighed. She did understand. That was her mother's way of instructing her to go and find Emerald.

Sapphire rose. "All of us?"

"No, Sapphy," Coral chorused with both mother and father as Lady Romeril was led out of the room.

Sapphire's shoulders slumped. "I really think it most unfair that I cannot be out in Society while you are having such—"

"You should not use that word, Coral," said Jasper quietly.

Coral rolled her eyes. "Micah uses it."

"Micah is a gentleman."

"Barely," Coral muttered under her breath, but as her father opened his mouth to continue the debate, she added, "I need to find Emerald."

It was not a very difficult endeavor. Emerald was in the parlor, the room kept for the family when they were not expecting visitors or preparing to go out. She had her nose in a book and jumped as Coral came in.

"I don't want to go," said Emerald instantly, panic on her face.

Coral hesitated. It was unfair, in a way. Emerald had no desire to be trotted out to find a husband, and Sapphire was quite literally chomping at the bit to be permitted to do so. It would be much fairer if the two sisters had been born in a different order; Sapphire the elder, allowed to dance and laugh and charm the world.

"You have to," Coral said softly.

Emerald did not attempt to argue. What was the point? They knew their place in the family and what was expected of them.

And so the de Petras women bundled up with pelisses against the cold wind and stepped outside, as Lady Romeril's words rang in Coral's mind.

"Better to start off with their income, why not! Far easier to filter out the bad 'uns!"

A small smile crept across Coral's face as she permitted herself to be helped into the carriage. Perhaps it would be a good idea to start with the question about wealth. It would certainly discount a great number of gentlemen.

Besides, if Emerald surprised them all and managed to get married before her, it would be Coral who would be forced to attempt to find a husband with Sapphire out on the prowl.

Opal nodded approvingly as she settled in the carriage opposite her daughters. "That is what I like to see, Coral, a beautiful smile. Just make sure that you use it when we arrive at Almack's."

A flicker of irritation seared through Coral's heart. "I do my best, Mama, and I have hardly struggled for proposals."

"No, just accepting them," said her mother tartly.

Coral caught her mother's eye, and they both smiled. They were very alike, really. The same sharpness of tongue, the same grit. The same determination to have things entirely their own way.

It was the only reason they clashed.

"You must try to attract the right sort," said Opal with a heavy sigh. "Despite your list. Goodness knows you have enough beauty to do so—"

"Mama, really," said Coral with a shiver of awkwardness. It was rather strange to speak to anyone about one's own beauty—not that she was particularly convinced.

She was pretty enough, she supposed. Her hair did most of the attracting needed, and once a gentleman discovered she was a de Petras—yes, *that* de Petras family—they were usually so intrigued it did not matter what she said.

Until the publication of her list, of course.

"Perhaps, tonight, do not ask about money," came the quiet suggestion of her sister.

Coral turned to glare at Emerald, but not before their mother chimed in, "An excellent suggestion! Yes, Coral, Lady Romeril's suggestion aside, perhaps if you could manage not to refer to your list—"

"I have the list for a reason," said Coral, drawing herself up as best she could in a moving carriage that did not appear to mind whether it knocked its inhabitants about as it hurtled down the streets of London. "I will marry a man who fits it, Mama."

Opal gave her daughter a discerning look. "Yes. Yes, you will."

Coral sighed. It was most irritating. *How old did one have to become to prevent one's mother from looking at you like...like that?*

As though you could not make your own decisions. As though anything you decided was foolish. As though it was idiotic to even attempt to make up one's own mind.

Well, she had stood by her convictions for two Seasons now, and she saw no reason to change her mind. Love, romance, that fluttery feeling everyone talked about…Coral had never found it. Not yet.

The point was, she had been clear in her intentions, and no one could ever claim she had not been open and honest with potential suitors.

"Ah, here we are!"

Coral blinked. So lost in her thoughts, she had hardly noticed they had already traveled the short distance across town to Almack's. The de Petras carriage was pulling up, struggling to weave its way through the numerous other carriages depositing their owners.

Opal tutted. "We are late!"

"I hate being late," said Emerald, and Coral could hear the fear in her sister's voice. "And everyone will look at us as we enter, all those eyes focused upon us—oh Coral, perhaps it is best if we do not go in at all!"

"Nonsense," said their mother before Coral could say a word. "Besides, if they do look over at us, there is no harm in that. Coral needs as many eyes on her as possible—eyes, preferably, who have not read that list!"

Coral shook her head but said nothing. There was no point.

The carriage door was opened, and a hand reached out to help them down. After waiting for her mother to descend, Coral turned to her sister. "After you."

Emerald shook her head, eyes wide, lips pressed together.

Coral sighed and descended the carriage without accepting the proffered hand. Her sister Emerald was so…so quiet. So shy. It was a wonder, sometimes, that she and Sapphire came from the same parents.

"Come on!" Opal's smile was fixed, false, and Coral remembered all too well just how many people could be listening now they had arrived at Almack's. Always better to assume that someone could gossip about what you said. Her mother's life had taught her that… "Come on, girls!"

Coral and Emerald wordlessly followed their mother. Emerald because she could not bring herself to speak, and Coral because she had nothing to say.

What was there to say? Almack's was a feature of all polite Society, which was why they attended, but there was no point expecting anything impressive or exciting to occur there.

There would be the same old boring ladies, Coral thought darkly as she allowed a footman to take her pelisse. The same old dull topics of conversation, the same dances, and if she was unfortunate, the same dull gentlemen to talk to, nothing of interest whatsoever.

The doors opened, and the three de Petras women stepped through. Coral blinked slightly in the brightness of the light—the chaperones of Almack's had evidently decided to spend a little more on candles this Season.

The dance hall came into view, and as Coral brought her hands together before her, demurely as her mother had taught her, she looked into the crowd of faces who turned to watch their entrance.

And saw a tall, blonde-haired man dressed in impeccable fashion staring right at her. He was…he was the most handsome man she had ever seen in her life. Blue eyes sparkled across the room, a slight smile on his face, and a most painful yet pleasurable jolt lurched through Coral's body.

Damn.

CHAPTER FOUR

THE REDHEADED WOMAN stared, unabashed, unashamed, as though she was a royal princess who had finally decided to grace Almack's with her presence.

Edward Barlow, Duke of Glaenarm, stared back. *What a woman.* It wasn't just her beauty, though that was difficult to ignore in a place like this, where ladies plastered their faces with goodness knows what, feathers everywhere, a strange desire to attract but accidentally leading to repelling the very gentlemen they were attempting to secure.

But not this woman. *This woman was…different.*

Red hair—no, that did not quite describe it. Edward had never seen a woman with hair so vibrantly colored. If he did not know better, he would have guessed she used some sort of dye— but surely not. There was nothing false about the woman entering Almack's.

Besides, it was not *how* she looked that had caught Edward's attention so, it was more how she *looked*.

How she looked out at those staring with an almost impetuous glare. How she did not seem to care that whispers were abounding about the place, as though she was the center of some sort of scandal yet had decided to hold her head high, as though she were an empress.

The way she looked at him…

Edward almost took a step back, the moment was so intense. He had not come here to look at the ladies. In truth, he had half hoped he would not be required to dance at all, let alone make dull, banal conversation.

*But this woman...*when their eyes met, it was as though Edward was pinned to the spot. As though they had been tied together by fate. As though every part of his life had been leading to this moment, dragging him inexorably to here, just so that she could look at him and he could look at her.

And then it was gone. Over.

Edward swallowed. The woman had dropped her gaze—no, that was not quite right. That suggested she had been cowed by the connection, and he could not imagine that woman being cowed by anything.

No, she had merely looked elsewhere, at another gentleman.

A curl of rage crept around Edward's heart at the mere thought. Which was ridiculous, of course. He did not own her, did not possess her. He was not even sure it was...

Coral de Petras.

The list he had read only that afternoon returned to his mind. All those foolish requirements, the categories that would make her a suitable husband, the way she wished to filter gentlemen out into good and bad...

To think it could be her.

Edward cleared his throat. He had not come here to find a wife. He needed no bride. He was here only as the friend of Maltravers and to meet this Coral de Petras, whenever she deigned to arrive.

He glanced at his companion, but for some strange reason, James Gresley, the Earl of Maltravers, did not look particularly stunned by the beautiful woman. Most unaccountable.

Well, he would probably never see her again, *at least not after tonight*, Edward told himself stiffly, trying to pull himself together. His heart was, most irritatingly, beating fast. Faster than it needed to.

Because he was not going to speak to her. Edward had no idea who she was and did not need such information. Certainly not.

"Who is that?" he found himself asking in an undertone to his friend.

Maltravers looked over. "Who?"

It was impossible that he could have missed her. Edward could still see the redheaded woman on the other side of Almack's, somehow conscious of her, even though he had not been looking for her. Not really.

She was standing quietly with the two ladies she had entered with. One surely the mother—there was enough of a resemblance there—and the other must be a sister. The mother appeared to be speaking with Lady Romeril. Edward shivered. *No woman deserved that.*

"Her," said Edward, jerking his head, grateful she was sufficiently far away. "The redhead."

Maltravers peered over at the other side of the room, and Edward was overcome by a desire to tell the man not to make it so obvious. Did he want the entire room knowing he was so…so enchanted?

For there was no other word for it. Edward may hate the fact that his entire body seemed attuned to the woman's presence, but he could not deny it.

He had seen his fair share of pretty ladies, of course. As a duke, it was an occupational hazard. How many times had Maltravers and other friends ribbed him for the way ladies seemed to gravitate to him in a crowded room, the man with the most impressive title?

But prettiness was nothing compared to the redheaded woman who had caught his gaze for a fraction of a second and was now seared into his soul. Edward did not understand it.

Shaking his head slightly as though his ears were full of water, he snapped under his breath, "Surely you know her, Maltravers, you know everyone in this place."

Maltravers, his dark eyes shining with mischief, said, "Why, of course, I know her."

It was enough to make him wish to pitch the blaggard out of Almack's and into the river—but his temper did not last long. It never could with Maltravers. The man may have had a difficult life, full of misery and misfortune, but that had never dampened his spirits. The man was a trickster, a true Puck.

"Very funny," said Edward darkly. "Yes, she has caught my eye, and yes, you know who she is, and I do not. Come on, if that is all the joke, I do not believe it to be much of a jest."

Chatter had leapt all around Almack's, now the redheaded woman and her two companions had entered the place. Edward half wondered whether he could just turn to anyone around him and inquire as to her name.

Maltravers took a step closer and dropped his voice into a hushed whisper. "That, my dear friend, is Coral de Petras, eldest daughter of Opal de Petras."

Coral de Petras. It had a strange, exotic taste in his mind. The woman who had written the list, the woman who had such exacting standards for a suitor…

Coral…well, the name suited her, of course.

"Yes, she is here, though I think it will be an interesting evening for her," said Maltravers with a shake of his head. Edward was rather startled to see his friend look serious for once. "I would imagine absolutely everyone here has read the papers, and it will not be difficult to guess that CP is Coral de Petras. The ladies will have their claws out tonight…I am not sure whether I would wish to exchange places with her."

She was standing with her eyes cast down demurely, as a young lady in Society should.

Lady Romeril said something, and in an instant, everything changed. Coral looked up, said something rather curt, though Edward could not hear from this distance what it was, and both her mother and Lady Romeril flushed.

A strange smile crept across Edward's face. *My word…if she could say something to offend or even silence Lady Romeril, then she was a formidable woman indeed.*

The desire to be introduced overwhelmed him like an avalanche, burying all his finer feelings. Part of him had almost decided that he had no wish to, that he would tell Maltravers he had not been serious about being introduced to the author of such a list.

But now…

Edward did not understand it, but then he did not need to understand it. He needed her—to be introduced to her. There was no point in letting his mind get away from him, even if his manhood was stirring to be closer.

He swallowed, trying to force down the sudden desire, but it was dampened rather than quenched. She was beautiful and clearly witty if the wry smile on her mother's face was anything to go by. And Maltravers knew her.

"How well do you know the de Petras family?" Edward asked.

Maltravers shrugged. "Rather well, as it happens."

Edward turned to him hastily. Rather well? The impression he had been given was that he had a passing acquaintance with them. "I beg your pardon?"

"Well, my father was friends with Jasper de Petras, the father of your beloved—"

"James Gresley, I will bury you—"

"Oh, don't get your cravat in a twist," said Maltravers with a laugh that made Edward feel a little ashamed of his momentary outburst. "I tell you, our fathers were friends. My father always thought very highly of him."

Interesting. Edward had only known the previous Earl of Maltravers for a few years before his untimely death, but the man had impeccable manners and a direct way of looking at the world. Anyone who befriended him was likely an impressive man indeed.

And Mrs. de Petras had raised an impressive daughter.

The thought flickered through his mind before Edward could stop it, but he did not attempt to. What could it hurt, thinking well of a pretty woman, from a distance? No harm at all. And it was not as though he had even been introduced to her. Not yet.

"And...and he had two daughters?" Edward found himself saying. The words just slipped from his mouth before he could stop them, curiosity overcoming his finer feelings.

"Three, and a son—I cannot see Micah here, though, more's the pity," said Maltravers with a sigh. "Perhaps it is for the best."

There was something there Edward did not like, something unsaid. A scandal, perhaps, or something rather unpleasant that Maltravers did not wish to say. He knew his friend well, even with the almost ten years between them.

Maltravers would not purposefully malign a man's character, but it was what he did not say that spoke volumes about this Micah de Petras.

"Scandal?"

A look of discomfort flickered across his friend's face. "Not with the son. He is the typical reprobate one would expect. Gambling, wine, women."

Edward nodded. Those were old yet common sins.

"No, it was the mother, actually," said Maltravers, dropping his voice even lower so Edward was forced to take another step toward him to make out his next words. "Or the father—the parents, whatever it was. My father never really told me, and Sapphy always said—"

"Sapphy?"

"Sapphire," corrected Maltravers, that inexplicable flush coloring his cheeks once again. "Their youngest. Anyway, she said it was a private matter, not one to discuss outside the family, and if she will not say anything, you know it is serious."

Serious. A serious scandal.

Edward sighed as he looked over at the beautiful woman who had so swiftly caught his attention the moment she had stepped into Almack's.

Well, it was always too good to be true. Scandal around a young woman, even as beautiful and captivating as that…she was certainly not an appropriate acquaintance for a duke.

Which was strange, considering her requirement that the perfect husband would have…what was it? No hint of scandal?

But perhaps that was understandable. If one's family had already weathered such a difficulty, it was easy to see why one would have no wish to suffer it for a second time.

"Yes, I heard most of Society stayed away from them for a time, except Lady Romeril," said Maltravers matter-of-factly.

Edward blinked. "Lady—Lady Romeril? Lady Romeril continued to hold them in her acquaintance?"

"Lady Romeril holds Mrs. Opal de Petras in very high regard," said Maltravers with a wide smile. "Interesting, isn't it?"

It certainly was. Edward was no stranger to hearing gossip about a young lady. Half the time it was not true, and in those situations where a small amount of truth could be found, it had been so extrapolated and twisted that it bore very little resemblance to the seed of truth which had started off the entire matter.

Perhaps that was true with this de Petras family. They still had their vouchers for Almack's, after all, though after Maltravers's words and seeing them make an immediate beeline for Lady Romeril, perhaps she was the reason they were still accepted here.

Curiosity piqued, there was little Edward could do to satiate it. *Coral de Petras.* An unusual name, an unusual family, by the sound of it—yet a family who had retained the good graces of not only Lady Romeril, but of the older Maltravers.

Edward drew himself up. Well, his decision had been made. It would likely be one he would regret, and there was absolutely no logic to it. No logic at all.

But logic was not what his body was running on anymore.

"You still interested in introducing me?"

Edward knew the moment the words out of his lips that Maltravers was going to exalt.

"You always used to say you did not wish to even come to Almack's!" crowed Maltravers, not bothering now to keep his voice down. Several people looked over, and Edward glared at his friend, who continued but in a quieter voice. "You used to say you had no wish to see plain-looking girls paraded in front of you while eating terrible food and even worse drink!"

"And nor do I," said Edward with a wry smile, "which is why I have not asked you to introduce me to any of the plain girls. I wish to be introduced to Coral de Petras—though I suppose we shall have to find Mr. de Petras first, of course. Goodness, I wonder what he thought of that damned list—"

But for some inexplicable reason, Maltravers was shaking his head. "No, it'll be Opal first—come on then, if you are determined to make a fool of yourself..."

Opal first? Edward did not understand, but as he and Maltravers pushed their way through the crowd, that did not matter.

No, what mattered was that in just a few moments, he would be standing before Coral de Petras. Edward's heart flickered, beating rather painfully against his chest as never before.

It made no sense. He was not here to find a bride—he had made that very clear to Maltravers—and to himself. He was curious, that was all. He could not be the only man in London to be curious about such a woman. *And he was not being introduced to Coral de Petras to marry her*, Edward told himself sternly. No, certainly not. He had no interest in such a thing.

He halted just before the gaggle of ladies as Maltravers cleared his throat loudly.

All three de Petras ladies and Lady Romeril turned—the latter eyeing him up in a rather blatant fashion.

"Well, well, what a fish to catch," said Lady Romeril with a smile and a wink at Opal. "I suppose I shall have to eat my words if that list delivers you such fine specimens. I shall leave you to it, my dear."

If it had been Lord Romeril who had said such a thing, Edward would have called him out immediately. As it was, he smiled painfully and hoped Coral had not heard her and got any ideas. He had no desire to be caught on the line of a pretty young lady, no matter how much her eyes flashed as she turned to look at him.

Edward's stomach flipped over. *Ah. That was not a good sign.*

"My dear Mrs. de Petras," said Maltravers smoothly, bowing low. "Miss de Petras, Miss Emerald."

The three ladies curtseyed, and Edward had to be careful not to stare. Opal, Coral, Emerald, Micah…what an interesting family.

"My Lord Maltravers," said Mrs. de Petras with a winning smile. "How pleasant to see you again. You are well, I trust?"

"I certainly am, I thank you," replied Maltravers cordially. "Why, it was only last week I…"

The conversation continued on, Mrs. de Petras and Maltravers chattering away happily, but Edward's impatience grew with every minute of chatter. This was intolerable! They had only stepped over here to be introduced to Coral—and instead, he was having to endure ten types of politeness!

Edward cleared his throat, and Maltravers glanced over with a mischievous smile.

Blast. He had been doing it on purpose, Edward realized, waiting to see how long it would take the duke to force the introduction.

"My, my, I quite forgot," said Maltravers still smiling, a man who had never forgotten anything so trivial in his life. "Your Grace, may I be so bold as to introduce Mrs. Opal de Petras, a longtime friend of the Maltravers family."

Edward saw in an instant just what mistake they had made. He should never have agreed to be introduced to the mother first—they should have waited for the father, wherever he was, to arrive.

As it was, Mrs. de Petras's eyes opened wide at the words "Your Grace" and very swiftly started to size him up.

Edward smiled weakly. *Of course.*

Mrs. de Petras curtseyed low, far lower than she had done for Maltravers. "Your Grace, such an honor to be introduced."

Her quiet murmur was polite, elegant, and with none of the gratuitous praise Edward had been forced to suffer from other mamas desperate to marry off their daughters. A small ray of hope rose in his chest. *Perhaps it would not be so bad.*

"And Miss Coral de Petras, and her sister Miss Emerald," finished Maltravers with a grin.

Edward watched as the two Miss de Petrases curtseyed. The younger, Emerald, fell into a curtsey as low as her mother—but the elder did not. As though not wishing to give him any feeling he was above them—though he was—Miss Coral de Petras lowered herself just enough to be recognized as a curtsey.

A wry smile tweaked at the corners of Edward's mouth. He had expected something interesting, after reading that list—but this was more than he could have hoped. *Oh, she was an interesting one, this Coral de Petras.*

"Mrs. de Petras, Miss de Petras, Miss Emerald," said Maltravers smoothly, "may I introduce Edward Barlow, Duke of Glaenarm."

"The pleasure is all mine," Edward said, bowing and hating how stiff his voice suddenly sounded. *Why did it always do that?* Whenever he wished to be eloquent and charming, his throat appeared to close up.

"How pleasant to meet one of young James's friends," said Mrs. de Petras, flicking out her fan and fluttering it before her. "Maltravers, I mean. It is so hard to get accustomed to the change of titles, do not you think, Your Grace?"

Edward smiled weakly. Well, she may not be determined to wed off her daughters immediately, but it was clear Mrs. de Petras wished to keep her options open—and he was now very much an option. There was no other way to translate that look at her daughter, designed to force her to contribute to the conversation.

His heart fluttered. Any moment now, Coral would speak,

and he would discover just how melodious was her voice, how delicate her praise…perhaps she could be entreated to join him in a dance…

"What is your income, Your Grace?" Coral asked pointedly, meeting his gaze and refusing to look away.

Edward's mouth fell open. Maltravers was laughing, beside himself with merriment, and Miss Emerald's face was crimson.

Only Mrs. de Petras appeared to have any presence of mind. "Oh, Coral, you must be careful, the duke will not understand your rather wry sense of—please pay her no attention, Your Grace, 'tis just a turn of phrase, one that I brought over to this country from Italy, it does not mean what you—"

"His Grace quite understands my meaning," said Coral sharply, ignoring her mother's frantic looks and not looking away from Edward. "Well, Your Grace?"

Edward stared at this woman who appeared to have no sense of decorum, propriety, or polite conversation. Asking a man his income was a rather delicate business, often left to the father of a young lady when it was clear the gentleman had an interest in her.

It was a conversation between men, about a man's world. Not something one simply bandied about in Almack's, for the whole world to hear!

And besides, he was a duke! One did not receive requests for financial information from—from people with no titles and no business knowing!

If it had been anyone else, Edward would have reacted quite differently. Why, if it had been a gentleman, he would have cut him most harshly and refused to have him permitted into his presence again. If an older woman, Lady Romeril say, he would have made a pretty quip about how it was absolutely none of her business, then left abruptly.

But Coral de Petras was no gentleman, nor an old woman. She was…beautiful. Young. Elegant. Independent, if that list was anything to go by. Powerfully determined in her own expression,

Edward could see that and appeared to have absolutely no shame.

He was intrigued. Edward could not help it; any man would be, or at least, any man with any sense.

While the noise of Almack's resounded around him and her mother's frantic attempts to make him forget what her daughter had said echoed before him, Edward stared at Coral—and she did not look away.

There was a determined air around her mouth that he found most alluring—and she knew it. Blast, he could see it in her eyes, the way she smiled. He could not stop looking, and she knew it.

"Me? I have an income of eight thousand a year, Miss de Petras," Edward said smoothly.

Turning to Maltravers who had an astonished look on his face—likely because he had never heard Edward speak so of the Glaenarm estate, one of the finest and richest in England—Edward continued, "Oh, you must not be so affronted, Maltravers. I am quite content to share the news of my wealth with Miss de Petras. After all, I must assume she inquired for a specific reason. Did you not?"

Edward turned and raised an eyebrow, hoping beyond hope Coral would not see the way his frantic heart was beating.

What was he doing?

"I did indeed," said Coral with a wry smile, "and I thank you for your honesty. Have you a house in the country?"

"I do indeed. Two."

"And a house in town?"

Where on earth were these questions leading? It could not be the list, surely, she would not be so blatant as that. It was most unaccountable, and yet Edward found a frisson of excitement rush up his spine. Well, when was the last time he had ever spoken so directly with a lady before? Had he ever?

"Naturally."

Coral raised an eyebrow, entirely ignoring the obvious embarrassment her family was suffering. "And where is it, pray?"

Edward blinked. She wanted to know his address? "Near

Mayfair."

She nodded as though that was perfectly reasonable. "Do you have a sister, Your Grace?"

A sister? The woman must be half-crazed, thought Edward, to think that she could interview him as though a footman for an open position!

"No, no sisters," he said with a wry smile. "No brothers either. I am an only child."

For some reason, this pronouncement made Coral's shoulders droop. An odd look of disappointment washed over her, as though he had sorely offended.

"I am afraid, in that case, you are of no interest to me."

*No interest to...*Edward stared at this remarkable, this marvelous woman. Who was she? Where did she come from? And why on earth did she believe a duke, even a siblingless one, was someone beyond her interest?

He had not expected it, in truth. Oh, he had known he had not fitted the list of requirements he had read in the newspaper, but he had assumed, deep down, that it was a joke. A way to attract the attention of gentlemen but not an actual prerequisite.

But Coral de Petras appeared to be genuine. She would truly discount a duke merely because he had no sister.

"No interest," Edward found himself repeating, a lurch of desire most inconveniently disrupting his thoughts. "No interest?"

"Oh, Your Grace, do not listen to a word she—"

"Yes, no interest," said Coral over her mother. She was still looking directly at him, as though she had nothing to fear by offending a duke, and Edward had to admit, it was intoxicating.

"You are looking for a very specific gentleman then, I take it."

Coral nodded. She stepped slightly away from her mother, who was smiling at her daughter's words, and Edward found himself stepping with her. He had to stay close to her, this marvelous woman who did not make any sense, who confused him beyond anything he had ever known.

"I am fixed upon the notion of marrying a particular man,

yes," said Coral blithely.

Edward's stomach twisted. "A wealthy man."

The vixen nodded. "Yes, at least five thousand a year, though of course even at that income a man's debts could greatly reduce his true value. A man who enjoys Mozart—"

"I hate Mozart," Edward found himself admitting, almost hypnotized by this remarkable woman.

"Ah, another reason you do not match the list then, Your Grace."

The list. The list! That damned list in the newspaper that Maltravers had shown him! CP, and all her necessities for a husband. It had been easy to pretend it was merely a quip, but now here she stood before him.

Coral de Petras.

What else had been on that list? Dark hair, which he did not fit; been to Italy, yes, though she had not inquired about that one yet...

But a love of reading? A sister? How could a man put up with such ridiculous necessities in a suitor?

His true value. Edward knew of course that dowries, money, wealth, income, riches, mortgages...all had to be taken into account when one wed. But to add so many additional require-ments to that inner list he was certain so many ladies had, so in this open manner, without any delicacy of phrase...

Oh, how he wished to play with her. To tease her, tempt her, prove to her she could fall in love with a man, any man, even if he had blonde hair—if he was charming enough.

"And of course, a gentleman must be fashionable," said Coral with a teasing smile. "And like dogs. I forgot to add that on the list, but my sister reminded me that it was important."

"You cannot think to find such a man," Edward pointed out.

Well, he could hardly help himself, could he? What sort of gentleman would this be, that he danced to the tune of a woman like this?

The beauty before him raised an eyebrow. "You think not?"

"No such man exists," Edward said firmly. "And if you found him, he would be a great bore."

"You are only piqued because you do not match my criteria," came the pert reply.

Why the little—

Oh, he was determined now. He would make this woman realize just how ridiculous she was being, how easy it was for a woman to fall in love with a passingly handsome duke. Like him.

He probably should not, but the temptation was too great. He would make her see just how easy it was to find a gentleman most unsuitable on paper, but rather delicious in fact.

Edward smiled. "What a shame I do not make the cut."

There—a flicker of desire in her eyes. Edward had seen it, he was sure, the moment he had smiled. She was interested in him, even if her words would deny it.

"Yes," Coral de Petras said slowly but with a hint of a smile. "What a shame."

CHAPTER FIVE

November 18, 1809

"HEN WHAT DO you know, she did it again!"

Coral sighed as she lounged on the sofa, her head tired from her mother's noise.

It was bad enough that she had been teased for her poor behavior at the time. And when they had returned in the carriage. And when they had got home. And the day afterward…

But now, to have the topic continuously raised again and again, days later, when as far as Coral could see she had only acted in good faith when speaking to a gentleman who may have got entirely the wrong idea about her…

"And to a *duke!*" Opal said with a teasing smile. "Honestly, Coral, I was most impressed. Turning down a duke!"

Coral rolled her eyes. *Her mother really could not let the matter go.*

"I saw that, Coral de Petras, and do not think you are too big and too grown-up for a good talking to!"

Her mother's tone was teasing still, but there was enough truth in it to wipe the smile from Coral's face.

She was only trying to do her best. Even if her mother's best focused entirely on, in Coral's mind, the wrong thing.

While it was quite acceptable to wish to be married…apparently, it was not as equally acceptable to inquire from a gentleman a few important details one needed to know before such a thing could take place.

It was nonsensical, in Coral's view.

The ceiling, newly painted just a few weeks ago in the latest Parisienne style, was the only thing Coral could be bothered to look at. She had attempted to read when she had entered the drawing room, perfectly ready to be polite and sensible, but her mother had followed her in here, and it had been naught but a jest ever since.

"What are we going to do with her?" her mother asked, arching an eyebrow.

Coral turned her head slightly and smiled at her father. Jasper de Petras was seated in an armchair near the fire, trying to look interested in his wife's words, when Coral knew her father simply did not care.

He had never encouraged her to marry. "You think I want my girls to leave me?"

That was what he always said, and it endeared him to her so greatly, Coral wondered wistfully whether she would ever meet someone she would want to leave her parents for. Her father, at the very least. One of the most easygoing and amiable men she had ever known—though Opal had once or twice dropped hints that he was a far more difficult man to live with than he ever let on.

"Well, my dear, I cannot think there is anything to be done," said Jasper mildly. "Coral has frightened away yet another suitor, and I agree, a duke would have been nice—"

"Nice?" Opal laughed as she rolled her eyes, and Coral hid a smile as her papa blinked at his wife. "Nice? Jasper de Petras, you are the most irritating, frustrating, nonsensical man I have ever had the misfortune to meet!"

Jasper smiled, a twinkle in his eye. "I know. And you married me."

In one swift movement, he grabbed his wife and pulled her

toward him. Opal shrieked but there was joy in her tone, and after being tugged unceremoniously to sit on her husband's lap, she kissed him on the lips.

"Mother!" cried Sapphire from the other sofa.

Coral merely smiled. It was strange seeing one's parents...well. Like that. It rather reminded one that there were certain activities that had to be completed for the four de Petras children to come into being in the first place, which was not a pleasant topic to consider.

But still, better that than the parents she had seen of her peers as she had entered Society. Why, she was not entirely sure whether Lady Romeril ever liked her husband, the way she spoke of the departed gentlemen, and there were plenty of gentlemen who spoke so disparagingly of their wives, she fairly flushed to hear them.

Not so with her parents. Whatever dramatic scenes may have taken place over the years, Coral could be in no doubt that her parents had married for love.

For love. Her heart twisted painfully. Yes, for love, and now that was a gift out of her reach. She would need to marry well, need to marry money, and the rest of the things on her list. A marriage that would weather scandal, for there would undoubtedly be more in the de Petras family if she was any judge.

Why, her papa had gone missing for seven long years when she had been a child, and the family had weathered the scandal that a second marriage between them brought.

A flash of a memory seared her mind, and though Coral knew she should not think of such things, she could not help it.

A pair of eyes—blue eyes. Eyes that flashed with intrigue and interest and something akin to desire but not quite. Eyes in a head that was remarkably handsome, and though she had only glanced at him once when she had entered Almack's, that glance had been enough to draw him to her...

Coral swallowed. She was thinking of Edward Barlow again—of the Duke of Glaenarm. She knew she should not.

Thinking of a man in such a way was scandalous, and besides, she had no intention of carrying the acquaintance forward.

Not for a duke who did not meet her requirements, no matter how handsome he might be.

"You two are disgusting," Sapphire said conversationally.

Their mama laughed as she wound her hands around her husband's neck. "Most probably, Sapphy, but that is my right as your mother."

"And I have no rights," said their papa cheerfully. "I gave them all to your mama when she was foolish enough to marry me."

"Foolish is the right word, I have been a fool for you ever since you turned up," Opal said with a laugh. "But that is what happens, I suppose, when one falls in love…"

Coral sighed and looked at the ceiling. *Love.* Now her dowry was impoverished, she would be marrying for an entirely different reason. She could only hope her mother's inheritance would serve the rest of the family; her siblings and their children…and perhaps one day her children…and their children…

A child with her red hair but Edward's eyes appeared in her mind, and Coral flushed at the very thought.

She should not be thinking of her future child, let alone one that shared a resemblance to a certain duke! James should never have introduced them. It was all a game to him, she knew.

Besides, she had been firm with the duke, had she not? He could be in no doubt as to her total lack of interest. She had been as sharp with him as she had been to all the others.

A mark of respect, Coral had told herself firmly, even as she had blushed that evening in the darkness of the carriage as they had returned home. She was only being polite, treating him the same as any other gentleman with more good looks than quality.

"You are looking for a very specific gentleman then, I take it."

"I am fixed upon the notion of marrying a particular man, yes."

Coral swallowed and felt a little shiver of regret tease at her heart—something she pushed determinedly aside. She had not made this decision lightly, only to be swayed by a handsome face, even if it did have a title.

A title was not enough. She required so much more than that… A gentleman, a man of honor, a man who could make her insides melt with just one kiss…

"Coral?"

"What?" Coral said, starting in shock at having such scandalous thoughts interrupted.

Sapphire blinked. "Nothing, I just…you looked very warm, that was all."

Coral pushed back a curl of hair and attempted desperately not to return to the rather hedonistic scene she had just been imagining with Edward. She certainly wasn't thinking about his hands around her. She shouldn't have been thinking of Edward kissing her, his lips trailing down to—

"Sapphire is right, you do look warm," said Opal with concern.

Coral swallowed. "I am quite well, I assure you."

This was ridiculous, she told herself as her family peered at her. She had no interest in Edward. It was very pleasant for him to have such an impressive title, she was sure, and there would certainly be some ladies who would accept his attentions, should he decide to pay them, merely for the pleasure of being called "Your Grace."

But not her. She had a far more sensible head on her shoulders and that meant she was not easily swayed by…by handsome faces and entitled men.

"Perhaps we should send for the doctor," she heard her father saying.

Opal's face brightened at that suggestion. "Oh yes, that lovely doctor—now, what was his name?"

"Doctor Walsingham," supplied Sapphire with a grin at Coral.

Coral glared at her younger sister, wishing it were Emerald seated there instead. Emerald never got involved, never egged on their mother—but then, that was Sapphy's way.

Sapphire returned her sister's glare by sticking out her tongue, though she retracted it swiftly as her mother looked over.

"Doctor Walsingham, yes, a nice man indeed," said Opal warmly, her gaze flickering to her eldest daughter. "I really think you would benefit from seeing him—such a charming man, such wonderful manners!"

Coral groaned. Her mother had never been this sort of person before. Had never obsessed over the potential suitors her daughters could meet with, never worried about a man's eligibility before they met him.

But since her third Season had begun, there was something rather…well. Desperate about her mother's attempts to marry her off. Perhaps it was because Sapphire could not come out into Society until either she or Emerald married—and the odds of her younger sister marrying before her were slight, to say the least.

A prickle of discomfort twisted her stomach. *It was so unlike her.* Unless her gentle quip the other day about desiring grand-children was far more than a jest…

"Mama, I do not need to see a doctor," Coral said firmly, twisting to put her feet back onto the floor. "I promise, I am not unwell, merely…merely warm."

Merely unable to stop thinking about a certain gentleman, she thought darkly, certain she would never speak these words aloud. *Merely thinking continuously about a man I have already decided I could never marry, but he was so…so handsome. So intriguing. So playful.*

"You are looking for a wealthy gentleman then, I take it."

Coral shivered.

Opal pointed a triumphant finger. "A shiver—a fever! My baby has a fever!"

"I do not believe Coral is unwell," said Jasper hastily, reaching out to lower his wife's finger that shook with the force of an accusation. "I believe she may just need a little fresh air—why do you not go out, Coral? Take Sapphire with you."

Her papa widened his eyes, a wordless message Coral was only too eager to accept.

"An excellent idea, Papa," said Coral, rising hastily to her feet. "I do miss Admiral, you know, we should get another dog. We never have sufficient excuses to go for walks. Come on, Sapphire."

"I don't want to go for a—"

"I'll point out all the gentlemen of the *ton* and tell you all their secrets," Coral said as she grabbed her youngest sister's hand and pulled her out of the room. Anything to get away from their mother when she was in this state. "Come on!"

As it turned out, Sapphire actually needed little persuasion. She was not a complete flirt, Coral thought wryly as they pulled on their pelisses and bickered gently about who was to wear the newest bonnet Emerald had purchased for herself but was not currently wearing. Coral won the argument but permitted Sapphire to have it because she pouted most irritatingly.

No, Sapphire was not a flirt exactly, but she was very definitely the baby of the family. So accustomed to getting her own way, Coral had swiftly found it was just easier to give her what she wanted rather than argue with her about it for an age.

"It does look far better on me, anyway," said Sapphire proudly as she placed the bonnet on her head, then turned instinctively to her sister for the ribbon to be tied. "It would look awful with your hair."

"It probably would, but now we'll never know, will we?" teased Coral, reaching forward as was her habit to tie her sister's ribbon.

Born without a right hand, Sapphire had never been treated any differently from the rest of the de Petras siblings, except in two regards. Firstly, she and her sisters had grown in the habit of tying her bonnet ribbons. Everything else, Sapphy did for herself. Secondly, she typically wore long gloves no matter the weather or Season, something her sisters would not have abided.

Besides, it was a little hard on her as she pulled the front door to and heard it click shut. Sapphire was so much younger than the other three de Petras siblings and was still treated like the baby she had not been for many a year.

"So?" Sapphire said eagerly.

Coral blinked as she joined her on the pavement. "So?"

Sapphire rolled her eyes. "Not five minutes ago you promised me gossip of the most delectable variety, and now you are ready to go back on your word!"

"I am not—come on, Sapphy, you know me better than that," said Coral with a laugh. Really, her little sister was the most rambunctious of them all. She had always thought it would be Micah who would drag them into scandal, but at this rate… "Let us go to Green Park. We can talk there."

The streets of London were busy, as always, but thriving in a way that was only felt at the beginning of the Season. Excited out-of-towners, arriving in their droves to rent rooms; lords and ladies returning to London townhouses, residences that had been closed during the summer months; more people than London appeared to know what to do with.

Coral breathed in happily. She had never lived anywhere else. Well, they had lived in Bath for a short time, but she could hardly remember the place now.

No, it was London where so much excitement occurred, where everyone came over the social calendar. She was sure to find the perfect gentleman she was looking for. Eventually.

The gate of Green Park was wide open, the paths busy with meandering couples, families, a few gaggles of gentlemen, who were pointing and chattering loudly at the ladies who passed.

Coral held her head high and wished for a very short moment that she had decided to keep Emerald's bonnet for herself. It was not that she was desperate to be desired, she told herself. It was more that it was more pleasant to be noticed.

But the lack of the bonnet did not seem to matter. As usual, her hair alone was sufficient to capture the gazes of many of those they passed, and she could even hear snippets of their comments.

"—de Petras? Surely not..."

"—hear what she said to the Duke of Glaenarm just last week?"

"That list! I am sure you read it, absolutely scandalous the way she made demands..."

"—spoke to him myself, and was astonished to hear..."

"No! Why the girl has no shame! Though of course, when one has hair like that..."

Coral ensured to keep her head high as they passed the whisperers.

Sapphire, of course, did not. She turned to stare after them, then turned to her sister. "You do not mind what they say?"

Coral shrugged. Trust the news of her conversation with the Duke of Glaenarm to spread like wildfire. Thankfully, no one outside the family had ever heard of her confrontation with the Earl of Chester.

"People will talk, no matter what," Coral said. "You know that as well as I."

For a small moment, Sapphire looked serious and nodded as she glanced at her arm.

It was not something that they spoke of in the family that often—not because they were ashamed, but because it was simply nothing to speak of. Sapphire's "stub," as she called it, was just a part of her. And that was it. Nothing more to be said.

Aside from having a little difficulty with bonnets and necklaces, Sapphy was the same girl of fourteen that you could find in the drawing rooms of many homes in London. But that did not stop people from staring.

Sapphire was yet to know just how cruel Society could be, and Coral could not help but wonder sometimes whether that was the true reason their mother had not permitted her to come out yet.

Little Sapphy needed to grow up before she was ready for such cruel looks.

"Who were they talking about?"

Coral was forced from her reverie by her sister's question. "Me, of course."

"Of course you, but who else?" asked Sapphire persistently. "This duke they mentioned—you did not really meet a duke?"

"They are not so impressive you know, Sapphy," said Coral as calmly as she could manage. "Just a gentleman, like any other."

Except his eyes were brighter, somehow, sharper and more intelligent. Except he drew her to him in a way she did not understand. Why, if Maltravers had not brought him over to be introduced, there was a very real chance Coral would have asked Lady Romeril to introduce her to him.

Heaven forbid!

But she had been unable to help it. Unable to keep away. Unable to stop looking at the man who was so much more than every other man who had attended Almack's that evening.

What kind of more, she could not tell. Just…*more.*

"Just a gentleman!" Sapphire sounded incredulous. "Why, if I ever meet a duke—when, I should say, for I am determined to meet as many as I can before I marry—then I will expect him to be far superior to all others! Was he not very superior?"

A smile danced across Coral's lips. "Yes, I suppose he was. When he—"

"Coral? Coral de Petras?"

Coral froze. No, she had imagined it. It was only because they were speaking of Edward—of the Duke of Glaenarm—that she had heard his voice. Fate would not be so cruel as to put the man in her path just as she was attempting to persuade her sister he was nothing special.

"Yes?" said the artless Sapphire, turning to the gentleman behind them. "And who are you?"

Coral turned slowly on the spot and flushed darkly as the duke appeared before her. *Damn. Damn!*

He was dressed in the most elegant coat and tails, his cravat woven into a knot of the height of fashion. *Irritating man.* It was as though he was purposefully attempting to tease her, to tempt her into thinking of him as a potential—but surely he could not have known he would see her today!

"Edward Barlow, Duke of Glaenarm," said Edward with a charming smile that made Coral's stomach twist painfully. "And you must be Miss Sapphire."

Sapphire's eyes brightened, and there was nothing Coral could do, no way to stop her, before she said, "Goodness, you're the duke then—and you know me!"

Edward's gaze flickered to Coral, and her flush deepened. "The duke?"

"Sapphy," said Coral hastily. "Why do you not go and—"

"Mama told me all about your conversation," said the irritating Sapphire, beaming at the duke, evidently thoroughly impressed to be meeting a real-life duke—moreover, one that her eldest sister had summarily dismissed. "I am sorry you are not perfect."

"Sapphire!" Coral hissed.

Mortification did not begin to cover it. She could feel her entire body tensing at the situation they found themselves in— the absolute nightmare Sapphire had created.

"This is why you are not out in Society," Coral muttered under her breath, reaching out for her sister's arm and trying to pull her away. "Because you cannot control your tongue!"

"Hark at you, telling me to control my tongue when you told the duke you wouldn't marry him," said Sapphire, pulling away her arm and gazing unabashedly at Edward. "I am sorry, Your Grace."

A smile was teasing across his lips. Coral wanted to melt into the ground and never be seen again.

"It is quite all right," said Edward to her little sister. "And you know, I did not actually propose to Miss de Petras."

His gaze met hers, and the heat rising in Coral's chest blossomed to her cheeks, surely now beetroot red. This was a disaster—she had to leave this conversation as quickly as possible!

Besides, it was not as though she liked him. Not as though

her heart had leapt with both fear and excitement when she had heard his voice. Not as though she was even more irritated now, more than ever, that she had allowed Sapphy to wear Emerald's darling bonnet…

"So, Miss de Petras," said Edward cheerfully. "Out husband hunting?"

Coral flushed. "No."

"No one is ever enough for my sister," said Sapphire conversationally, as though it was perfectly normal to discuss one's expectations for a sister's husband in the middle of the Green Park on a November afternoon. "I am sure she quizzed you most heartily, Your Grace, you'll know all about it."

The flush was darkening, going deeper and deeper into her soul, and Coral wished to goodness she had the power to separate Sapphire from Edward in this moment.

Edward was smiling—a knowing smile, a kind one, but one full of mischief nonetheless. "Well, Miss Sapphire, I do know a little about it, but not all. I can imagine it is quite difficult, Miss de Petras."

Coral swallowed. *Why was her mouth so inconveniently dry?* "I only recently placed the ad."

She had kept her gaze defiant as she had spoken, and Edward did not look away. There was something there, something powerful, something she did not understand. Something she was not sure she wanted to.

"I understand," said Edward breezily. "I could help you hunt for a perfect husband if you would like. I know everyone—at least, everyone worth knowing."

Coral's breath caught in her throat. The idea of the first man to truly take her breath away helping her to find the perfect husband…one which would not be him…

It was painful. Why, she could not tell, but it hurt, the idea that he could so easily look past her and farm her off to another man. *Had he no desire for her at all?*

"No, thank you."

"Sapphire!" Coral hissed. "I think I can answer the gentleman very well without your help!"

Sapphire blinked owlishly at her sister. "But I do not think you actually wish to marry a man who meets that ridiculous list, Coral."

Coral could feel Edward's gaze upon her and wished to goodness they had never attempted to escape their mother's wrath by coming here. It was better, surely, to listen to her whitter on about Doctor Walsingham and all the other eligible gentlemen than suffer this!

"Our mother thinks Coral is too much of a romantic," confided Sapphire in a loud, carrying voice to the grinning duke. "And so do I. I do not think she will actually wait to marry a man who ticks all those boxes."

Coral swallowed and looked into the teasing eyes of the duke she was already beginning to care far too much for. "Your Grace, I accept your offer."

She ignored her sister's gasp beside her and looked fiercely into the gentleman's eyes. He had to see she had no pretentions upon him, at any rate.

Edward nodded, his smile still dancing on his lips. "Very well. Let the hunt for the perfect suitor begin."

CHAPTER SIX

November 19, 1809

EDWARD WAS NOT usually a fool.

It was something he prided himself on. True, he was a duke, but that did not make him infallible, and he had worked hard to ensure he lived up to the name he had been born with. Being a Glaenarm did not just mean everything was handed to one. He had been expected to work for it, to know his worth and value, to ensure they increased due to his labors.

Not actual labor, of course. Not with his hands. He was still a duke.

He knew about the world, knew the chaos, knew what people were and who he was.

Which meant it was totally inexplicable why he found himself standing outside Don Saltero's Chelsea Coffee House forty full minutes before he and Coral—Miss de Petras—had agreed.

Edward swallowed, the busyness of London swarming past him just behind his back. He was a fool indeed, though he could not understand why. He knew precisely the time it took him to walk to the coffee house from his London townhouse—situated as it was right in the most elegant part of town.

So why on earth had he decided to leave it not five minutes, not ten minutes, but almost a full hour too early?

Even with some dawdling with a flower seller at the side of the road, half in a mind to buy Coral a flower, then deciding against it, Edward had managed to find himself significantly early for their rendezvous.

Edward smiled, despite the rush of panic in his lungs. Well, what harm could it do, really? Either he managed to persuade Miss de Petras that she cared for him, a man she considered ineligible because he did not meet all the points on that damned list, or…or he did not.

His pride told him he would be successful. Why, it would surely only take a few minutes with her in a coffee house, which was more than respectable enough for a meeting. Coral would be unable to cope under his charm, Edward was certain. She would crumble like one of the pastries he was also determined to have.

"Very well. Let the hunt for the perfect suitor begin."

Edward's stomach lurched, and his heart did that strange twisting thing it was starting to do more and more, now he came to think about it.

Yes, it was all so simple…unless, of course, it was he who ended up losing his heart.

He pushed away the thought as he stepped into the coffee house, the heat and chatter blasting across him like a wave. Edward surely did not have to worry about that. Coral de Petras was pretty, yes, and arresting in a rather charming sort of way.

But he was a duke, and she was a miss. A mere miss, indeed, from a family with a scandalous past. No, he was surely in no danger.

Edward nodded at the man who quickly took him to his favorite table—right in the corner, away from the gossiping ladies who always sat in the center, in the hope they would be seen by as many gentlemen as possible, yet close to the window so Edward could see who was coming and going.

It was his pet haunt, the obvious choice when he had to suggest a meeting place to Coral for the beginning of their husband hunt.

"Not at my house," Coral had said hastily, and Edward had tried not to smile at the idea of what Opal de Petras would say if a duke arrived at her front door, asking for her daughter.

Edward pulled out his pocket watch and glanced at it as the man brought over a large steaming pot of coffee and a large cup.

Half-past ten. He was eager. Too eager. Perhaps he would have a cup of coffee to steady his nerves. Just a simple cup of the hot, sticky sweet liquid, and he would be ready to meet with Coral, without his heart being affected at all.

But for some reason, the coffee appeared to have the opposite effect than Edward was hoping for. Instead of calming him, his senses were heightened, his heart beating faster, the strange sense he was about to embark on something most exciting flooding through his veins.

This was madness. Madness! He should not be agreeing to meet with young chits in coffee houses to tease them about finding perfect husbands!

Edward was in half a mind to rise to his feet and leave, but just at that moment, the door to the street opened and the most beautiful woman stepped in.

He blinked. *Coral de Petras.* How had he already forgotten, in less than four and twenty hours, just how beautiful she was?

No, beautiful was not the right word. Radiant. Resplendent. The English language did not appear to contain the right descriptor for a woman who was able to make an entire coffee house quiet for a moment as she appeared, as though dazzled.

Edward swallowed. He was certainly dazzled by her. In all his years in Society, he had met plenty of ladies, but none of them looked like her. Looked at him like her. His heart fluttered as pride rose, pride that she was looking for him, had arranged to meet with him. The whole place would see that he was her choice.

Coral de Petras looked around for a moment, evidently unsure of herself, but then she glanced over in his direction, and Edward smiled as their gazes met.

Oh, Lord, it was a good thing this was all a jest on his part, or he would find himself in trouble. Edward had never felt this strange stirring in his stomach before. Never known himself to be so enamored with a woman. Never found her so…interesting.

Coral made her way around the tables and patrons, her rather old-fashioned gown a brilliant red to match her hair. Edward found he could not take his eyes off her. Why would anyone wish to look away from such a picture of perfection?

"Good morning," said Coral lightly, stopping by the table. "I thought I was early, but I see now I may have mistaken the time."

Edward gaped. Words would come, he knew, but at this moment he had no idea what those words would be.

Coral raised an eyebrow. "Do I have to pull out the chair myself?"

"Wh-Oh, yes, of course," said Edward hastily, jumping up so quickly his chair tipped over.

Clenching his jaw and hoping no one saw his foolishness, Edward gently pulled out the chair Coral had so pointedly been standing beside and waited for her to step into it.

It was only a moment—a flash of scent, the sense that Coral was incredibly close to him, that if he only leaned forward, he could place a kiss on the back of her neck. Taste her.

And then it was over. Coral had leaned down, and Edward quickly moved the chair in, hating that he was so easily over-whelmed by her. By the sheer force of her presence.

Swallowing any words which may have arisen from such an intense encounter—one that Edward was certain he had entirely fabricated—he returned to his side of the table, righted his chair, and sat upon it.

"You did not wait for me," said Coral blandly.

Edward smiled nervously. *Why—what right did he have to be nervous?* "Well, as I am not courting you, Miss de Petras, I thought you would not mind if I started my coffee before you."

He glanced away, just for a moment, to catch the eye of the waiter, who nodded and immediately started piling a fresh coffee pot and a plate of pastries onto a tray.

Coral had raised an eyebrow. "How very straightforward of you."

Edward shrugged, hoping she could not see just how desperately he was attempting to stay calm in the conversation. "I am a matter-of-fact man, Miss de Petras, and I believe you are quite of that nature. I thought it only reasonable to be as direct with you as you have been with me."

She was impressed, he could see that, and Edward hated how much he relished seeing her admiration.

Oh, if only she had been some pretty, airheaded thing he could have charmed in twenty minutes and bedded before the night was out. It would have been so easy then.

Perhaps too easy. Perhaps that was one of the reasons why Coral de Petras was so fascinating. If she had been coquettish, attempting to attract him merely because he was a duke, then would he have found her so delectably fascinating?

"Your gown is very...very nice," said Edward lamely.

Very nice? Very nice? What did he think he was playing at, spewing such rot?

Coral raised an eyebrow. "I know it is most unfashionable, more my mother's era than my own—but I like it. I like its drama, its ribbons."

Edward nodded, not trusting his voice to say anything. Well, he could not argue with that.

"You and I know this is more business than pleasure," Coral pointed out as the coffee and pastries arrived at their table. "But other people do not. You are not afraid of unseeing eyes believing that you are courting me?"

Edward hesitated. It was a good point, one well made. That was the trouble with coffee houses, of course, they were rife with gossip, both intellectual and base.

Anyone seen meeting in a coffee house was presumed to have some sort of close relationship, even if that was one of friendship or family. But here they were, the two of them, with absolutely no intentions toward each other—*at least, not from her side,* Edward thought darkly—and it was perfectly possible the gossip would rush through the *ton* before they finished their pastries.

Blast. He should have foreseen this, should have considered just how it could look.

Edward smiled, as though a million thoughts had not just rushed through his head. "Oh, I do not believe we are in much danger of that, Miss de Petras. After all, I am sure most of Society is aware now of your requirements for a suitor, and as you know, I am not in the running. Your requirements for a husband are quite clear, and I do not fit them."

He watched, rather sadly, as Coral's shoulders loosened, the tension she had evidently been holding released.

If only it was not so easy, Edward thought darkly, *to convince a woman that you had no wish to court her. By God, he would have to be careful.*

"Well, there is some logic in that," she admitted, pouring her coffee. Edward supposed he should have offered to pour it himself, but there it was. "So, with that understanding confirmed between us, Your Grace—"

"Edward."

Coral blinked, placing down the coffee pot with a startled look. "I beg your pardon?"

Edward wished to goodness the words had not slipped from his mouth, but what he could do now that they were said?

Besides, they had come from a deep place within him. The part of him which had called her Coral, before her sister just yesterday. It had been daft of him to give into that craving, that need to speak her name, but now it had emerged again.

"Edward," he repeated, not looking away. "I would like you to call me Edward. I would like to call you Coral, too, if I may."

He watched her carefully, saw the signs he knew all too well—the flush of the cheeks, the way her eyes looked away from him, the twisting of her fingers together, as though she had been caught in the act.

And so she had. Edward could see, even if Coral wished to hide it, how pleasant she had found hearing her name on his lips.

So, he was right. He was not the only one at this table finding the other most delightful. If only he could get her to admit it…why, then the real fun could begin.

"Coral?" she said a little uncertainly.

Edward shrugged, as though he requested this intimate favor from ladies all the time. "It is your name, is it not?"

Yet he knew he was asking for far more than she could give him in this regard—at least, far more than she had expected.

But Coral continued to surprise him. "Well then, Edward, to business. You mentioned yesterday in the park—and by the way, I must take this opportunity to apologize."

Edward blinked. He had become so entranced by hearing his name spoken by her that he could not make out what on earth Coral needed to apologize for.

Apologize? For agreeing to meet with him? For spending time with him? For speaking his name in such a seductive way, he was certain he wouldn't be able to stand up for a few minutes while he tried to think of ice-cold baths and long hikes up glaciers?

"My sister," said Coral with a wry smile.

Edward laughed. "By God, I never thought to meet anyone like her in my life!"

"She is entirely incorrigible," Coral said, shaking her head, "and I do not believe this will be the last time I have to apologize for her behavior. It is certainly not the first."

"She is a woman with her own mind," said Edward warmly.

After all, she was only a chit of a thing really, and it had been mightily funny to watch Coral burn with embarrassment as her younger sister had chattered on. He had been in half a mind to tell her to bring Sapphire along with her, but desire had won that argument. Edward wanted Coral all to himself.

"She is a girl who does not know her place," said Coral with a dry laugh. "But I admit, she is a darling."

"I did not see her at Almack's, so I supposed she was not out."

"Not for her lack of asking, of course, but my mother would not think of such a thing. Not while Emerald and I are unmarried, though, in truth, I think Sapphire's tongue needs a little taming first."

Edward nodded. It was the same story the world over in a family of sisters, though he was surprised it had not been their father, Jasper de Petras, who had put his foot down. Obviously, Opal de Petras was a force to be reckoned with.

"But we are not here to discuss my wayward sister," said Coral, taking a deep breath. "You know my situation, Your— Edward."

Your Edward. Edward clenched his jaw to prevent himself from asking her to repeat that. *Dear God, the sound of that on her lips*—the only way it could be improved would be if she were to moan the words…

But no. He must not think of such things, must not permit his mind to meander.

"I do indeed, Coral," said Edward, a teasing smile unbidden yet growing on his lips. "You are in need of a perfect husband."

"Need…need is a strong word," said Coral delicately, lifting the coffee to her lips and smiling. "Want. Want is probably more accurate. But can you help me, Your Grace? I am certain you mix in some of the finest circles."

Edward almost laughed. It was amazing, the way this woman spoke about men as though they were the weather. He had never encountered anyone who could speak so calmly, so directly. As though it did not really matter. As though everyone should be so open with their financial histories, their family tree, and details about their estates.

It was a good thing he was absolutely rolling in money and with a title, or he may find himself put out by her tone.

"I do indeed, and many of those fine gentlemen are here," Edward said, lowering his voice. *It would not do for someone to overhear him, after all.* "I chose this place especially, for it is one of the most popular places for those of a certain quality to while away a few hours."

Coral perked up at these words. "Truly?"

With anyone else, Edward would have considered them mercenary to speak so about gentlemen of eligible age. It would have sickened him to see a lady so eagerly hunting after them, desperate it seemed, to find one who would marry her as swiftly as he could.

But he had asked a few pointed, yet hopefully, nonchalant questions of Maltravers after their meeting with the de Petras family at Almack's, and Edward had been rather surprised at what he had been told.

Firstly, the de Petras family was by no means destitute, so Coral could not be looking to marry to offset any familial debts.

Secondly, Coral herself had a sizeable fortune—a dowry of forty thousand pounds. Edward assumed gentlemen would be crowding her, instead of Coral seeking a suitor.

And thirdly, the Earl of Chester had made an approach at the end of last Season—and been rejected.

Now, Edward was not the sort of man to pry into another man's circumstances, but Chester had made it abundantly clear at the beginning of that Season that his income had swelled to near six thousand pounds a year. He had a title, an impressive estate— there was that strange scandal about his sister. Perhaps that was it?

"Truly, there are many fine gentlemen here this very moment."

Coral's gaze flickered on either side of him. "Who?"

There was no malicious hunger in her words, not eagerness to tempt a gentleman. Just plain facts, as ever, from the woman who was fast becoming the most complicated and intriguing woman Edward had ever met.

He pointed at three by jerking his head. "The blue waistcoat and yellow cravat. The one who hasn't yet removed his top hat. The young one—there, eating the ridiculously large pastry."

Coral looked elegantly over her coffee cup, and Edward

found himself hating them, each and every one of them.

How dare they receive the gaze of Coral de Petras and not appreciate it for the gift that it was! How they could sit there, sized up by the most beautiful woman he had ever seen—and yet do nothing about it?

It was unfathomable.

Edward's heart skipped a beat painfully as Coral's gaze returned to him.

"Can you introduce me to the one with the yellow cravat?"

Rage, unbidden and untamed, roared in Edward's chest at her request. She wanted to meet one of them—immediately, just like that. She had made her choice and now wished to proceed.

It was unconscionable. He had been certain he would have so much more time with her. Time to quiz Coral on her true motives, understand her, make her laugh, if he could. Oh, how he loved to hear her laugh. She had laughed at the memory of Sapphire, but he had not yet made her smile.

And it appeared his opportunity to do so was already over. Why, she had made her choice and already wished to leave him.

The jealousy was bitter in his throat, and Edward was unable to do anything but ask rather bluntly, "Why would you want to be introduced to old Orrinshire?"

Coral blinked, as though he had said something rather imprudent. "Is that not the entire point?"

Edward swallowed. "I beg your pardon?"

A smile danced across Coral's face as she leaned toward him. Edward attempted not to look at her bodice, the way her breasts swelled as she took a breath to speak, but he could not help it.

Damnit, he was a man, after all.

"Edward," Coral said in a low voice, her smile now delicious and mischievous, "I was not toying with you, I promise. I am not here to seduce you. I am here to gain your insight into the wealth and value of the gentlemen around me, and if you cannot do that, then I suggest that you and I part ways. This was not, after all this, a trick to woo me, was it?"

Edward swallowed, almost hypnotized by the woman before him. Tempting as it was to reveal all, to beg her forgiveness, to beg for a good number of things, he knew that would be the end of their acquaintance. An acquaintance that was only just beginning.

And that left him with but one choice.

"Wh-Why would I do that? I do not make the cut, so I cannot hope to win you."

Coral hesitated, and Edward's hopes rose at that moment as they never had expected before.

Then she nodded and leaned back in her seat. "Precisely. No hope to win me whatsoever. So, when shall you introduce me to his lordship?"

Edward took a deep breath and allowed it to slowly leave his lungs. This was going to be harder than he thought.

CHAPTER SEVEN

November 28, 1809

"**—a**ND WHERE IS Micah?"

The question echoed around the de Petras house, and Coral's fingers paused at the pianoforte, her heart twisting painfully as she waited for the reply.

The door to the hall was open, otherwise, she would never have heard the question. Her mother's voice, tired and slightly irritated, went silent as she evidently waited for a reply.

Murmurs, words that Coral could not make out—but she recognized that voice. Mrs. Clarkson, their housekeeper for as long as Coral could remember, sounded apologetic. Awkward. Embarrassed.

Coral sighed heavily and turned back to the sheet music on the pianoforte as she practiced a particularly difficult section of this sonata. She had never enjoyed playing the harpsichord or the pianoforte. Her fingers had never done what she had wanted, but years of furious practice meant she could at least play three pieces of music adequately well, by heart.

That was all she had needed last Season, but of course, now that they were entering a new Season, everyone would know those pieces. To impress, she would need something new.

Coral's brows furrowed as she tried to extricate her thumb

before launching into a new octave, but it was a tricky business. Such a shame. She knew that Mozart piece better than the back of her hand, but she could not face the humiliation of playing it again in the drawing rooms of polite Society.

She had to demonstrate she was at least partially accomplished.

"What do you mean, borrowed money from the bureau?"

Coral winced. Her mother's voice had not become more emotional, to the contrary, it had become sharper, more aggressive—more certain of itself.

Trust Micah to do something as foolish as take money from Mama's bureau. He had never been one for following the rules, and Coral had always known that if one of them was to get into trouble, it would probably be Micah.

Micah was going to be in a great deal of trouble when he eventually returned home—but then of course, depending on how much money he took, he could be gone for days. He had taken his own rooms in town, to a great familial uproar, but it meant he could avoid them for weeks at a time now.

A heavy sigh billowed from one of the chairs in the drawing room, and Coral looked over to see Emerald placing a book in her lap, her ear clearly attuned to the argument that was happening in the hallway.

"Five hundred pounds!"

Both the sisters blanched. Coral could hardly believe it! Such a sum—it was a quarter of the year's income! Five hundred pounds—they lived on two thousand pounds all year, their family of six. With their father's shipping business all but destroyed, the last thing they needed was money disappearing. And Micah had taken such a sum?

"What was he thinking?" Emerald breathed, eyes nervously glancing to her sister.

Coral swallowed. She had no wish to speak ill of Micah, nor to set her sister against him—Micah had done plenty himself by acting so deceitfully.

By the time he came back home, tail between his legs—for the money would not last, not the way Micah spent it—there was going to be a significant conversation with his mother. And Coral, probably, too.

Her stomach lurched painfully, and a wave of nausea threatened to overwhelm her, but Coral pushed it aside.

That was the trouble with being the heir, of course. Her mother would undoubtedly drag her into the sorry mess, and she would have to sit there, awkwardly, watching Micah be shouted at for his misdeeds.

"I do not believe he is thinking at all," murmured Coral darkly. "In fact, I would say he is being led astray by—"

She halted her words hastily as a figure crept into the room through the door from the parlor—but it was only their father.

Jasper smiled weakly. "Is she still going?"

Coral glanced at the door, where harassed words still slipped through.

"—done everything we could for that boy, and how does he repay us?"

Coral nodded. "I believe it will be a little while before she is finished."

Her papa nodded and sat opposite Emerald with a sigh. "Hindsight is a wonderful thing, girls. Sometimes I wonder whether I was too hard on him."

Coral pursed her lips but did not say anything. It was not her place to criticize her parents, and in this situation, she felt no need to. She and Emerald had turned out well, and though Sapphire was…headstrong, there was no real ill in her.

No, it was Micah. He was the only de Petras who truly threatened their good name. Perhaps it was a good thing he was absent from the family home at the moment. She would hate for Edward to meet him and form such an impression of them…

But that was foolish, wasn't it? Edward was not the gentleman she was attempting to attract, it was…what was his name? The man with the yellow cravat…

Coral swallowed as a rush of desire filled her—but not for the man whom she had forgotten the moment she and Edward had left the coffee house.

No, it was the duke himself who had entirely overtaken her mind in the days since that conversation. Oh, there had had others. A chance meeting in the park, a few snatched words in the street. Coral had not been able to think of any other reason to detain him, something she had bitterly regretted when she had returned home.

Which was completely ridiculous, she told herself firmly. After all, it was not the duke whom she had her sights on. He was not suitable, as he himself had told her. He was not the gentleman she should be trying for.

Still…

"How is the duke then?"

Coral started. It was as though her father had seen right through her mind into her thoughts and decided to bring them out into the light—most inconveniently for her.

"The duke?" she repeated lightly as she played for a little more time.

She did not want to have this conversation. Not with Emerald here, the dismayed shouts of their mother still heard.

She knew what they wanted, her whole family. They were determined for her to catch the duke. But she had been clear, right from the beginning, with them and with Edward. She had told him, clearly, that she had no interest in marriage to a man who did not fit a simple list.

Had she not ascertained that for sure at their last proper meeting?

"Edward, I was not toying with you, I promise. I am not here to seduce you. I am here to gain your insight into the wealth and value of the gentlemen around me, and if you cannot do that, then I suggest that you and I part ways. This was not, after all this, a trick to woo me, was it?"

Emerald, however, rolled her eyes. "How many dukes are

you in conversation with, Coral, that you cannot recall which one we are talking of?"

Coral caught her father's eye, which had a mischievous glint within it, and steeled herself for the conversation to come. "I will not marry him, Papa."

"Did I say you should?" asked her father mildly.

"No, but I know what you are thinking," Coral warned, "and I tell you again, I will not marry him."

"Who are you not marrying?" asked Opal distractedly, entering the room with pink cheeks and rather red eyes.

Coral looked at the pianoforte keys. She hated seeing her mother after she had been crying. It was rare now, thank goodness, but it brought back painful memories.

"Coral here has decided against that nice Edward Barlow, Duke of Glaenarm," said her father in a teasing tone Coral did not appreciate. "Poor man."

"Poor man, indeed," said Coral dryly, turning her hands back to the pianoforte and attempting to continue practicing.

Opal sighed heavily as she sat beside Emerald. "Now, Coral, you do not have to be coy with us. We know."

"I am not being coy!" said Coral defiantly.

Besides, they could not know. She had not told anyone, even Em, how Edward's face had appeared so disobligingly often in her dreams. How she had found herself comparing every other gentleman they met with him—and found them wanting.

How she had found herself hoping, against all hope, that when they had been invited to the Earl of Marnmouth's card party a few nights ago, Edward would be there. How disappointed she had been when he had not.

Which was foolish of her, on two counts. Firstly, because a duke with no established presence in London nor interest in cards could not possibly hope to keep up in the card games at Marnmouth, his spending more prolific than anyone Coral had ever met.

And secondly, because she did not care about Edward. Not at

all. He was just…just a handsome man she had taken a liking to, that was all. *She did not actually care for him.*

"You have not mentioned him much," said Emerald quietly.

"There!" Coral halted her playing, bad as it was, to point a triumphant finger at her sister. "You see!"

"And you only ever don't talk about a gentleman," continued Emerald, a faint flush appearing on her cheeks as all eyes in the room turned to her, "when you really like him."

Coral opened her mouth to refute the slander but found words were entirely failing her—which was most unfair. How dare Emerald be right. How dare her sister know her far better than she had expected.

Jasper tried to hide a smile, but Coral could see it. She glared at her father, who had the decency to look away.

Opal, however, could not be so easily cowed. "Interesting. So, you do like him, Coral? Why not wed him—he is a charming sort of fellow, and you would be a duchess!" A light appeared in her eyes that Coral had never seen before. "Coral de Petras, Duchess of Glaenarm."

"I hardly think Edward—any duke, for that matter, would accept me keeping my name," said Coral, hating herself for the slip-up and hoping none of her family had noticed. *She really must remember not to call him Edward.* "Let alone accept taking my name."

It was a shrewd look her mother gave her, and for the first time in the conversation, Coral dropped her gaze.

"So, you have thought about it then?" asked her mother quietly.

Coral sighed heavily. There was only one way to end this conversation, and she hated to do it, but her mother left her no choice.

"You think a duke would wish to align himself with our family, once the news of Papa's shipping disaster gets out? With Micah running amok in the streets?"

The moment the words were out of her mouth, Coral regretted it. She should not have been so eager to use whatever tactic was possible to halt her mother's suppositions—but then, she had heard them near on every hour of the day for weeks, ever since she had first made Edward's acquaintance.

The effect was sharp and instantaneous. Emerald drew in an intake of breath, and their father's face lost all evidence of merriment. Opal's eyes became steel.

"I am sorry, Mama," said Coral quietly. "I should not have…I am sorry."

That was one of the things she loved so much about her mother. As long as one gave an apology—a genuine one, it could not just be a matter of course—then Opal de Petras was, usually, swift to forgive.

But not forget. Though her mother smiled briefly and inclined her head as a silent acceptance of Coral's words, none of the warmth seeped back into her voice as she spoke.

"Well, I suppose I do not have time for any more questions. My guests will be arriving for luncheon at any moment."

Emerald looked up hastily. "Guests?"

"Just a few friends," Opal said placatingly, before shooting a concerned look at Coral.

Coral examined her sister closely. She could not understand it; Emerald was pretty, clever, and usually light-hearted. Though she was young, one would have thought she would be snapped up for a wife almost the moment that she had entered Society last year.

After all, she did not have to bear the weight of the de Petras name.

But Emerald's inexplicable fear of crowds, her hatred of being in company, had restricted her ability to even speak to a gentleman—and it was growing worse. Last year, Emerald's first Season, she had agreed albeit reluctantly to attend all the events her sister had.

But this Season, Coral had gone alone to almost every invitation they had received. It was unfathomable.

"You do not have to join me if you do not wish," said Opal hesitantly. Coral could hear the same confusion in her voice that nestled in her heart. "I would like it if you did, but only if you are comfortable, naturally."

Coral watched the war within her sister's features—the desire to please their mother, her absolute terror of being around others.

"I…I think I will—"

The doorbell rang, cutting off Emerald.

Opal rose and smoothed her gown. "Go along with your father, Emerald. We can talk more about this later."

"Oh, so I am not attending luncheon either?"

"You are keeping Emerald company," said her mother pointedly. "And Sapphire, too, if you can find her."

"Well, what about you?" asked Jasper, a genuine look of concern on his face. "You cannot be expected to bear the brunt of representing our family on your shoulders."

Coral should have known it was coming. She should have seen the signs immediately, rushed out of the room before the words could be said, escaped just as Emerald already had—but it was too late.

"Oh, I won't," said Opal breezily. "Coral is accompanying me."

"What?" Coral played a discord, her fingers stumbling over the keys at the news of her sudden luncheon engagement. "Mama, truly?"

"It is time you took more of an active role in this family," said Opal firmly. Their first guest had arrived. "And while you are unmarried, you may help me with it."

There was just a bite of reproof but Coral said nothing. What was there to say? When one lived under one's mother's roof, one did what one was told. *Up to a point.*

"Fine," she said heavily, rising to her feet and moving to the center of the room, ready to welcome their first guest. "But do not expect me to find the conversation of your friends interesting.

It is all weddings and marriages and—"

"Ah, Your Grace," smiled her mother warmly at the gentleman who had just entered the room. "So glad you could come."

Coral's mouth fell open. It was Edward. Edward, here, in her house. *What did he think he was playing at?*

"What are you doing here?" she found herself asking.

"Coral!"

"Your mother invited me," said Edward with a charming smile, ignoring his hostess's scandalized hiss at her daughter. "And very grateful I was, too, to receive such an invitation."

Coral blinked, hardly able to think, certainly not speak. This was wrong, somehow, and she could not explain it. A strange merging of two worlds—her secret plan with Edward to help her find the perfect husband, and her family.

The two had always been separate. She had always intended them to stay that way. But how could she do that with him here?

She turned to glare at her mother, who had a rather self-satisfied, smug look.

"What a kind thing to say," Coral said sweetly. "Here, let me show you the spectacular view we have here from our windows—there is the doorbell, Mama, please do not let us prevent you from attending to your guests."

Grabbing Edward's arm and frog-marching him to the window away from her prying mother's ears, Coral glared at the man who had the audacity to accept her mother's invitation.

"Honestly, what were you thinking?" she hissed.

Warm, welcoming chatter and gracious replies echoed behind them as more of her mother's luncheon guests arrived, but Coral paid them no heed. She was far more interested in the gentleman beside her.

The gentleman with a warm, engaging smile that seemed too knowing for her liking.

Coral suddenly realized she was still holding Edward's arm and dropped it hastily, as though it burned her. Perhaps it had. She certainly felt very warm.

"Did my mother truly invite you?"

"And why would you think otherwise, Miss de Petras?" Edward said in a low, almost laughing voice. "I am sorry, I could not help myself. When I received her invitation, I thought it was the perfect opportunity to…to spend a little more time with you. To get to know you better. I half believe that was her intention, in truth."

Coral narrowed her eyes. "Oh, yes? And why would you want to do that?"

After all, had she not made it abundantly clear she had no interest in him as a person? He had discounted himself most grievously from her list of potential spouses by his honesty, and though Coral may wish that things were different…

No. She could not think like that—she would not. Edward Barlow, Duke of Glaenarm, was not a potential husband. He was merely a means to an end, and she must ensure she did not forget it.

"How else will I help you find the fabulous husband you seek?"

"Why help me?" Coral asked quietly.

He raised an eyebrow. "What do you mean?"

"Well," said Coral, lowering her voice and hoping to goodness her mother's guests did not entirely mistake their tête-à-tête for something far more romantic. "You are a duke."

In her mind, that quite explained her meaning, but it appeared Edward did not understand. A furrow appeared in his brow—a furrow, Coral realized with a sinking feeling in her stomach, that made the man even more attractive.

Damn.

"I am a duke," he said, "but I do not see how that has any bearing on the matter."

"But should you not be—oh, I do not know—looking for a bride yourself?" asked Coral quietly. "I mean, you have a fortune, you are not…not ill-looking. Should you not be looking for a bride?"

"Like you, you mean?"

Coral flushed. She had not intended that at all, far from it, but now he had pointed it out, in any other normal circumstances, they could have been a perfect match.

But that was not the situation they were in. Desperately trying to remind herself she promised to marry a man who reached the heady heights of her list, Coral forced herself to stay calm.

"No, not like me, I wish to marry a man who is far more than just a gentleman, you know that," said Coral as coldly as she could manage. "But I mean, do you not have friends, family to see? Why spend your time in London seeking out a husband for me?"

She had attempted to keep as much suspicion as she could from her tone, but Coral could see she had not entirely managed it.

That did not seem to matter, however. Edward grinned. "You know, being a duke can be so dull. Nothing but bowing and scraping, listening to dull people talk about dull things that do not concern me. But this? This is…interesting."

Interesting. What did that mean?

Never before had Coral wished to see through the hidden meaning of a gentleman's words as much as this. Her gaze raked over his face, half-jesting, half-serious, and she wondered just how much she could trust a man who spoke like this.

Besides, he made her feel…strange. The room was now full of people chattering away, but that could not account for the sudden warmness of the room.

Could it?

It certainly couldn't be Edward.

Coral's eyes met his bright blue ones, sparkling in the sunlight pouring through the windows, and her stomach lurched—but it was not the painful lurch of disappointing news or further evidence of Micah's disgrace.

No, it was far more…pleasant than that. She could think of

no other way to describe it, and it was most irregular.

Coral glanced at her hands, steadied her breathing, which had become jagged for some reason, then looked up at him, firm in her resolve.

"So," she said in an undertone. "Are there any eligible bachelors my mother thought fit to include on her invitation list?"

Turning ever so slightly to look at those in the room, Coral saw to her disappointment that most of her mother's guests appeared to be ladies of more mature years. Trust her mother to point her directly toward a duke.

Edward chuckled, and a shiver of pleasure rushed through Coral's heart.

"I do find it interesting that you are so determined to marry someone who meets such lofty expectations that even a prince may not meet it, Coral," Edward said in a low voice. Something strange plucked at Coral's heart as he said her name. "I mean to say, why go to such extraordinary lengths? You are a lady, your dowry is not insufficient—"

"My dowry—what do you know of my dowry?" said Coral curtly.

They had all promised, had they not, that the news of her father's misfortune would not be repeated beyond the family, hadn't they? The last thing they needed was more scandal. That was her mother's decision, and so that was what they had agreed on as a family.

How could she expect him to understand? No one did, at least, she had never met anyone who had. The idea of her mother being the head of the family, it was unheard of here. Her family was so…so different. Perhaps it was that way in Italy, where her mother had come from, but as far as she knew, the de Petras family was the only one like it in the whole of England.

Coral knew she could not even attempt to explain it.

"A father's place is at the head of the household," the man had said rather stiffly, and Coral had seen his interest in her fade away with every passing moment. "But for you, it is…your mother?"

Coral bit her lip as she looked at Edward, clearly curious, yet not pushing her to speak. There was no easy way to explain this, and she certainly had no wish to do so in her mother's drawing room.

Not if Edward was going to prove himself to be as dull and staid as all the other gentlemen she'd had the misfortune of opening up to.

It appeared, however, that Edward saw her hesitation and understood it. He glanced about the room, as though looking for something in particular, and Coral watched his eyes alight on the door to the parlor.

He turned back to her, taking her hand in one swift movement that made Coral gasp, though she attempted to hide it. Edward placed her hand on his arm and winked.

"Coral de Petras, how interested are you in attending your mother's luncheon?"

Coral's heart was pounding painfully in her chest, which did not make sense, for she had no interest in Edward. No interest at all. No desire to have his hand once again on hers.

"None whatsoever," she found herself saying in a whisper.

Edward's smile broadened. "Excellent. Come with me."

CHAPTER EIGHT

EDWARD DID NOT have a plan. But that was how he liked it.

He had no idea of the layout of the de Petras house. For all he knew, the door he was making for could lead to a cupboard.

But as he opened it and slipped through, Coral on his arm gave him the strength he had not known he needed. Edward felt as though he was striding through the world with supreme confidence, a power he had never known before.

A parlor appeared before him as Coral quietly shut the door behind him.

"This is your plan?" she whispered, a teasing smile on her lips. "Hide in the parlor?"

Edward swallowed. It sounded ridiculous when she put it like that. It was not as though he had a plan, precisely, other than escaping the warm whispers behind him that pointed out, quite proudly, that her daughter was having a private conversation with a duke.

That could only be Mrs. de Petras, and it was clear her daughter would never speak freely while in her mother's presence.

Just why it was so important to Edward to hear Coral speak openly…he could not put it into words. He just knew, somehow, by the teasing look on her face, that he must. Had to unpack the wild ideas that whirled in that mind, for he could see something astonishing was happening in there.

"But should you not be—oh, I do not know—looking for a bride yourself? I mean, you have a fortune, you are not...not ill-looking. Should you not be looking for a bride?"

"Like you, you mean?"

Edward looked around and spotted a door that surely led to the hall. Well, he had pulled Coral away from her mother's luncheon. There was already going to be gossip aplenty in the room behind them. They may as well give them something to really talk about.

"Come on," he said again, this time pulling Coral to the hall.

Edward grabbed his greatcoat and top hat, which had been placed delicately by, he assumed, the housekeeper, in pride of place, right by the door.

"Where is your pelisse?"

Coral's mouth fell open. "You cannot be serious."

"Why not?" asked Edward in a low voice as he pulled his arms through the sleeves.

To do so, he had been forced to remove Coral's hand from his arm, and he had never noticed before just what a lack there was when he was not touching her.

Not that he could think about that. How obvious did Coral de Petras have to make it before he realized she had absolutely no interest in him?

"But my mother!" Coral hissed, glancing back down the hall and coloring slightly as she spoke. "She will think...well, she will think that we—"

"Let them think what they want," Edward urged, discovering he would be most distressed if Coral did not come with him. *To lose the opportunity to speak with her, to spend a little time with her without mother nor sister nor gawping watchers in a coffee house...* "We know the truth, after all."

She hesitated just a moment longer, and Edward found himself considering additional arguments that would encourage her to come with him.

By Jove, he had never had this trouble before! Ladies had always been tripping over themselves to speak with him, to take a turn about the room with him, to spend any time with him whatsoever.

Yet here he was, trying to persuade a woman as lovely and as independently minded as Coral to depart with him!

"We are only going to the park," Edward said in a low voice, placing his top hat on his head and praying to goodness he could persuade her. His pride—nay, his very being was determined to have her. *On a walk with him, that was. That was all.* "Are you afraid, Coral de Petras?"

He had not intended his words to be so teasing, but that was how they emerged. A smile crept across his lips as he saw the indignation rise in Coral's eyes.

There it was—the sparking, independent young woman who had accosted him so boldly at Almack's when she had inquired as to his income. There was the woman who had so enchanted him in that moment, who Edward had been unable to let slip through his fingers.

Even if it was against his better judgment.

"Afraid? Me?" Coral said, pulling a pelisse from the coatrack without looking at it, and forcing her arms through it with such violence, Edward was almost certain she had ripped a hole in it. "Never."

Never. Edward grinned as he opened the door and bowed as Coral stepped through it. Now there was a woman he could spend…well, at least an hour with. The day with.

The rest of his life with?

The thought flashed through his mind before he could stop it, and Edward cleared his throat as he, too, stepped out of the house and into the street, pulling the door shut behind him. As though his slight cough could dislodge from his mind the sudden realization that Coral de Petras was a rather special woman indeed.

She was waiting on the pavement, eyebrow raised. "The park, I think you mentioned?"

Edward nodded, attempting to get his bearings. The chilly November wind was nothing to his greatcoat, of course, but he certainly felt much warmer than he could remember when he had approached the de Petras house.

If only he hadn't sent his carriage away—but then, perhaps that was all to the good. A chance to walk, a chance to spend even longer with this bewitching woman.

"The park," Edward said, offering his arm and finding a ridiculous spurt of joy pump through his heart as Coral took it without question.

There was something so natural about the movement, something Edward forced himself to disregard. He was not on the hunt for a bride, and Coral de Petras was certainly not someone he could marry. Not with that hint of scandal mentioned by Maltravers—and where was that brother he had mentioned? He had seen neither hide nor hair of him, all about town.

"We used to walk here all the time."

"You did?"

Coral flushed. She had not intended to speak aloud. "We used to walk the Admiral here often."

"You…you walked an Admiral?"

"What? Oh, no," she said with a laugh. "Admiral was our dog. Papa still misses him, I know, but it's been too difficult to think about getting another dog. Emerald and Sapphire beg for one, but still. His heart is with Admiral."

Edward smiled. He rather liked the image of Coral, Emerald, and Sapphire walking a retired Admiral up and down the London streets.

"Oh, I love winter," Coral said impetuously.

Edward raised an eyebrow as they started along the pavement. "I would have thought you more of a summer child."

"Oh no, that is definitely my brother Mi—my sister, Emerald, I would say," said Coral, correcting herself hastily.

Edward could not help but notice the sudden change. There he was again, this Micah fellow, whom no one appeared comfortable to talk about. What sort of mischief had the lad managed to get himself into, then? From what Maltravers said, the boy was more than twenty years of age. Old enough to know better, whatever he was doing.

"I just love the wind," said Coral, her face softening and all the tension Edward had seen in the drawing room of her house melting away as the breeze tugged at her fiery red curls. "Don't you feel immensely more alive when it is rushing through you?"

"I certainly feel more aware of my body, if that is what you mean," replied Edward dryly.

Coral glanced at him, her gaze moving up and down, and Edward was suddenly more conscious of his body than any wind could ever have made him. What had possessed him to say such a thing? Coral was hardly a prim young miss who wouldn't say boo to a goose, but honestly! The way she looked at him, as though she was marking him for a country fair!

"I suppose that is partly what I mean, yes," she said eventually as they came to a crossroads and carefully crossed over, narrowly avoiding a barouche driven by a shouting young man, a gleefully giggling lady beside him. "But I think it is more than that. The sensation that one is out in the wild, as much as London can be described as wild. As though anything could happen. As though the winds of fate were moving you along your path, and one's decisions, though important, were having far less of an effect than one originally thought."

Edward stared as they turned a corner and approached the park where he had met the two de Petras sisters only a few weeks ago.

What a woman. It must be easy for people to underestimate Coral de Petras. After all, she was a gentlewoman, pretty to look at, and from a family of pretty sisters.

But Emerald and Sapphire did not hold a candle to their eldest sister. Something came alive in Coral when she spoke, as though poetry had never held truth until this moment. Edward could not understand how she was suddenly able to relax, her voice becoming clearer and more certain with every step they took further from her house.

Ah. Perhaps that was it. Her family.

Try as he might, Edward had to admit, as they entered the park and started walking a little more slowly along one path, he was intrigued. Curious. Interested.

Interested in Coral de Petras.

But not as a potential bride, of course. Edward told himself silently it was precisely the opposite. He had intended to tease her into falling in love with him and had somehow found himself offering to point her in the direction of a potential suitor who would match her.

But how could there ever be a gentleman to match the wild and delectable Coral de Petras?

"So, your list," he said briskly. She was the one supposed to be admiring him, not the other way around. "It is long and varied—far more varied than I would have imagined."

There was a teasing look in her eyes. "You disapprove?"

"You certainly never struck me as a fortune hunter," Edward found himself saying. "At least five thousand a year, I think that's what you said. Why is a specific income even on your list?"

Coral laughed, leaning into him as they passed another promenading couple, and Edward's loins lurched with the sudden closeness. "No, I suppose in a way, I suppose I am not a fortune hunter. Money has become...well. More important than I originally thought."

This was so opposite to everything Edward felt he had seen in Coral that he could not help but be surprised—a feeling that was evidently painted on his face, for she laughed.

"There is no reason to look like that!"

"You can see why I am surprised, though, can you not?" asked Edward, trying to keep his voice calm and wondering why on earth it was threatening to quiver with every word. "You are, after all, seeking a husband with quite a prodigious amount of wealth."

Coral shrugged, and Edward attempted not to look at her breasts. *Dear God, he was in trouble.*

"I am not so sure about that," Coral said lightly. "Yes, I seek a gentleman with a sufficient income—"

"Sufficient income!" Edward could not help but exclaim. "What was it your sister said you rejected last Season—six thousand a year?"

"Six thousand a year is nothing if the estate has debts of nigh on three thousand a year," said Coral dismissively, as though she had taken a careful look at the accounts of the Earl of Chester and evidently found them wanting. "I am no simpleton, Edward, even I can do the sums on that one."

He had to admit she was right. There was many a gentleman, and a nobleman to boot, who had an income impressive at first glance, but debts pouring out of his ears.

But why did a lady of such an upbringing know about such things—care about such things? From what he had seen of the de Petras house, they were fairly wealthy, but Edward could not comprehend how a daughter, after all, would know about such things.

"Tell me," he said quietly. "How does someone like you know about such things—care about such things?"

Coral glanced up with a wry smile. "You mean a woman?"

Edward hesitated. "Well. Yes."

It did not appear to be a trap, and he was rewarded for his honesty by a laugh from his companion.

"You ask complicated questions, *Your Grace.*"

"I did not think I did, *Miss de Petras*," teased Edward, though his heart twisted painfully at the honorific she used. It was strange, after hearing himself called Edward by her, it was actually quite bizarre to hear her revert to such formality. "It is not such a complicated question, is it?"

Coral did not answer immediately but looked ahead of them along the path. "There."

Edward looked, though it was an effort to drag his eyes away.

Just along the path, about twenty yards ahead of them on the left was a bench. It was empty.

"Let us sit there," said Coral with a heavy sigh Edward did not understand. "And I can tell you a little of the story, though, in truth, I do not know it all. You'll have to keep it to yourself though. I am not really supposed to be speaking of it to anyone outside the family."

Curiosity piqued beyond what he could endure, Edward asked before they reached the bench, "About why you wish to marry a rich man?"

"About that, and why I know so much about money, and…other things," said Coral with a mischievous smile. "It is a good thing you do not wish to marry me yourself, that is all I will say."

As Edward slowly lowered himself onto the bench, mind whirling at what Coral could possibly mean, he found to his disappointment that it once again meant a separation between the two of them.

But they could hardly sit on a bench together arm in arm. Edward knew that, knew what it would look like. Why, the news that they were engaged to be married would circulate through the *ton* faster than he could imagine—perhaps reaching Mrs. Opal de Petras before they did.

But the fact was, and Edward was finding it more and more irritating, he wanted to sit close to Coral. Wanted to still feel the weight of her hand on his arm. Wanted to see, if he was quiet, if he slowed his breathing, whether he could feel her pulse. Feel the strength of her desire by how her heart fluttered.

The fact that his own heart was fluttering most painfully was neither here nor there.

Coral was smiling serenely out at those who walked past.

"Perhaps we should have found a more private place to talk," Edward muttered.

Coral laughed. "What, and be discovered accidentally, and create rumors all over London neither you nor I would wish?"

A dark part of him wished for that, Edward knew, but he could never admit it. Never say to the woman beside him that he had intended her to fall in love with him herself, just to show her that her precious list could not capture the true essence of a man.

It had been a foolish idea, one Edward almost regretted. Would Coral be smiling at him, charming him, attempting to win him if she knew?

"Fortune hunting," said Edward firmly, more for his own benefit than hers.

Coral raised an eyebrow. "Do you have to call it such a term? I prefer to focus on my list."

Edward could not help but laugh. "Have you always had such requirements? I mean, this is your second Season, is it not?"

"Third," said Coral lightly.

This surprised him. "And you have traversed through two entire Seasons and only received one proposal of marriage, never finding the perfect gentleman?"

What was wrong with them all? Were there no sensible men in England, that Coral de Petras had managed to enter her third Season with only one measly proposal?

"Not...not exactly," said Coral quietly, her gaze dipping to her hands clasped in her lap.

Edward edged ever so slightly closer. Well, a few inches could not hurt, could they? No one would even notice, but he did. He could feel the difference, feel it in his bones. Knew that with every inch that he crept closer to Coral, his heart pattered most inconveniently.

"How many then?"

"Almost twenty," Coral said cheerfully, though she kept her voice down.

"Almost—"

"There is no need to shout, Your Grace," Coral said with a wry smile, teasing as though he were her servant. "Most of Society knows about them. They do not need to be informed."

With great self-control, Edward shut his mouth and said no

more. *Almost twenty proposals?* If he had not been on the Continent the last few years, dealing with his father's final affairs, then surely, he would have heard all about them—but twenty?

Well, he could not blame the poor sods who tried it. Just to be in Coral's presence was to feel oneself losing grip of one's control. But twenty? Was there not an Englishman in the world good enough for her?

"I have heard tell your dowry is near forty thousand pounds," said Edward slowly.

It was a gamble, true, but Coral had always been marvelously blunt with him. Perhaps it was time for a little return of that honesty.

A nervous laugh was initially all the response he received.

"Well?"

Coral grinned, her fingers twisting in her lap belying her nerves. "Most gentlemen do not ask such things. Especially dukes. Were you not taught any manners, Edward?"

There it was again, his name on her lips. Edward fought the desire to crush her against the bench and show her just what sort of manners he had been taught. Perhaps if they had loitered in her parents' parlor, he would have done.

As it was…

"You were the one who asked about my fortune," Edward pointed out as a gaggle of schoolboys in the uniform of the Westminster School scampered past them. "I follow your lead, Coral."

Follow her lead. Edward tried to push aside the thought of just what he could do if she permitted him to kiss her, tempt her, tease her.

"I suppose that is fair," said Coral with a shake of her head.

"And your father?"

There it was again—that shadow that crossed Coral's face whenever her father was mentioned. Edward could not understand it. He had heard little ill of the man, except some guff about him being misplaced for a time, but what man hadn't escaped his family for a few days?

"My father has little say in the matter."

Edward nodded sagely. "Yes, I know a few families where the wife rules the roost. Lady Romeril, for instance—"

"As impressive as Lady Romeril is, the situation is not quite the same," Coral said delicately. "Oh, this is always so difficult to explain…"

Though tempted to interrupt her thoughts, to tell her he was a relatively bright man and able to understand quite a great deal, Edward managed to hold his tongue. There was an odd expression on Coral's face, half embarrassment, half pride. What did it all mean?

Then she took a deep breath, as though she was about to dive into a deep pool. "My family…we are different."

Whatever it was that Coral thought so strange, it would be all the easier for him to comfort her once she had explained.

"Most families," continued Coral, smiling as she looked at him, "are headed by a man. The father. His children take his name, until daughters are married and take their husband's name. Sons retain the name, and the eldest inherits."

Edward nodded. *Well, naturally. That was how it was done.*

"But not in my family."

A frown creased his forehead. "No?"

Coral shook her head. "No, in fact, quite the opposite. 'Tis my mother who is the head of the family. She was born a de Petras, and my father took her name—we all did, and when I am married, my husband will take mine. He will become a de Petras. I am the heir of the de Petras family."

Edward stared. Astonishment did not entirely cover it, for he was having a difficult time taking it all in. *A woman, lead a family? A woman, give her name to her husband? A woman, inherit?*

"I…I have never heard of such a thing," he admitted.

A crease of concern appeared between Coral's brows. "I know."

"I do not mean it is a bad thing," Edward said hastily. "I

just…goodness. So, you are the heir."

Coral nodded. "That was all very simple, until…until a few weeks ago."

He leaned forward. A few weeks ago? Just before they first met, then. What could have changed in this strange family to make the situation even more complex?

She sighed. "I should not really be telling you this, but…my father owns a shipping business."

Edward nodded. So Maltravers had said.

"Three ships moving cargo about the place, mostly in Europe, though I believe he intended to set out on an expedition to India at some point, see if he could get hold of some rare spices. Though that plan will have to be shelved, now."

There was a look of remarkable pain on her face, pain he had not seen before.

Coral took a deep breath. "Until the storm. All three ships were lost."

Ah. It was all starting to become clear now—at least, as clear as something remarkably confusing could be.

"My mother's inheritance, though substantial, cannot bear the burden of all four dowries—"

"Four dowries?" Edward interrupted, unable to help himself. "I thought you only had two sisters?"

She laughed at that, gently under her breath, as though he should have worked out the problem. "As I am the heir, it was decided that Micah would be given a dowry, something to help him establish his own household whenever he married. But, there is no longer sufficient funds."

Edward tried to wrap his mind around the idea of a man having a dowry and pushed it aside. *A problem for another day.*

"If I marry a wealthy man," said Coral with a wry smile, "there will be enough for Em, Sapphy, Micah—all of them would have dowries. I wanted a love match, so I decided if I had to sacrifice that, I would at least have my minimum requirements met…and so I wrote the list."

Understanding started, slowly, to dawn in Edward's mind. The sudden focus on money, the long list, the determination to find an absolutely perfect gentleman.

Now he knew more about the family, it was starting to make sense. Why Opal was the one referred to for all decisions, why the siblings all looked up to Coral so—why, in truth, the brother Micah appeared to be so wayward. It must be an odd thing, thought Edward, to see one's sister inherit in your place.

And of course, that was why Coral wished to marry a wealthy man. He could see it now: the concern for her siblings, the weight of responsibility that sat heavy on her shoulders.

"You take a great sacrifice upon yourself."

Coral laughed dryly. "I suppose I do—but then, would not any eldest do that? Would not any heir see what they could do for their siblings, then do it?"

She was a brave woman, he could not help but think. He could see the pain tugging at her temples, the way she clasped her hands tightly in her lap. It pained her, to give up the chance of a true love match, but she had made her decision and that, it appeared, was that.

"But...but you *could* marry anyone," said Edward slowly. "I mean, you are the heir. You have the choice."

For some reason, a flush tinged his cheeks as he spoke. He knew how that could sound, and he did not mean it that way. *Did he?*

Coral's cheeks, too, had darkened at his words. "I suppose I could, but after finally deciding on a love match, to have that taken away from me...I must marry a wealthy man, a man who does not mind I have no dowry of my own. And after all, money solves most problems."

It was so unlike what Edward had been expecting, he blinked and waited to see if the words changed their flavor. But they did not.

"Money solves most problems?" he repeated slowly. "That is not what I would have expected to hear from the lips of a young woman."

Edward's gaze drifted to Coral's mouth, then wished to goodness he had not permitted such a thing. Now all he could think about was how they tasted, their softness, how he could crush them beneath his own and take—

"I think it is a rather pragmatic approach," Coral said with a heavy sigh. "Money has power, does it not? We crave it, seek it, hoard it. It allows us to cross many difficulties, solve many problems, and remove barriers."

Ice sank into Edward's chest as Coral's eyes rested on him. Yes, he was more than wealthy enough to solve almost all his problems with just a wave of his checkbook. Why, he could not recall the last time an insurmountable issue could not be surmounted by a large amount of gold.

"I-I suppose so," was all he managed.

He was fighting off the desire to take her hand in his now. The chill of the day had only increased as the wind had, but Edward knew that was not the reason. No, he wanted to touch her, feel a connection. Match the intimacy on the outside with what he felt within.

"Well," Edward said, clearing his throat and hoping to goodness that she had not seen the warring emotions in his eyes. "We have the entire park full of potential suitors. Shall we?"

He rose and offered his arm. It was a small compromise with himself, a way to be connected to her without crossing a line he certainly should not cross.

Coral rose in a delicate swish of silk and smiled as she took his arm. "We shall."

Edward's manhood twitched at the mere suggestion of desire—but something else did, too. His heart. Most painfully and most uniquely.

Ah. He was only now starting to realize just how much danger he was in.

CHAPTER NINE

December 5, 1809

CORAL HEARD HIM before she saw him, of course.

It was always the way with Micah. Even as a small boy—and Coral had to admit, it was difficult to see him as a man and not the delightfully adorable child he had once been—Micah had always been able to get away with murder.

It had been one of the few bones of contention between the three siblings, four, once Sapphire had come along.

Coral had always been filled with a sense of righteous indignation when she saw, time and time again, that Micah was able to do almost whatever he wanted, and neither of their parents saw fit to punish him.

"I do not understand!" she could well remember saying, stamping her foot—a habit which she had thankfully left behind in childhood. "I was never allowed to—"

"Well, you are a girl, my dear," said her mother once, looking at her with a sort of sad smile that Coral had not understood at the time. "You will be held to higher standards out there in the world."

And Coral could remember frowning, not quite understanding her mother's words. "Is that because I will inherit?"

And her mother had sighed, pulled her close, and hugged her

tightly. "In a way. Do not think on it now."

Coral had much time in the intervening years to do just that, and she had to admit that in a sad way, her mother was right. Ladies were expected to be far better behaved than the men around them—and being a de Petras made that all the more complicated.

Still, it did not explain why Micah felt able to cause such a ruckus whenever he returned back home.

"Micah de Petras!" Coral shouted from the parlor, where she had been lazily reading a book on the sofa and half thinking about how desperately she had wished to kiss Edward and how right it was that she had not done it. "Come in here and stop making so much noise!"

The crashes and bangs in the hall halted, and then the door burst open.

"Coral!" beamed her brother, seemingly unaware of the absolute havoc he had been causing, running up and down the stairs like a maniac. "You are in good spirits."

Coral scowled waspishly over her book at her brother. Tall, handsome like her father but with their mother's eyes, Coral had once overheard her parents talking about how Micah would break many a heart when he was older.

It appeared their predictions had come true. There never seemed to be a time when Micah was not in some sort of trouble with a lady, his name coupled with countless other ladies in the gossip sheets.

One day, she would be the matriarch in her mother's place, and it would be her responsibility to keep Micah in line.

Heaven help her…

Micah slammed the door behind him.

Coral winced. "Is it possible for you to move about the house without causing avalanches?"

Her brother threw himself into a chair and peered at her book. "Avalanches? You're not reading another Mrs. Radcliffe, are you? All those Swiss alps and adventures and nonsense."

Coral carefully put aside the book she was reading—it was a Mrs. Radcliffe, as it happened, but that was complete chance, for she read a great number of novels—and glared. "You are incorrigible."

"Micah Incorrigible de Petras, that's me," said Micah cheerfully, as though he had not just been tramping about making an awful racket.

Coral threw a cushion at her brother, who most irritatingly caught it, and placed it behind him on the chair.

That was the trouble with brothers, though admittedly she did not have a varied experience. They seemed perfectly designed to irritate one, beyond what was reasonable or manageable.

Coral sighed. Only eighteen months younger than herself, a tall strapping man—one who several ladies of her acquaintance had delicately asked about—yet still he seemed to have nothing better to do than tease his sisters.

Well. Almost nothing better to do.

"Any new proposals? he asked. "Or have you made it impossible to find a husband now?"

"I will marry whomever I wish, and he had better tick off everything from my list or there will be no wedding," Coral said sharply, pushing all thoughts of Edward from her mind.

It was getting more and more lamentable that the duke did not meet her requirements, it really was. Their long walk around the park had descended not into husband spotting, but rather talking about each other. She was actually starting to care for him. It really was most disagreeable.

"You're in a foul temper suddenly, sister dearest."

Coral rolled her eyes. There were only two situations in which her brother started using phrases like that, and it was never good news. If only she could let out all this frustration, and shout damn to the world.

"What is her name?"

Micah raised his eyebrows in protest. "I did not say there was any such person! Really, I do not know where you get your ideas from."

"I was not born yesterday, you idiot," said Coral good-naturedly. *Well, it was difficult to be angry at Micah for long.* "Come on, there is always a woman in your life, whether a young lady you should absolutely not be touching or a mistress—"

"—a mistress I absolutely should be touching," finished Micah with a wicked grin.

A shameful flush tinged Coral's cheeks as she looked away. She had never…inquired, that was the polite way to put it, about her brother's exploits, though she had heard enough on the rumor mill to get a general idea of the thing.

Gentlemen of the *ton* were accepted to have previous…entanglements before one settled down, but Micah was taking it too far. He appeared to have several mistresses, all dancing around for his affections. And Micah still managed to get a few of the ladies of the gentry into rather sticky situations.

He had not been forced into matrimony yet, Coral thought darkly, *but it was only a matter of time…*

"I do not want to know anything about…about that," Coral said primly, wishing Emerald was here to be even more embarrassed than she. "I merely meant…I do not suppose you would ever introduce me to one of them?"

Her words wiped the smile off Micah's face. "One of my mistresses? You cannot be serious, Coral!"

Coral found, rather to her surprise, that she was. "Well, you spend so much of your time with them, we hardly see you. Gambling halls, dens of iniquity—"

"Sounds delightful, doesn't it?"

"—and your mistresses take up all your time," Coral continued doggedly. She sat up a little to look at her brother more directly. "Honestly, Micah. Do you not ever miss us? Do you not wonder what you are missing?"

Her words appeared to have, finally, struck home. Micah's smile had not reappeared, and he glanced at his hands before resolutely meeting her gaze again.

"Sometimes," he said quietly. "Not with you, gadding about finding husbands—"

"One would be more than enough," interrupted Coral with a sigh.

Micah continued as though she had not spoken. It was always the way with them—talking over each other, half-listening, half-not. It was enough to drive her father up the wall, but their mother had always laughed and said it was the Italian in them.

"—and Emerald is too quiet to be taken anywhere, there is no point in trying," Micah continued.

"And Sapphire?"

There it was again—that slight quiver of shame Coral had spotted earlier. So, her brother did have an idea of how he was disappointing the family, then.

"Sapphire is but fourteen years old," Coral said, pressing home her advantage. "She would benefit from another sibling around the place, trying to keep her in line."

Micah snorted. "You are not afraid I would lead Sapphire astray, into some of my more bad habits?"

Coral glared.

"Not like that!" Micah said hastily, putting his hands up in mock surrender. "The day I take any of my sisters to my favorite gambling den is the day I get shipped out of the de Petras family once and for all! Not that it would matter…"

His voice trailed away, and a strange vulnerability flashed across his face.

Coral breathed out slowly. She knew she would get to it eventually, the real reason Micah was always spending their mother's money and dashing about the place, never staying too long anywhere.

"Does it truly upset you?" Coral asked quietly. "Me being the heir, I mean, instead of you. As it is for every other family."

There was no maliciousness in her brother, but Coral saw the truth before he spoke.

"It is hard," he said heavily. "Lord knows I try not to get

too…too prickly about it. That is the way it is, the way I have always known. You get the money, the name—"

"It's a good thing we don't have a title," said Coral, trying to make him laugh.

It did not work. "You cannot understand what it is to be with one's friends, see them inherit, make decisions, not having to listen to their mother or their sister," said Micah with a sad sort of smile. "Oh, you and Mother are great sorts, Coral, do not misunderstand me…but still. I am alone in this. If I am to gain any wealth and power, I will have to become a self-made man."

Coral nodded. There did not appear to be much else to say, Micah had summarized it so exquisitely.

It was strange. Yet at the same time, it was just as strange for her, but in the other direction. No ladies had the burden of maintaining a family's reputation, not as a whole. No other ladies had received lessons not only in French and art but in household management, stocks and shares, interest rates for bonds, rental prices in Bath…

And she…she would have to find a gentleman who was not only willing to accept that, play second fiddle to her all her life…but would take her name, too.

"You are my little brother," began Coral gently.

Micah chuckled as he shook his head. "Damnit, woman, I am not that much younger than you!"

"You will always be my little brother," Coral said as she joined his laughter. "I am sorry, Micah, but that is just how it is! I will always remember you as the small boy who refused to eat his vegetables. No matter how big you grow."

She had believed her words nothing more than a jest—a continuation of the fine humor she had managed to find in him. But somehow, Coral had crossed a line.

Micah rose abruptly from his seat, a scowl once again across his forehead. "You may think I am nothing but a boy to order about, Coral, but I think you will find that I am making my own way in the world, without the benefits of the de Petras name. I'll see you later."

He had stormed over to the door before Coral could cry, "When—when, Micah?"

The door slammed, and moments later, the front door echoed it.

Coral leaned back against the sofa. Every time she thought she understood him, that she was beginning to make him understand… for some reason he took offense at what she was trying to do and stormed off.

Tension was building in her temples, and she raised a hand to massage them. Being the head of this family was impossible, and she wasn't even the sole one in charge yet. Her mother had managed it for decades, but how, Coral was not entirely sure.

She could not even get her brother to talk to her for more than twenty minutes.

Fresh air. That was what she needed. All this being cooped up indoors, this close to Christmas—it wasn't right.

Within ten minutes—Coral had placed a bonnet on her head, a pelisse over her shoulders, and a fur stole over it for added warmth.

Winter had arrived quickly in London. Most mornings began with snow, though it was often melted by the time Coral stepped outside.

Today, however, the snowfall had been thick enough to leave just over an inch on the pavements. Thankful she had pulled on her winter boots rather than the soft delicate soles she had been preferring until a week ago, Coral breathed in the cold air and started walking.

There was no particular direction that she encouraged her feet to go. There were few streets or paths Coral did not know. But only after five minutes did she realize where her unconscious mind was taking her.

Green Park. Where she had met with Edward, where they had talked, sat on that bench, gone husband-hunting…

Not that it had led to any introductions.

Coral halted, a woman almost walking into her after the sudden change in pace.

She could not go to the park—at least, not that one. The chances of seeing Edward there were high, to be sure, but she could not permit herself to see him. Not after her thoughts had decided to be so disobliging.

No, it was best she went somewhere which did not remind her so strongly of the duke she was starting to want but absolutely knew she could not have.

Resolutely changing direction, Coral strode instead toward Regent's Park. It was a little farther, to be sure, but she would value the exercise—and the opportunity not to have her mind turned once again by a certain duke.

The instant Coral stepped into the park and saw a few riders going along the green verges, a voice called out her name most familiarly.

"Coral—Miss de Petras?"

Coral's stomach lurched, and joy rose in her heart, unable to be battened down. It was Edward. There he was, inexplicably precisely where she had supposed him not to be. Even better, he was striding toward her in a most delightful way, a smile on his face.

"Why, I thought you usually frequented Green Park," he said, bowing as he reached her.

"Did you not go there because you wished to avoid me?"

What had possessed her to say such a thing? It was unconscionable, and Coral waited for the misery of shame to flood through her.

But it did not come. Edward's eyes merely twinkled as he said, "I can neither confirm nor deny that I was avoiding you, Coral. Besides, the last thing I would wish to do is make a fool of myself for you, would I?"

For an instant, Coral wished she could encourage him to do just that. *Be a fool. Be a fool for me. Show me what it is to desire me. Show me what it is to be kissed...*

Not for the first time, Coral's gaze drifted over to Edward's mouth. He had a strong jaw, a handsome one that seemed to be perpetually smiling.

But what if it wasn't? What if it was kissing her, passionately, devotedly, stirring passion in her that Coral had never known, never expected—

"Coral? Coral, are you quite well?"

"Perfectly well, I thank you," Coral managed to say, pulling herself away from the delightful image of Edward kissing her and blinking up at the real Edward who was perturbed by her silence. "I was just…just thinking."

That winning smile was back on Edward's face. "Husband hunting?"

Heat seared Coral's cheeks. She had entirely forgotten she had been given the address of that gentleman, whatever his name was, the one with the yellow cravat she had espied in the coffee house.

He had seemed to be a perfect match—very wealthy, little debt, a delightful sister, a marvelous place in the country, a love of reading, and a little older than she and, therefore, hopefully, willing to accept her rather unusual terms for matrimony…yet in all that time, Coral had never called upon him.

It was strange. At no point had she even thought about him until Edward reminded her.

Why was that, Coral wondered. Perhaps she was not as interested in him as she had thought—though that made little sense. It was not as though she currently had any alternatives at present.

"Take a walk with me," Coral said firmly.

Edward raised his eyebrows.

Coral giggled at his response. "You know, sometimes I wonder why you have never married, Edward."

She took his arm, and that odd yet familiar tingling returned, quivering all over her body. Why was it that she only felt it when in close proximity to Edward, more when she was touching him?

Many layers of fabric lay between them, yet she was utterly

unable to shrug off the feeling that she was being…well. Intimate with him.

"Oh, I never found the right person," said Edward as they started to meander slowly along the path. "Until now."

Until now? What did that mean? Coral blinked up, a strange sort of jealousy soaring through her. Had Edward met someone—a lady who had caught his eye?

The idea of Edward finding another lady attractive…it had never occurred to her. Which was foolishness, of course. She was not going to marry him, so why not someone else?

"I have been thinking about what you said."

Coral shook her head slightly and tried to force a smile. "Which bit?"

"All of it, I suppose," said Edward cheerfully. "Most particularly the bit about your husband taking your name, de Petras. 'Tis most unusual."

"My father certainly thought so, he has told me about it," said Coral with a small laugh. "I do believe the Earl of Maltravers—James's father, I mean—thought him entirely without his wits when he announced it."

"I can see why," said Edward dryly. "There are few men who would consider such a thing, much less do it. Your father must be a strong and principled man."

Coral's heart fluttered painfully. This conversation felt dangerous, intimate in a way she had never discovered before. How was it possible to speak in such a way to a man she had only known a few months?

Yet, it did not feel that way. On the contrary, there were few gentlemen, few people, Coral had felt able to be this open with. Something within Edward encouraged her to speak openly, and she was a rather blunt person to begin with.

That was why when Coral opened her mouth, the most scandalous question emerged. "And would you?"

Edward almost tripped, but he managed to hold his balance. "I beg your pardon?"

"Would you?" repeated Coral, not sure why she was doing this to herself, but certain that she had to ask the question. "Would you consider it, much less do it? Are you a strong and principled man?"

Her heart was pattering painfully and fear, joy, and hope mingled within it. Coral could hardly breathe for waiting for Edward's response. It was not as though Edward was a true contender for her hand, after all. He simply did not satisfy her list.

But the thought occurred to her, and it was a heady one, that Edward could satisfy her in other ways…

Edward stopped, turning to face her but not dropping her arm. Coral found herself pulled closer to him as they stood on the path, a little way from anyone else. His eyes met hers, serious and bright blue, almost flashing in the wintery sunlight.

Coral swallowed. Something in her wanted him, wanted him as she had never wanted a man before. What would it be to kiss him, to be held by him? To know that she was his world, his everything, that nothing in the world mattered as long as they were together?

For a moment, Coral found herself leaning ever so slightly toward him. It was madness, it was glorious, it was going to happen—she was going to kiss him, then—

Edward smiled. "There is a ball coming up, near Christmas Day."

Coral blinked. "Wh-What?"

"A ball," Edward repeated. "I think the Duke of Axwick is holding it, though goodness knows why, the man is so miserable. I thought you may wish to attend."

"A ball…the Duke of Axwick," said Coral stupidly.

Why was it so impossible to get her mind to work? Something odd had happened, something she did not understand and would need to spend time understanding later.

But right now, Coral knew she had to say something. She blinked, and the handsome Duke of Glaenarm swam in and out of focus before her.

"I can certainly gain an invitation for you," said Edward easily, a teasing smile tugging the corner of his lips. "For all of you, except Sapphire, for which she will have to forgive me."

Coral smiled weakly. "All of us."

"There'll be plenty of eligible gentlemen there," Edward said, lowering his voice. "Plenty of stupid ones. Easy to control."

She had to laugh at that. "And you think that is the sort of husband I want?"

The smile that had been dancing on Edward's lips disappeared. "Isn't it?"

Coral swallowed. A few weeks ago, she would have admitted that it was; that a malleable husband was just the sort of thing she wanted.

Now? Now she was not so sure.

She took a deep breath. "A ball. Yes. Marvelous. I'll go to the ball."

CHAPTER TEN

December 15, 1809

"**I** SHOULD NEVER have invited her to that damned ball!"

Edward knew he should not permit his irritation to get the better of him. Knew it was shameless to say such things in public and knew he had created this entire situation for himself; If there was any justice in the world, he would just have to swallow his regret.

But he refused, on all counts. It was ridiculous, it was infuriating, and now he was stuck in precisely the situation he had promised himself he would not get into.

He was truly starting to care for Miss Coral de Petras.

"Well, it was your idea," said James Gresley, Earl of Maltravers, fairly.

Edward glared. "How dare you be so calm and rational."

His friend shrugged, the snow, which had settled on his shoulders as they had walked to the haberdashery, now starting to melt.

"I do not see what the problem is," said Maltravers easily, pulling a drawer and peering inside at the buttons within. "You wanted Coral to be at the Axwick ball. You invited her. You even went to the trouble of speaking to Axwick and ensuring the whole family could attend."

A knot tied itself even tighter in Edward's stomach. When his friend put it like that, he was even more of a fool than he had thought in the first place.

What had possessed him to do it? There he had been, standing in the park, absolutely freezing before Coral had arrived but then dangerously warm once they started walking together...and the words had just slipped out of his mouth.

"There is a ball coming up, near Christmas Day."

It wasn't even his ball! Oh, Edward knew it would be foolish of him indeed to attempt to host a ball this season, not now he had spent so much time with her, apparently helping her to find a perfect husband that did not exist.

"I still do not know why Axwick is hosting a ball," said Edward bad-tempered as he opened a drawer and glared at the gold gilt buttons within. "The man has never been known to throw a ball before."

"I would imagine it is on behalf of his sister," Maltravers said easily.

Edward glared once again at his friend. Here he was, in a time of desperate need, and his friend was being so...so reasonable! It was enough to drive a man to distraction.

"What I do not understand is," continued Maltravers without a care in the world, "after going to all this trouble to ensure Coral was invited, and her family—remind me, did you include Sapphire?"

Edward raised an eyebrow. "No. Why?"

"I just thought she may enjoy being included on the invitation, that was all," said his friend lightly.

A little too lightly. *Just why was Maltravers attempting to be so nonchalant about the youngest de Petras?*

"She is not out, as far as I am aware."

Maltravers shook his head, carefully avoiding his friend's eye. "No, no, I suppose it would have been far too outside the order of things for Axwick to invite a lady who is not officially out. Even for a duke."

Edward stared at his friend. There was something going on, something he did not precisely understand. He had never noticed it before, and perhaps it was a relatively new development in his friend—but was that a flush coming across his cheeks?

"What on earth has got into you?"

"Into me?" said Maltravers hastily, poking a finger into Edward's chest. "You are the one inviting ladies to other people's balls, then panicking about it days later!"

Edward sighed. The man spoke too much truth to refute it—and besides, they needed to keep their voices down. The haberdashery was busy this time in the Season, and the chatter of ladies, giggles of children, and the gruff voice of a gentleman at the counter attempting to find a button to match his waistcoat thankfully covered much of their conversation.

Still. The last thing he needed was for someone else to hear his foolish attempts to…

To what? Impress Coral?

Edward snorted and turned away from the buttons to look at the rolls of material available for waistcoats and cravats.

He was not looking to impress Coral, not really. Not in any greater way than he tried to impress everyone.

It was part of being a duke. One had to be impressive, otherwise what was the point in the title? Just about anyone could call themselves a duke. You needed to be able to tell a duke from a mile off. Something in the way he dressed, the way he held himself. The way he conducted himself with the ladies.

Edward's stomach lurched. He was not doing too well there. After telling himself he was only spending time with Coral to make her care for him—*only*, he had assured himself, *to demonstrate to her that a fine income and a sister and dark hair and a love of Mozart was not the only way to learn to care for a person*—he had instead…

Well. He was not in love. Edward cleared his throat and picked up a sample of material in a dark navy blue. No. He was not thinking about Coral almost every minute of the day. Not thinking about where she could be, what she was doing, and whom she was speaking to.

Not hating whoever it was who was speaking to her. Not wondering what this delightful navy silk would look like next to her fiery red hair.

Not wondering what she would look like in nothing, her hair falling softly past her shoulders—

"Glaenarm!"

Edward started. Blinking, he saw Maltravers was staring at him as though he had become a man possessed, and there were two elderly ladies on the other side of him, evidently attempting to pass him but waiting patiently for him to notice and move aside.

He hastily stepped to the right. "My apologies, ladies."

One of them smiled knowingly, but the other tutted under her breath.

Maltravers waited until they were firmly on the other side of the haberdashery before laughing. "You have lost at least one potential bride there, Glaenarm."

"Very funny," said Edward dourly. *As though any woman could take the place of Coral in his heart...*

Blast. He was well and truly sunk.

There was nothing for it. He would have to attend this ball, kiss Coral—only the once—to get her out of his system, then never see her again.

It would not be too hard. Only the very end of his life as he knew it. Only the depths of misery he had never known before at the very thought of his life stretching on, forever, without the light that Coral brought.

"What was it you wanted in here?"

Edward blinked. Maltravers was still standing before him, and most upsettingly, Coral had not magically appeared. It was most irritating.

"Material for a cravat," Edward said firmly. Yes, that was it. For some reason, none of those in his dressing room in the house seemed good enough.

Which was madness. He had over five and twenty, for goodness' sake. So why, suddenly, were none of them sufficient to wear to a ball that Coral was attending?

"Well, they all look much the same to me," said Maltravers with a shrug as he turned to the rolls and rolls of fabric. "Blues, greens, reds…cannot your valet do this?"

Edward sighed. It was a reasonable question. Such a shame he did not have a reasonable answer. "Yes, I suppose he could, but…well. I wanted to choose it myself."

He knew the moment the words left his mouth he had made a mistake. The mischievous smile that never seemed to be too far from Maltravers's face returned in earnest, but this time, there was an altogether-too-knowing look that accompanied it.

"I see," Maltravers said triumphantly. "You want to impress her!"

"I do not want to impress her," lied Edward swiftly. "Wh- Whomever *she* is."

Blast. It was hardly a resounding success, his lie, and he was almost certain Maltravers had seen right through it. Edward turned away to look up a different shelf of material and tried to tell himself, in no uncertain terms, to get a grip.

This was foolish. He had never felt like this before about any lady of his acquaintance, had never felt feelings like this, never known what it was to have one's mind entirely taken over by desires like this.

Oh, he knew of it, of course. He had seen the lovesick fools at the club, had heard their sighs and moans about how they simply could not go on living unless a certain miss treated them kindly.

Edward had always thought them ridiculous. It usually passed in a year or two, but the time of suffering appeared to be very great. It was not as though he had vowed he would never be one of them, nothing so dramatic as that. He had just never thought he would be.

And now…now Edward knew better.

Forcing aside all thoughts about how delightful and wonderful Coral was, how glorious it was to be in her presence, and how witty her tongue was—and perhaps what else it could do—Edward picked up another piece of material.

"Perhaps this one," he said vaguely.

Maltravers appeared at his side and wrinkled his nose. "Really?"

Edward placed it back without another word. This was intolerable. How was a man supposed to do anything, think anything, get anything done, when one's heart and mind were so affixed on another?

"You want to impress her!"

Yes, he wanted to impress her. Though Edward would never admit it, not aloud—and certainly not to Maltravers, nor in public—the desire to impress Coral, to make her feel the same about him as he felt for her…it was growing with every passing day.

If only she did not have this ridiculous list. If only she could see beyond it, see what a match they could be, see how his lack of aptness should not in any way prevent them from being together if they…

But perhaps not. Edward found it impossible to tell Coral the truth now—after spending so many days together in discussion about the right person to marry, after their walks together, after making her laugh and seeing the way her eyes glittered when she looked at him…

Would she have been so open, so unguarded with him if she had known he had been attempting to gain her affections? Would she have happily sat with him in the coffee house, gone for walks in the park, if she had thought he was pursuing her?

Edward swallowed. All these thoughts were nonsense, of course. Declaring his affections for Coral would mean nothing but rejection. She had made herself perfectly clear, had she not, that she felt comfortable with him precisely because he did not fit her list of conditions?

Edward's stomach turned. No, that he would not do—but he was starting to get himself into real trouble, his heart truly affected. Days were either filled with Coral or filled with longing. Edward hated the weakness within him, how swiftly he had found himself caught.

"And you have traversed through two entire Seasons and only received one proposal of marriage?"

"Not…not exactly."

"How many then?"

"Almost twenty."

Only now did he understand just how Coral had received so many proposals. Any gentleman who spent more than ten minutes with the woman became intoxicated! It made Edward wonder how on earth Maltravers had managed to remain immune…

"What about this one?" his friend said, pointing at a bolt of dark green silk. "I think I can get it down, wait a moment…"

Edward stared at his friend but said nothing. *Perhaps Maltravers was not immune. Perhaps he was one of the casualties—perhaps even…*

"Maltravers," Edward found himself saying, "have you ever proposed marriage to Coral de Petras?"

Maltravers's fingers slipped, pulling down the entire rack of fabric. Festoons of blue, white, yellow, red, and orange fabric appeared to fall from the sky, billowing out, covering the haberdashery.

Shrieks rang out as ladies were covered by the falling fabric, and somewhere to his left, mainly under a large bolt of black satin, was a laughing Maltravers.

"What on earth have you done?" Edward said, laughing himself. Well, it was so ridiculous—only a man like Maltravers could do such a thing. "You fool!"

"It was hardly done on purpose now, was it?" chuckled Maltravers, pulling the bolt of fabric from him and looking gleefully across the haberdashery, which resembled a rainbow.

Edward caught sight of the haberdasher, spluttering in outrage at the destruction of his shop, and sighed heavily. "I hope you have enough coin to pay for all this."

That wiped the smile from Maltravers's face. "You cannot think—you honestly believe he will require me to pay for it? All of it?"

Edward shrugged. "If he cannot sell it, I am afraid you will have enough material to last you the end of your days!"

"Absolutely not," said Maltravers firmly. "I shall send my seamstress over to help him tidy if that is what he requires, but I cannot consider—"

"James! Edward, what on earth are you doing here, coated in fabric?"

Edward's stomach lurched, and the knot which had been such a bother in his stomach started to loosen as the warm glow of Coral's presence washed over him.

There she was, standing on the other side of the haberdashery, thankfully not covered in material—though there was a smile on her face that Edward both adored and did not like.

"It was not me," Edward said hastily. "It was Maltravers! James!"

A gentle shove on his shoulder told him Maltravers did not appreciate having his guilt loudly broadcast around the shop, but it was too late.

"Maltravers?" The haberdasher was still struggling to get through to them, but the look on his face told Edward he was going to continue trying, come what may. "Maltravers!"

Maltravers sighed heavily. "Now you have got me into trouble, Glaenarm—are you happy now?"

"Yes," said Edward simply. Well, what else could he say? Coral was here—a chance meeting that had lifted his spirits and his heart rate. "Go on, talk to the man."

Grumbling under his breath about faithless friends and what one should do to them when betrayed, Maltravers forced his way through the fabric over to the counter.

Coral, on the other hand, stepped over to Edward, whose lungs tightened with every step closer she got.

She was so…so elegant. While others struggled through the fabric constricting their path, Coral was somehow able to just lightly meander over to him as though it was nothing. As though she could walk on air.

Edward swallowed. He was starting to know the feeling.

"Hello," he said, nerves overtaking him at the last second, reducing his carefully constructed welcome to a single word.

Coral smiled. She looked marvelous. Edward was surprised she was not mobbed on the street as she made her way here, she was so fetching.

Blast. He truly needed to calm himself, or he was certain he would start to say things he was thinking, the truth instead of the trick he was playing on her. All he had to do was make her admit his feelings for him…

"You have come to buy some fabric?" Coral asked, an eyebrow raised.

"Nowhere near the amount Maltravers has upended, I assure you. Just enough for a cravat."

She nodded, as though that was to be expected. "Perhaps you are more fashionable than you give yourself credit for."

His stomach lurched most painfully. "Perhaps I am. Perhaps I meet other requirements on your list, too."

He should not have spoken. Coral raised an eyebrow with a teasing laugh that told him in no uncertain terms that she greatly appreciated his joke.

If only it had been one.

"Edward—Your Grace, I mean," she said, suddenly conscious of where they were. "We have spoken on this, you do not match the list."

"Perhaps not," Edward found himself saying, heat pounding through his veins. "But have you ever considered that you may one day meet a man who does not meet your list, but improves upon it?"

Her eyes met his, shining in the sunlight pouring through the haberdasher's window, and Edward's stomach lurched most painfully.

What was she thinking? Did she understand what he was saying, what he was trying to say? Did he even understand what he meant?

"I think not," Coral said quietly.

Edward did his best not to permit his shoulders to sag overly much. They were in public, after all, and even if they had been alone, he did not wish Coral to see just how devastated he was by her words.

No, they needed to talk about something else. Quickly.

"Yes, a cravat," he said firmly. "And what about you? A new gown, perhaps?"

Coral laughed as she shook her head. "No, I thank you. I came for a ribbon only."

She lifted her hand, and Edward saw what he had not seen before—a delicate fold of navy blue silk. The same silk he had pondered over not twenty minutes ago and tried to consider what it would be like against her hair. Her hair and her naked body.

Heat rushed through Edward's body as he tried to calm himself, but he could not help it. The image of Coral, naked and squirming under his touch, appeared once again in his mind.

Oh, if only he could bed her, just once, purge her from the system and find himself free of her. Edward could not understand it but knew he had never failed to remove a woman from his system in such a way.

Surely Coral would be just the same?

"And...and what will your plan be?"

Coral frowned slightly. "My plan?"

Edward nodded. That was it, talk of the ball—the perfect distraction from the growing need to touch her. "Your plan of attack, as it were. After all, there will be a number of gentlemen there who fit your criteria, and you will need to decide how to approach them all. How...how to attract them."

Why had his voice grown so hoarse at the end of that sentence? Edward hated himself for the weakness he was showing, but he could not help it. He had to have her, and soon.

"Oh, that will be easy," said Coral with a smile. "I will simply look dazzlingly beautiful, of course."

She laughed, as though her jest was remarkably clever, but Edward did not join her. He merely looked at her, pain filling his heart.

Yes, that would be sufficient. Any gentleman not staring at Coral with her sparkling eyes and navy blue ribbon drawing even more attention to her fiery red hair would be a fool indeed. She would have the entire ball eating out of her hand.

"You are not laughing."

Edward shook his head slowly as Maltravers's argument with the haberdasher reached new heights. "It is not funny. I do not laugh at the truth."

Coral looked startled by his words, her eyes meeting his—and for the first time, Edward was left in absolutely no doubt.

She wanted him. She desired him in a way she did not quite understand, he could see that now, and if they had been anywhere else, Edward would have fulfilled the unspoken, desperate cry of her heart and shown her just what pleasure could be found in his arms.

Would that spark Coral's desire enough for her to rush into his arms?

But just as he was considering how he could create such a situation, Edward's lips opened of their own accord and said something he had certainly not intended to say.

"May I have the first dance?"

Coral's lips parted in surprise, just for a moment. "The—the first dance?"

Edward nodded. He could no longer trust his lips, it seemed, not while he was so focused on hers. Oh, to taste of those lips—to show Coral just what she was starting to mean to him...

"And how am I supposed to meet the perfect man if I am

dancing with you?" Coral asked with a raised eyebrow.

Edward swallowed. What he wanted to say—that the thought of her dancing with anyone else was enough for him to reach for his dueling pistols and call the devil out for even thinking of touching her—was probably not the right thing to say.

At least, not yet.

"I…I could make them jealous," he said in a flash of inspiration.

"Now, really, that is absolutely not what the fabric is worth!" came the exhausted cry of Maltravers from the counter.

Coral smiled. "Jealous, you say?"

He had to secure it, the first dance at Axwick's ball. Then if the evening did not pan out how he had wanted, well, he could not be blamed for it.

It would all depend on that first dance.

"Jealous," he said as firmly as he could manage. "After all, you will be dancing with a duke."

"A duke that I have made quite clear I will not marry," Coral pointed out.

Edward grinned. "They don't know that."

She examined him closely, and for a heart-stopping moment, he was sure she had finally seen through his pretense and was ready to censor him for attempting to steal her heart when he knew she had decided against him—right before she fell into his arms to accept the lovemaking she so desperately wanted.

But instead, she nodded. "I suppose you are right. It is agreed then. We will dance the first—oh Lord!"

Coral's eyes had drifted over Edward's shoulder, and for a moment he thought Maltravers might have done something foolhardy. Punched the haberdasher on the nose, for example.

But as he looked around, he saw nothing vexing—he did see Mrs. Opal de Petras walking into the haberdashery, however.

"Goodness, we cannot have my mother thinking that—well," said Coral hastily, smiling but stepping away from him.

Edward followed her instinctively, hating the idea of her

leaving. "But—"

"I will see you at the ball if not before," said Coral cheerily. "Goodbye, Your Grace."

She was gone before he could say another word. Looking helplessly after her, knowing he was wretched and lost without her, Edward sighed heavily, shoulders sagging. Now he was only left with—

"Five guineas, and that is my final offer!"

CHAPTER ELEVEN

December 23, 1809

THE DUKE OF AXWICK'S townhouse was far more impressive than anything Coral had ever seen. Tall columns surrounded its doorway, and a line of carriages was waiting to deposit their inhabitants beside it. The de Petras carriage waited in line, as expected, and Coral's heart pattered softly yet with an increasing pace as the carriage drew slowly nearer and nearer.

The Duke of Axwick's ball.

Few people had ever been to the place, let alone attended a ball there—at least, not in this duke's time.

She had never attended any event hosted by a duke; the most impressive invitations were from Maltravers, and they did not count. Even an earl ceased to be exciting when a friend of the family.

"Almost there," said Opal under her breath. "Almost at the door."

Coral glanced at her mother. It was unlike her to be overwhelmed. Coral could well remember a time in her first Season when someone had made a rather inappropriate remark about her gown—unfashionable as it was—and Opal had actually taken the gentleman by the collar, marched him to the door of Lady Romeril's home, and pitched him out. Not without muttering a few dark warnings about returning and darkening doors, either.

Lady Romeril had applauded her mother when she returned, and Opal had only flushed a little. Coral had been mortified. Opal had explained later that she and Lady Romeril had an understanding about riffraff, whatever that meant.

But tonight, her most splendid necklace resting on her collarbones and an inordinate number of pins in her hair, Coral thought her mother looked…well, ruffled.

"Do not expect too much," murmured Jasper.

Coral smiled. Sometimes she underestimated him. She was not the only one who could feel her mother's tension, then.

"I am not expecting—"

"Yes, you are, and you will only find yourself disappointed," Jasper said in an undertone, a smile on his face as the carriage rumbled forward. "I have it on good authority the Duke of Axwick has no wish to be married, and I see no reason to doubt a gentleman's word."

Opal visibly deflated. "Oh."

That was most disappointing. She had never met the Duke of Axwick in person, of course, but from what she knew of him, he seemed a most delightful gentleman. Likely to complete the list, too.

Coral nudged her sister Emerald to ask her whether she truly thought the Duke of Axwick had no wish for marriage—but Emerald was looking out of the window, her hands tight fists of anxiety in her lap.

"I had no idea there were so many people," she whispered. "The Duke of Axwick's ball is popular, then?"

"Not so, my dear," Opal said hastily, throwing a smile in Coral's direction. "The guest list is, for a duke's ball, rather limited. I am impressed, Coral, you must have made a fine impression on the duke to receive an invitation."

Coral frowned at her mother. Had she not been entirely clear, right from the beginning, that the Duke of Glaenarm was not going to receive any encouragement for advances—not that he would make any. Not now she had been so clear about it.

A small prickle of regret curled around her heart, but she pushed it aside. It was all to the good, she was sure, that Edward had absolutely no ideas of courting her.

"Indeed, I had not even realized you had met the duke," said Opal with a wide smile. "You charmer, Coral, you kept that very close to your chest."

Coral blinked. *Not realized she had—her mother had invited him to her very own luncheon!*

And then the pieces fell together.

"Oh, Mama, you are mistaken," said Coral warmly, hoping to correct her mother's misunderstanding as swiftly as possible. "It was not the Duke of Axwick who invited me to his ball, although, of course, he did approve the suggestion. No, it was the Duke of Glaenarm."

She should have kept her mouth firmly shut. Coral could see a glowing light of excitement appear in Opal's eyes at the mention of Edward.

"The Duke of Glaenarm!" Opal beamed. "You have not given up on him then, that is most excellent."

"Mama, no," Coral attempted to say, but she was completely overrun.

"He is a most excellent fellow, I do declare, and so handsome! And you know a title can cover a multitude of shortcomings, and your dowry is—"

"My dowry is gone," interrupted Coral curtly, trying desperately not to look at her sister. "You think I would not impoverish myself so that my siblings have the chance to make a good match—a love match?"

Opal had the good grace to look abashed. "Well…well, you did not have to—"

"I think we are almost there," said Jasper hastily, drawing the awkward discussion to a close. "Yes, here we are."

As he spoke, the carriage door was opened by a footman in a most impressive livery. It was unfortunate that it was on the side

Emerald was sitting. Her eyes widened, her surprise at being the first expected to descend from the carriage obviously overwhelming.

"I will go first, if you do not mind, Em?" her father asked in a low voice.

Emerald appeared to be unable to speak. Coral bit her lip as their father descended the carriage, gently yet firmly declining the necessity of a footman at all, putting his own hand out to help his daughters down.

Her sister was two and twenty, yet still, she treated any social occasion as though it was personally designed to offend her. There was nothing for it, of course; Emerald had always been a shy child and had grown into a woman who would rather stay at the sidelines than speak to a single person.

No, that was not quite right, Coral thought as she smoothed her skirts and looked at the Axwick house. *Emerald would rather not be at a social occasion at all.*

"Well, here we are," said Opal breathlessly, her smile returned. "In we go!"

The hall of the Axwick home was resplendent, and Coral tried not to let her amazement show as she allowed her wrap to be taken by a footman. Emerald stammered something about making sure she got it back to the unfortunate servant who was attending her.

"My, my, you are dressed beautifully, Coral," said Opal approvingly, just before they stepped into the ballroom which a footman was indicating. "Remarkably well, actually."

Coral rolled her eyes. She could almost hear the unspoken words from her mother: *are you here to impress a certain someone? A certain duke, by any chance?*

"All the better to eat them with, Mama," she said sweetly.

Her mother opened her mouth to undoubtedly reprove her nonsense, but it did not matter. Firstly, because Coral herself had felt the indignity of the words and had flushed a little at her audacity.

Eat them with! Such a sensuous thing to say, and in public, too!

Not that her sister had heard a word. She was hurriedly whispering something to their father, who was evidently attempting to calm her.

And secondly, because at that very moment, the footmen opened the double doors to the ballroom, and the de Petras family were hit with a wave of sound, music, laughter, and curious eyes turning in their direction.

"Mrs. Opal de Petras, Mr. Jasper de Petras, Miss Coral de Petras, and Miss Emerald de Petras!"

A loud voice just to the left shouted their names, a man wearing the same livery as the footmen. *They were officially announced.*

Coral swallowed. She was not as nervous as Emerald, nor as forward as Sapphire, but even she found this overwhelming. For all the talk that a select group had received invitations, it certainly felt as though the whole of the *ton* had received one.

The Axwick ballroom was large; in fact, thanks to its mirrored design, it was hard to tell just how large it was. Countless ladies in elegant empire-line gowns, feathers and ribbons in their hair, stared at the approaching de Petras family. Gentlemen halted their conversations to turn and look, their chatter rising in volume.

"Oh, I would much rather go home," whispered Emerald under her breath as the four de Petrases walked forward, Opal inclining her head to a few people she evidently knew.

"Do not be silly, Emerald," Coral hissed back, trying to keep a smile on her face as she did so. "It is just a ball."

"Just a—"

"Emerald de Petras, control yourself," Opal said with a sympathetic look. "You are fortunate, indeed, to be invited to such a place, and if you think for one moment I will let you depart without even dancing a single—"

"Let us stand over here, out of the way of the doors," said Jasper calmly, offering his arm to his wife.

Opal closed her mouth, took her husband's arm, and the four

of them moved to the side, collecting in a group by the wall where a bracket of candles glimmered.

"I would rather have stayed at home," said Emerald in a low voice as soon as the four turned in as a circle.

Coral's gaze had slipped past her sister's shoulder and across the ballroom. There were plenty of faces here she recognized—some more familiar, and more friendly than others—but one was missing.

Where was he?

"—part of being a lady in Society," her mother was saying in a low voice as she gently fanned herself, appearing to all the world as though no debate with her daughter was happening at all. "And the sooner you become accustomed—"

"Lady Romeril!" announced the man.

Coral was remarkably glad they were turned in upon themselves, making it almost impossible for Lady Romeril to see them. Whether or not she was an old friend of her mother's, she had no need for the woman's acerbic tongue tonight.

"Why could not Sapphire have come instead of me?" Emerald said earnestly. "She wishes to attend such things while they are nothing but—"

"Sapphire? Here?" Jasper could not help but laugh. "My dear girl, she is not out!"

The same old argument. Of course, they had not thought to have it at home, nor in the carriage; they had to have it right here, before the entire Axwick party.

But it was surely not the entire party. *Edward was not here.*

A slight pang clutched at her heart as Coral's eyes darted about the place in search of him. It was most unaccountable; he had specifically asked her to come, had made it all good with the Duke of Axwick himself, had extended the invitation to the entire de Petras family.

They had not been able to find Micah, to her mother's great shame, and Sapphire had considered it most irritating that her mother had not permitted her to come out into Society purely for this ball, but still.

That did not explain where Edward—

"—cannot behave yourself, I will have no choice but to—"

The double doors to the great hall opened once more, and the incredibly loud gentleman spoke again.

"Edward Barlow, Duke of Glaenarm!"

All four of the de Petrases' heads turned.

Coral could not help it. The entire ball seemed to be a waste, somehow, if Edward was not in it—which was ridiculous, because as they had agreed, she was only here to hunt down a husband with a sufficient fortune.

If only her sister and parents had not been so equally eager to see him.

"We are here for Coral, after all," hissed Emerald under her breath. "I assure you, no one would notice if I—Coral?"

Coral did not reply. She was already stepping away from her family, away from their gossiping and worrying, toward the gentleman whose presence she had been longing for, even if she had not recognized the emotion at first.

Her heart leapt as he grinned. *Edward.* Was there ever a man so handsome? Coral was not the only woman, she could see, transfixed by his presence—but she alone received his smile.

"What kept you?" she asked in a low voice as she reached him.

Edward bowed, a look of astonishment on his face. "I had not realized you were waiting for me."

The words came tumbling from her mouth. "I have been waiting for you since the moment I arrived."

She flushed at her forward words, but there was no point taking them back. They had been spoken, and if she was not very much mistaken, they were warmly received.

"I make it my business never to arrive at a ball until right before the dancing is to begin," Edward said lightly. "Shall we?"

As though the musicians had been waiting for his very words, they struck up their first note, indicating a country dance. Coral took the proffered arm and once again felt that tingle of expectation rush through her.

Which was only for the dance, of course. It could mean nothing else.

Firmly looking away from her family, who would undoubtedly be embarrassing her mightily for dancing the first with a duke, Coral felt a little bereft as Edward placed her in the line of ladies and then released her hand.

It was strange. In the months she had known him, Coral was starting to become…well, dependent on him, truth be told. She liked his presence. Needed it, whenever she could have it.

Which was ridiculous. Edward was becoming more friend than a flatterer. More like Maltravers, a friend of the family, than a gentleman wooing her.

Why, she would feel nothing at all when they danced together, she was sure.

So, when Coral stepped forward and clasped hands with Edward, she gasped as his touch sparked something hot and thunderous.

Did he feel it, too? Coral looked amazed into Edward's eyes but saw only something she did not understand. A small smile teased his lips, but he said nothing as his hands moved to her waist, throwing pleasurable ripples through her body that Coral had not expected.

It was her imagination, surely—but as the music continued and she stepped along the row with him, his hands by her waist, her hands up against his chest, Coral found to her great surprise that her heart was racing, and…

She swallowed as the contact ended, the dance separating them as they turned away and stepped around the lady and gentleman to their left. This was impossible. She was not—she did not have feelings for Edward!

Feelings were what would grow once she found her perfect husband, Coral knew—yet at this moment, she was not entirely sure what she knew.

The dance brought them together again, and this time Coral

was eager for his touch, desperate to be close to him, and was rewarded with a strange warm tug just below her stomach as Edward placed his hands on her waist again.

Coral tried to speak, tried to say anything, but she could not. Desire was rushing through her body. She could name it, even if she did not understand where it had come from.

Desire. Desire for Edward. Desire for his touch. Desire for more…

Mind clouded with desperate sensations Coral had never felt before, the dance whirled forward, faster and faster, and Coral found herself crying out for more, more of this heady momentum that seemed to be pitching her and Edward toward—

The dance ended.

The music stopped, the ladies on either side of her curtseyed as their partners bowed, but Coral could not move. Her heart thundered, her pulse roaring, and there was an ache in her body that had never been there before.

Edward did not bow. He was looking at her, all smiles gone from his lips, as though something truly astonishing had happened. Coral tried to swallow, but her mouth was dry. She needed to say something, needed to bring this spell they were under to an end, whatever it was.

But she could not. Neither could he unless she was much mistaken. Perhaps she was. She certainly did not understand quite what had just happened there.

But not knowing what to think did not mean she did not know how to feel.

And she wanted him. *Edward.* As she had never wanted a gentleman before.

Oh, she had read about this in books, romances that tore a woman from her family, her friends, everything she knew, because she simply had to be with the man before her.

Coral had never given it much credit. She did now.

"I…" Coral cleared her throat as best she could, but still, no words came out. She smiled weakly.

Edward stepped toward her, closing the gap as the other couples drifted away.

"Coral," he murmured quietly.

She felt it rush through her, the need in his voice. What did it mean? How could they have shared something so intense, so special, before so many people? Before the entirety of the Duke of Axwick's ball? Before her family.

The thought was like cold water, dousing her all over and bringing her back to her senses. Her family was here—and if they were to see her and Edward standing here like fools, doing nothing, saying nothing, they would certainly get a most incorrect view.

Completely incorrect. Nonsensical, in fact.

"I should return to my family," said Coral quietly.

Edward nodded slowly. "Yes. Yes, I suppose you must dance with other gentlemen."

Coral tried to smile, but there was something wrong with her jaw. "Yes. I must find my perfect husband, after…after all."

Why did her words feel so stilted? So false? When she spoke them to Edward, they tasted bitter.

"Yes, I suppose you must," said Edward with a laugh that sounded a little harsh to Coral's ear. "But before you do that, let me show you something."

Instead of offering her his arm, he took her hand in his and started leading her across the ballroom, away from her family.

Coral cast a look back and saw the surprised look on her sister's face, the approving nod of her mother—but before she could even sigh with the predictability of it all, Edward increased his pace and she was forced to turn.

Edward clearly knew the Axwick home well, for he pulled her to a nondescript door that creaked open as he turned the handle.

Coral gasped as they stepped outside into the garden. Icy lawn cracked beneath their feet, and the chill was truly quite astonishing.

"Edward!"

Edward closed the door and pulled her further into the garden without saying a word.

Coral's heart beat faster, confusion governing her. The garden? What on earth could Edward need to show her out here, in the garden, in the evening, in winter?

"Edward?"

He halted at the sound of his name. They were standing underneath a tree, its branches bare yet glistening as streams of candlelight escaped through the ballroom windows.

There was a strange look on his face, and Coral took a hesitant step closer to see him clearer. A look she did not recognize, a look of…hunger?

"Well, here we are," Coral said helplessly. "What was it you wanted to show me?"

"This," said Edward, a growl in his throat.

Before Coral knew it, before she could do anything or say anything to prevent it—even if she had wanted to—Edward had grabbed hold of her arms, pulled her toward him, and crushed his lips on hers.

Her very first kiss. This was perhaps not the circumstances in which Coral had expected to receive it, but that did not matter. Sparks of pleasure shot through her, pleasure that only increased as Edward tilted her head gently and teased her lips open, his tongue ravishing her mouth and causing that ache she did not understand to shift and grow within her.

Coral lost herself in the kiss, in Edward, in the passion he poured down on her. Fingers entangled in his hair, and her body pressed up against him, she lost all sense of time and place as the kiss continued on into eternity.

Eventually, painfully, the kiss ended.

Coral blinked up at him, eyes dazed. He had kissed her. Edward had kissed her—and most thoroughly, too.

"Wh-Why did you want to…to show me that?" Coral stammered, heart racing.

"So that when you kiss one of your perfect husband candidates," said Edward in a low voice, eyes fixed upon hers, "you know. You will know what it should feel like."

Without another word, Edward strode away, slamming the door to the ballroom.

Coral half leaned, half fell against the tree trunk as her legs quivered with unresolved passion. *What on earth?*

CHAPTER TWELVE

December 28, 1809

HE WAS A damned fool. He had been born a damned fool, he was certainly living like a damned fool, and he would surely die like a damned fool.

Edward stared endlessly into the blaze in the library grate. The fire had been built up high that morning, and he had been feeding it ever since, ignoring breakfast, ignoring luncheon, focused on nothing else but his own misery.

He was an idiot. Even the supposed joys of Christmas had not been able to dull the aching irritation within him. At himself. All because of his own stupid actions.

"So that when you kiss one of your perfect husband candidates, you know. You will know what it should feel like."

Edward groaned into the silence of the library. He had given orders he was not to be disturbed, naturally, so he could stay here and think on his own stupidity in peace. He had thought, for a time, that if he could just get it through his system, he would stop feeling as though he had been an utter cad.

"Wh-Why did you want to…to show me that?"

A reasonable question and one that Edward, at this moment, simply could not answer. What was it for? Why had he taken it upon himself to do something he knew would be anathema to his soul? He was not one to go about kissing ladies who did not expect it.

The image of Coral's face, eyes wide in shock yet without approbation, appeared in his mind.

Edward's manhood twitched.

Damnit. It was all Axwick's fault. If the man had even been present, then perhaps he would have felt some sort of decorum, would have been able to control himself, prevent himself from making such an ass of himself.

As it was...

"I suppose you must dance with other gentlemen."

"Yes. I must find my perfect husband, after...after all."

"Yes, I suppose you must. But before you do that, let me show you something."

Edward sighed heavily.

It had been a tease, at least at first. He had only intended to give the woman a small peck on the lips. Just something to make her flush. Just something to make the day different, to remind her of the stakes she was playing with.

That she was playing with? Edward almost laughed at the thought. No, the moment his lips had touched hers, he had been lost. Overcome with desire, but more than desire, something akin to real feeling. Edward had been unable to stop himself.

Perhaps she was the one playing with him.

It would certainly explain a lot. Perhaps she considered him a suitable candidate, even without a sister or that damnable dark hair, and was just waiting for him to speak. That would explain why Coral was always in his thoughts, in his dreams, twisting and turning, always out of reach as his fingertips grazed her skin.

Edward cleared his throat and looked longingly at his drinks cabinet. It was far too early to indulge, and he was not going to capitulate just because he had lost his heart to a woman who evidently did not want it.

There. He had thought it, the words he had been trying to avoid for so long.

He cared for her. Though she had done nothing to attain it, Coral's mere presence, her joy, her teasing wit, her beauty had been enough to attract him. More than attract him. Cause Edward to make foolish, rash decisions.

And at the end of the day, if she had any desire for him at all, would she not have written to him? Visited? Done something to see him?

Five days, Edward thought miserably. Five long days—to be sure, including Christmas, but still—since that kiss, that heady kiss he could not stop thinking about…and he had heard nothing.

Not a peep. Not a whit. Not even a hastily scrawled note, one he had dreamed about, covered in ink splotches and declarations of love…

Edward forced himself to sit up straight and pull a book from the shelf behind him. He was being ridiculous—no, worse than ridiculous. He was being idiotic.

What was the first thing Coral had said to him?

"What is your income, Your Grace?"

He had to smile, even if his heart was breaking. Coral had always been clear about what she wanted from a gentleman, had made it so public she had caused more gossip than Edward had ever heard, and it was not his place to decide if that was right or wrong.

Were not other ladies just as mercenary, yet far more coquettish? Did they not preen and strut about, hoping to attract the most impressive of gentlemen, yet giggle and laugh when it was suggested to them, as though they had never thought of such a thing?

At least Coral had been honest.

Edward glanced at the book that he had picked from the shelf. *Arcana Naturae, Ope & Beneficio Exquisitissimorum Microscopiorum*. Dear Lord.

He placed it back on the shelf and leaned back in his chair, trying not to let his thoughts wander to Coral. To what she could be doing right now. To whom she could be talking. Perhaps a gentleman at a card party, or a gentleman in the park, or a gentleman at a tea party…

In short, anyone but him.

Edward's jaw clenched, but it was no good. He had to do something, but precisely what, he was not sure. Sending a note himself was a surefire way to encourage Mrs. de Petras into thinking he had some sort of intentions toward her daughter.

And he did not. Probably.

Yet the desire to see Coral again was growing most painfully, preventing Edward from thinking or doing anything that may be described in any way as helpful. He had found himself waking in the night in a cold sweat, with the strange sensation that he had been expected to do something and only just then remembered what it was.

"Wh-Why did you want to…to show me that?"

Edward clenched his hands as he attempted to slacken his jaw. He was developing a headache from all this tension, but what was he supposed to do? He could hardly just turn up outside the de Petras house and demand to speak to Coral, then…

What?

There were not words for what he was feeling. A stiffness in his body that he was not close to her, a desperate need to know where she was, whether she was safe and happy.

And, of course, the rather strident need to possess her, body and soul, in his bed.

Edward cleared his throat. Perhaps that was a particular impulse that he should, in all faith, attempt to quell.

Above it all was this strange sense, one Edward had never felt before, that it was not his place to do anything. She was a de Petras, after all—how had she put it?

"I am the heir of the de Petras family."

She was the one who would be leading the de Petras family in the next generation—a strange thought, one Edward had considered for some time. Coral was the one who would be the head of the house, with all the financial responsibility that came with it. She was the one who would give her name to her future husband… Unless they could reach a compromise…

Edward de Petras, Duke of Glaenarm. That would never do.

Clearing his throat violently, as though he was almost choking, Edward shook his head. He should not have even thought that. It seemed a ridiculous thing. Dukes did not relinquish their titles or names.

Pushing the tantalizing idea from his mind, he rose from his seat and paced along the bookshelves, looking for a tome that would adequately distract him from foolish thoughts. It appeared, however, that there was no such book in his library. It was most inconvenient. There was clearly a need to restock his library with more interesting books.

Or my life, Edward thought wryly, *with less interesting women.*

But the idea of removing Coral from his life was a repellent one, one that made his entire mind rebel. No, if he was not to have Coral in his life there would be little point, as far as he could tell, in living.

After their tête-à-tête by the tree outside, that kiss which had rocked Edward to his boots and made it almost impossible to think, he had left the garden, left the ballroom, left Axwick's place entirely.

But perhaps he had been too hurried. Perhaps Coral had entered the ballroom desperately searching for him but had instead been introduced to an idiot who by some chance actually met the conditions of her list. One she had danced with, laughed with, and introduced to her parents…

"No," whispered Edward into the silence of the library.

Surely not. But there was no reason why not. It was not as though Coral was beholden to him, not as though she had made any promises to him. Nor he to her.

Edward dropped heavily into the armchair by the fire again as regret poured through him. Not for kissing her, that would be a memory he took to the grave, one he would treasure.

But leaving like that, without so much as a kind word. Edward could not explain it, save his mind had been whirling, his senses overwhelmed by just how much he'd wanted her.

It had taken a great deal of self-control not to push her against that tree trunk and take her precisely how he wanted.

"Your Grace?"

Edward started. His eyes had drifted closed as he had lost himself once more in the memory of that kiss, the dozy warmth of the room encouraging him toward slumber.

But he could not sleep. The library door had opened, entirely without him hearing it, and now a footman was standing before him, peering at the duke.

Edward cleared his throat as he sat straighter, glaring at the unfortunate footman as though it were he who had been caught in a rather foolish position.

"Yes?" he asked aggressively.

The footman took the tiniest of steps back, perhaps an inch. Guilt rushed through Edward—was it not enough that he was miserable, but he had to make everyone around him miserable, too?

"A visitor for you, Your Grace," said the footman in his best announcing voice.

Edward frowned. "A visitor? Now? I said I was not to be—"

"Miss Coral de Petras, Your Grace," said the footman, bowing as he stepped aside to reveal Coral standing in the doorway.

Edward almost tripped over his own feet as he rose hastily, heart pounding as he took in the sight of the most beautiful woman in the world.

Coral de Petras. She was wearing that gown he was becoming so fond of, the red with gold feathers embroidered across the bodice. Out of fashion, yes, but it suited her. He had a slight suspicion it was not the gown, but instead, its wearer that was becoming so damn dear to him.

"Coral," he said blankly.

She curtseyed low, as was due his rank, and Edward stared in astonishment until he realized the footman was still there. He was standing to the side it was true, but curious eyes flickered over them.

Edward smiled weakly. He should not have said Coral's name—he should have called her Miss de Petras. But how could he after what they had shared?

"That will be all, thank you," he said curtly to Frost, the footman.

For the first time ever, Edward thought Frost was about to disagree with him, request to stay to watch whatever this strange scene was going to be—but with a glare from his master, the footman bowed low and slipped out of the library.

Edward's smile disappeared. What on earth was he supposed to do now?

Coral was equally silent, her eyes downcast, as though she had come with bad news.

Edward's stomach lurched. Had something happened? Had she decided it was simply not possible for the two of them to spend more time together? After his rash kiss, his silent declaration of affection she evidently could not return, was she here to ask him to stay away?

But then why come at all?

Edward swallowed, tasting the fear in his throat. Whatever reason had spurred Coral to come here, it was surely not good. That meant he had to have it over with as soon as possible.

"Won't...won't you sit down?" he asked awkwardly.

"I won't," she said quietly.

The tension in Edward's stomach knotted tighter. Why did she not just come out and say it? He had offended her. She had not wished for the kiss, and he had entirely imagined her enjoyment.

All the intimacy between them, the easy conversation, the way Edward had always felt entirely himself when he was with her...it was all gone. Over. Done for.

There was nothing for it now but to apologize, receive her staid acceptance, which would not be honest but at least polite, and then wave her goodbye as she left him.

Forever.

"I…" Edward cleared his throat. This was ridiculous, he had never had such trouble speaking to anyone before, let alone a lady. "I feel I ought to—to apologize."

That got her attention. Coral lifted her gaze, meeting his with absolutely no emotion. Oh, how Edward hated to see her so cold, so aloof. He had never realized how precious their connection was until he had lost it.

"Why?" asked Coral quietly, taking a step toward him.

Had this been love? It was certainly heartbreak, that Edward did know. To hear her speak like that to him, as though he was nothing, as though they had shared nothing, were nothing to each other…it was anathema.

But then, he had not asked for any promises, had he? He had given no assurances—in fact, they had been quite clear to each other that they had no desire for each other at all…

"This was not, after all this, a trick to woo me, was it?"

"I should not have kissed you," Edward said awkwardly. "I…it was wrong of me."

Coral was still gazing at him, curiosity across her face. "Why?"

She took another step forward. Edward's heart, traitorous as it was, gloried in the closeness between them but knew it meant nothing. Why, he'd had Coral in his arms just a few days ago, and had been kissing her the best he could—and still he had not convinced her. Not stirred her to anything.

"You know why," said Edward quietly.

Coral took a final step toward him so that she stood but a few inches from him. "No. I know nothing of the thought. All I know is that I have not been able to think of anything else save that kiss since you strode away from me."

Edward's jaw dropped. He could not have heard her correctly. Coral had not said those words—not Coral de Petras, the woman who was so determinedly hunting for a husband who would be more eligible for a princess!

But no, his ears were not deceiving him—and nor were his eyes. Edward took in the sight of Coral, her cheeks pink, evidently a little astonished at herself for speaking so plainly…but she had come here, had she not? She had said those words.

"All I know is that I have not been able to think of anything else save that kiss since you strode away from me."

A better man would have stepped away from the tantalizing woman, forced himself to have a conversation about the matter, and probably ended their time together with nothing more than a respectful bow.

Edward was not that man. Unable to help himself, driven by desire and desperation in equal measure, he answered in the only way he knew how—with his lips.

Coral appeared to welcome his sudden movement—at least, she lifted her hands to his face to pull him closer, moaning slightly as Edward kissed her reverentially, his hands not on her waist, which would have been scandalous enough, but on her buttocks, drawing her in, drawing her closer.

Edward lost himself in the passion. This was what he had craved, who he had craved. Coral, pure and simple. Just her and her hunger, for there was certainly a great deal of it. She clung to him, and Edward gripped her tight, determined never to release her.

The kiss ended almost as soon as it began, and Edward groaned with the need of her, but as he lowered his lips to hers once again, Coral leaned back slightly.

"Is this what it feels like?" she asked, wide eyes gazing up at him with complete trust.

Complete trust. Edward swallowed, trying to think clearly but unable to as his fingers tightened around the taut and soft buttocks of the woman who was fast becoming everything to him. *Everything.*

"What?"

Coral blinked, a nervous smile creeping across her face. "Caring about someone."

Edward almost groaned aloud. *Oh, to hear those words from her mouth…to know that she cared for him just as he cared for her…*

Well, perhaps not entirely the same. Edward hardly knew himself what these sensations were, overpowering his heart, molding it into a new shape, changing him from the inside out—into what, he did not know.

He did not care. Not while Coral was in his arms. Was it not enough that he cared, that caring for Coral was going to become the primary reason for his existence?

"Yes," Edward said, lowering his head to nuzzle Coral's neck, glorying in the way she trembled at his touch. "Yes, this is what it is to care for someone."

"I…I like it," she gasped.

And that was when he lost almost complete control. Capturing her lips once again, Edward's desperate hands tilted her toward him, groaning in her mouth as he felt the press of her against his throbbing manhood.

Oh, if she were not a lady of the ton, *and he were not a gentleman, just what delights he could show her…*

But it appeared Coral did not particularly mind that she was a lady of the *ton*. Before Edward knew what was happening, Coral had forced him to take a few steps back until he was pressed against a bookcase, her ardor overpowering her, just as it threatened to overpower him.

Edward moaned, tightening his embrace around her and teasing open her lips, desperate to taste of that innermost sanctum—well, not that one. *Not yet.*

Her passion sparked his own. Feeling her desperation to be touched made him touch her more, one of his hands moving to her waist, then creeping to her breast. Coral moaned, tilting her head back as his finger found her nipple, just waiting there underneath the delicate satin—

And then she pulled away.

Edward blinked, his sight seemingly lost for a moment. As it came back, he realized he was leaning heavily against the bookcase, shelves the only thing keeping him upright, his mind spinning with the fiery encounter he had just enjoyed with a woman who had said not a month ago that she could never consider him as a potential husband.

"Edward, I was not toying with you, I promise. I am not here to seduce you."

"Is this what it feels like? Caring about someone."

Edward swallowed, but it was Coral who spoke first.

"I...I do not know what to do with...with all these feelings," she said helplessly.

Her hair was mussed, half-fallen from its pins, lips pink, eyes wide and full of lust.

Yes, she wanted him. Edward's manhood jerked to see the desire within her, but he could not give her what she wanted. Not yet at least.

He managed to laugh, though it was a jagged one. "Neither do I."

Coral breathed a laugh, pushing her hair back with her hands and looking around the library as though desperately seeking to distract herself. "You...this place. It is far more impressive than I had expected, I must say."

Before he could think, his tongue had rattled on without him. "Even though it's in the wrong part of town?"

His teasing made her flush. "There is more than one good part of town, I think. Perhaps I should add a requirement to the list."

Edward grinned. "The ever-expanding list?"

"I should require a certain standard of décor. I demand it from their fashion, why not their home?" Coral said with a gentle laugh.

He could not help it. That damned list, always getting in the way, always separating them when was it not obvious that they were perfect together? Was it not clear that without that list, they would be engaged already?

"So now you have seen my impressive house, does that mean I make the list?"

Her eyes caught his, and Edward's stomach lurched painfully. How was she able to look at him with such intensity, as though she could see deep within his soul?

For a moment, a moment that simply did not go on long enough, in Edward's opinion, Coral hesitated, torn. He could see it in her eyes, the way she held herself. something drew her to him that was inexplicable—certainly not compatible that her list.

But—

"N-No," Coral said gently. "I am afraid you don't. I...I should go."

"Don't go," said Edward instantly.

She smiled, and he found he could not regret his eagerness.

"I do not want you to go," he admitted quietly.

"And I do not want to," said Coral quietly, "but I told my mama that I would be but a few minutes to speak to a friend. She will be expecting me, now, at the theater for a matinée."

A few minutes to speak to a friend. Well, Edward knew that he had to accept that, even if he did not wish to. So, Opal de Petras had not been informed of her daughter's journey here—and he was a *friend*, was he?

He was not aware of any friends who kissed each other senseless against library bookshelves.

"Coral—"

"Goodbye," she said, turning to go with a great deal of reluctance yet not enough to make her stay. "Edward."

His name rang out in the library long after Coral had gone, after Edward had fallen into his chair, legs no longer able to hold him.

What was he going to do with her?

CHAPTER THIRTEEN

January 2, 1810

"...a ND NATURALLY, WHEN I saw the thoroughbred, I just knew I had to have him. I mean, the flanks of the beast! I had never seen an animal like it, and so I told my trainer, though he did not believe me at first. Jenkins, I told him, I know you are my trainer but I know a good horse when I see one..."

Just before Coral had entered into her first Season, Opal had instructed her daughter on the best way to yawn without anyone actually knowing one is yawning. It is something particular about the jaw, the way one keeps it closed.

Coral had not understood at the time just why her mother was taking all this time to teach her a skill she would surely never need. She was about to enter Society, after all—a place packed with interesting people, thrilling conversations, card parties, balls, dances...

"...and of course, I was right!" said the gentleman before her triumphantly, as though he had demonstrated something both charming and highly amusing. "The horse won!"

Coral nodded blithely, trying to transform the growing yawn into a smile. "Indeed."

"Indeed, he did, and a marvelous race he ran, too," continued the eager gentleman, whose name Coral had forgotten the moment he opened his mouth. "Why, when the first corner was turned, I admit, for a brief moment I was slightly concerned I had overshot myself. Third in the line and looking as though no ground could be taken…"

Coral allowed the words to wash over her, as though she was listening to some second-rate pianist play her least favorite Mozart.

Well, he was probably not the most boring person in the world, though that was hardly an accolade worth celebrating. How was a gentleman so…so dull?

That was the trouble with Lady Romeril's card parties, her guest list was primarily designed to make her look impressive.

And that was why Lord…Lord Whomever, the gentleman seated beside her on the sofa, was treating her to a rather unimpressive tale of all the horses he had purchased. He had a title, to be sure, and Coral was sure most young ladies would have given their back teeth to have so easily caught his attention. He was handsome, had at least five thousand a year, had been to Italy, had dark hair…

In fact, the irritating man fitted the bill perfectly. He ticked off everything on her list.

Coral sighed, trying to keep her boredom hidden. It really was most unfair. The first gentleman she had ever met who could actually have been a potential suitor, if not for…

Well. He was so dull.

It was only now that Coral started to realize there was something ineffable about a person. Something that could not precisely be captured in a list. It was most unfortunate.

There appeared to be no one better to speak with at the card party, however, which was most distressing, and so Coral allowed herself to be monopolized by a man who seemed eager enough to impress, even if he was not sufficiently managing it.

If only the man could distract her from thoughts of…

A memory poured into her mind. It was never far away, every instant drawing her back. The moment she and Edward…when they had almost admitted something like affection for each other…

"I…I do not know what to do with…with all these feelings."

Coral swallowed. She was not too close to the fire, yet felt most inexplicably warm. That was what happened when one remembered the tight grip of Edward's hands on her buttocks, the way his fingers knew precisely what they were looking for as they quested for her breast.

"…but of course, I sold him in the end, one cannot hold onto a beast like that for too long, the odds on his success dwindle with every passing month, and I believe I got a good price for him, studded out somewhere—I took two of his fillies, wonderful mares, for my own stables you know…"

Coral nodded, as though she could not hope but hear more of the inane chatter about horses for hours and hours upon end.

She had never been bored in Edward's presence, far from it. Now she considered it, there was always an undercurrent of unpredictability in her interactions with the Duke of Glaenarm. She loved it, enjoyed it, found him rather amusing…

But now she had to suffer through the conversational ineptitude of other, lesser gentlemen. Coral could not help but wonder how she had not recognized his value before.

Edward Barlow, Duke of Glaenarm. A man like no other.

In fact, and Coral was loathe to admit it to anyone save in the quiet of her own mind, she was beginning to wish Edward was not lacking in other areas that her list highlighted.

An Edward who had a love of reading, of Mozart…one with all the same charm, the same looks, the same witty quickness, the same manner which made Coral wish to do something reckless…the same Edward she knew—but with a sister.

Oh, what a suitable match that would be.

Coral forced the thought from her mind. It was merely carelessness, permitting her thoughts to wend towards an ideal Edward, an Edward who had been to Italy and was, therefore, an appropriate choice for her.

The perfect man. Her mother had told her, more than once, that he did not exist.

"But you found Papa," Coral had said, not a month before this Season had begun.

And her mother had smiled that knowing smile that told Coral there was far more to her parents' marriage than she could ever dream of, and said, "Your father was not made for me, Coral. That is not how it works. When one finds someone to love, one has to love all the imperfections, all the mistakes, all the things one might decide to change."

"And then change them, over time?" Coral had said eagerly.

And Opal had laughed and shaken her head. "No—it is not he who changes, my dear, but you. Your heart changes. You learn to love what you did not believe you could love before."

Coral had not understood her mother's words at the time, and she was not entirely sure she understood them now. How was it possible to love the foibles and irritations of a gentleman's character? How could one come to accept the fact there would be parts of him one did not like?

It was not such a problem with Edward, she thought wistfully as the gentleman before her started wittering on about a mare he had purchased only last week. There were no faults within Edward's character, nothing that she would wish to change.

Only a few aspects of his life, but that was sadly beyond her ability.

If she had no siblings…

But Coral forced that thought away. Another reality she could not change; yes, if she had no siblings, she could marry Edward and they could be happy together.

Assuming he would agree to take her name, of course.

"…tried to buy her from me for a thousand pounds! I said a thousand pounds? Only a king's ransom could convince me to part with such a horse, and we had at it, I can tell you, over bridge…"

But as it was, she had three siblings, each of them requiring a dowry. Now that their father's income was gone, she'd had to make this difficult choice. And she would make it again if she had to.

Coral's gaze flickered over to her sister Emerald, seated at a table playing a game. It appeared she was losing, but Emerald would not mind. It would mean the attention was away from her. If Emerald were ever to marry—something that appeared less and less likely with each passing month—she would need her dowry.

"...Miss de Petras?"

Coral blinked. The man before her now looked a little despondent, and she realized he'd been waiting for a reply from her which had never come.

"So fascinating, my lord, the way you have so expertly navigated the complexities of horse breeding," Coral said with what she hoped was a winning smile. "I am impressed."

The gentleman beamed as Coral thanked her lucky stars that decorum meant she could call him "my lord" without having to worry about remembering his name.

"Thank you, Miss de Petras," said the gentleman, moving an inch closer.

Coral pursed her lips. *Now that would never do.*

She was just about to give the man a gentle reproof—nothing too harsh, but just enough to put him back in his place—when a head of blonde hair caught her eye.

Her breath caught in her throat. *Edward.*

Coral's entire body quivered. It seemed impossible his mere presence was sufficient to warm her, to shake her, to make Coral feel desperately eager to be close to him again. But it was. Moreover, Coral knew precisely what this ache in her stomach and just below it meant, now she had accosted him so scandalously in his library last week.

She wanted to be kissed by him. Touched by him. Loved by him. But first...

"—and you see, once I realized the power of the stallion—"

"My lord," said Coral swiftly, interrupting the fresh tide of information about horses that she would never want to hear again, "I am sorry to say that I cannot marry you."

The gentleman blinked. "I…I beg your pardon?"

"I am sure you are a very amiable gentleman, and one who will make an excellent husband," said Coral as gently as she could manage while she tracked Edward's movements around the room in her peripheral vision. "And I know you are considering me as a potential bride, and I must tell you, my lord, that the idea is entirely out of the question."

The man's jaw had dropped. She was sorry to do it, so definitively and so publicly, *but really*, Coral thought, *it was kinder to tell him straight away.*

It would never do for the man to generate hopes she could never fulfill.

"I do not understand!" The gentleman looked genuinely affronted, though Coral could not see why. "I was given to understand you were interested in a gentleman with a specific list, a list you had the gall to put in a newspaper, and that criteria I fill!"

Coral flushed. "Be that as it may," she said crisply, "you do not fulfill my requirements."

"B-But I am a lord!" stammered the gentleman. "And I am wealthy, I have been to Italy, I love Mozart! I have three sisters! I have my own townhouse here and manor in Cambridgeshire, with an income of five thousand a year!"

"And a mortgage on that property, with debts of two thousand a year and rising fast, if your obsession with horse racing is anything to go by," said Coral succinctly.

Edward was standing in the corner, talking to a young lady Coral did not know. She said something and he laughed, and Coral wanted to rage over there and stop him from doing whatever it was he was doing.

"I am sorry, my lord, I truly am. But I published this list to attract the best of men, but also to hold myself to account. I am sure you understand—I would be a fickle woman indeed who went against her own word," said Coral with a brief smile. "You will have to excuse me."

It had taken all Coral's self-control to stay away from Edward as long as she had. Leaving behind the spluttering lord, she stepped lightly around the room until she was a few feet from Edward.

He glanced up. He saw her. He smiled.

"You will have to excuse me, Miss Marnion," Coral heard him murmur to the lady he had been speaking to before he stepped away from her and toward Coral.

Coral's heart twisted in a strange sort of delighted victory.

She and Edward halted by the side of the room. Coral could feel the gazes of at least three people upon her. Really, when were her mother, sister, and that dratted Maltravers going to mind their own business?

"I did not realize you were invited to Lady Romeril's card party," Coral said lightly with what she hoped was a winning smile.

Edward matched her smile. "I was not."

Coral laughed. He really was the most mischievous man she had ever met! "You are bold indeed to defy her."

"Perhaps not bold enough."

Coral's breath caught in her throat. Edward was looking at her with such intensity, such force, it quite took her breath away.

She knew what she wanted. She had known it the moment she had pushed Edward into that bookcase and reveled in the way he had touched her. She was an innocent, yes, but she knew what a gentleman and a lady could share. She knew she wanted it, wanted to share it with Edward, all sense of decorum and propriety be damned.

But how to ask for it...

Coral glanced at Edward and saw the same desire in his eyes. He wanted her, and she wanted him, and the only thing keeping each other apart was decorum. If only she could tell him...but Coral did not have the words.

It was for women like Micah's mistresses, she thought darkly, *to know that particular vocabulary.*

But her body was aching for his touch, desperate for it. Desperate for him…

"Perhaps not bold enough."

Coral swallowed, knew what she was about to say was scandalous—that if anyone else heard her, she would be thrown out of polite Society immediately. She found, to her astonishment, that she did not care.

"If you were bold enough," she whispered, not looking away from Edward's eyes, "I would say yes."

His gaze dropped to her mouth, to the way her lips parted, and Coral shivered at what she had just suggested. Did he understand? Did Edward follow her meaning—would he accept her invitation?

"Follow me," said Edward quietly, his voice just a breath. "To the hall, a few minutes after I have gone. Follow me, Coral."

He was gone before she could say a word, taking her breath with him. Coral blinked; she could hardly believe what had happened. But Edward had indeed slipped into the hall, and he expected her to follow him when no one could connect the two disappearances together.

Coral's chest tightened as her heart twisted with excitement. Were her cheeks flushed? Could anyone guess what had just occurred between them?

"You look remarkably warm, Miss de Petras."

Coral jumped. There was Lady Romeril—how had she managed to get so close to her so quickly? Or, and the thought was a perilous one, had she been close the entire time?

Had she, in fact, overheard her conversation with Edward?

"Warm? Yes, I suppose I am a little warm, Lady Romeril, I thank you," Coral said in her most aloof manner.

Lady Romeril laughed. "You do remind me of your mother sometimes, you know."

Coral glanced over at her mother, still near the fireplace.

What would her mother say if she knew just what Coral planned to share with Edward in just a few moments?

But she had to push that thought aside. She had made her choice, and it was Edward. She did not understand it, would unravel it later when this ache within her had been sated.

"In fact, I remember when your mother came to me in great need during a rather interesting scandal that—"

"You must excuse me," said Coral vaguely, not taking in a word. "Lady Romeril."

Lady Romeril's splutters followed her across the room, but Coral paid them no heed. All she could think about was reaching the hall and finding Edward. Of being with him.

The hall was empty and dark, and Coral gasped as a hand reached for her in the darkness.

"Hush," came Edward's quiet voice from the gloom. "Are you ready?"

Coral nodded, hardly trusting her voice. *Ready? How could she be ready?* She was not entirely sure she knew what he was proposing, whether he had understood her desperate and unspoken wish.

"If you were bold enough, I would say yes."

But it appeared he did. Stepping almost silently across the hall, Edward's hand pulled her inexorably toward the staircase. Only one of the steps creaked as they crept up, no sign of any footmen or servants to hinder their path.

Coral's heart was thundering so loudly, she was certain the entire household including the card party downstairs would hear it—would come out to ask them where they were going.

But they did not. In fact, she and Edward were entirely uninterrupted as they crept along the upstairs corridor, and not a thing happened as Edward opened a door and pulled her through it.

They were in a bedchamber. A guest bedchamber, from what Coral could see. The bed was made but hidden by a large coverlet, intended to keep the dust out. There was no candle in the room, but her eyes acclimatized to the darkness, and she could see such desire on his face.

Instinctively, Coral took a step backward, her heels touching the now closed door. "We...we should not do this. Not here. Anyone could catch us."

Edward followed her, pinning her against the door with his chest, and Coral gasped at the intensity of the contact. "Do you want to stop?"

Coral swallowed. His lips were just above hers, tormentingly out of reach, and she knew if she just leaned forward an inch, she could close that gap, taste him, feel the intense pleasure that roared through her body whenever Edward's lips were on hers.

"I said," Edward repeated slowly, lowering his head and kissing that delicate spot just beneath her ear, "do you want to stop?"

"No," Coral whispered.

"Louder."

"No," Coral said, fearful someone would hear them, fearful Edward would stop.

He raised his head. "Good. Because I want you, Coral. I have wanted you since the moment you walked into Almack's and cut me down to size."

Her questing fingers tightened around his lapels, bringing him closer. "I did no such thing."

"I have never felt so entirely out of control with a woman in all my life," Edward murmured, lowering his head once again but this time kissing her collar bone.

Coral gasped, her back arching against the door to bring Edward closer, her mind spinning with unadulterated pleasure. "Never?"

"Never," groaned Edward, capturing her hands with his and pushing them to the side so she could not stop him, as though Coral would want to. "Never, Coral. You possess me, consume me—you control me. I am yours."

Coral moaned, unable to take the sensations any longer, knowing she was just as much his as he was hers. She belonged to him, she could see that now, and no other gentleman would ever come close—no one.

It appeared her moan did something strange to Edward, unblocking the dam of self-control. Growling under his breath, he crushed his lips upon hers, and this time there was no gentleness, no reverence, just desire and lust and a need to be close.

Coral's hands struggled under his, wanting to pull him closer, wanting to touch him, but Edward's hands were strong, and she quivered in the intensity. Somehow the restriction heightened the pleasure roaring through her body, and the ache inside her grew, warming and filling her.

"Coral, I want you," Edward moaned into her mouth.

Coral knew precisely what answer he needed to hear. "And I want you."

Edward released her hands, stepping just an inch away from her, leaving Coral feeling bereft at his absence—but then she saw what he was doing.

Edward's fingers fumbled at the buttons of his breeches, and Coral stared in amazement as he thrust them down, revealing himself in all his nakedness to her.

She swallowed. *Well, she knew, in theory, what...but that was...*

"Are you sure?" Edward breathed heavily, gazing into her eyes.

Coral could see the desperation there, see the hunger—but also the respect. The need to know she was truly accepting this rebellious lovemaking, that she was willing to cross the line with him.

The ache between her legs tingled. "Yes—yes, make love to me, Edward."

With a growl, Edward covered her body with his once more, and this time Coral's fingers were free to tangle themselves into his hair, pulling him closer. His hands appeared to be otherwise occupied. Coral could just about make out something he pulled from his waistcoat pocket, then he was putting something over himself, and all of a sudden, Coral gasped.

He had lifted her. The strength in his arms lifted her bodily from the ground, Edward's strong hands on her buttocks, her skirts billowing as her legs instinctively moved around him, pulling him closer, her ankles meeting behind his back.

Edward groaned. "This might hurt, Coral."

She braced herself at his words, not knowing entirely what he meant—and a cry did escape her lips, but it was not one of pain.

Pain? Oh, no. Nothing could be further from the sensation she was feeling as Edward pushed aside her skirts and entered her, his manhood gently easing into her wetness, and the ache that had been building twisted with sweet agony that she desperately had to feel again.

"Did I hurt you?"

"Hurt me?" Coral said, eyes hazy with desire. "Love me, Edward. Just love me."

As though to prove she was well, she kissed him, trying to show him with a shy, teasing tongue just how much she wanted him.

Edward groaned in her mouth and thrust into her, causing ripples of delight to shower through her body. This was everything…this was glorious…this was more than she could ever have hoped for.

How did anyone manage to stop themselves from doing this all night, all day?

"More," Coral moaned, clutching at his neck and holding on for dear life as Edward thrust into her again and again, deeper each time and building a rhythm that was echoed by her heartbeat. "More, more—damn!"

It was too much—far too much, and the curse word she had never intended to say burst from Coral's lips as ecstasy, pure and fantastic, overcome her body, shaking it as pleasure roared through her, her eyes closing, holding onto Edward for dear life as she lost all control.

"Coral!" Edward thrust hard into her several times, burrowing his head in her breasts as he shook.

They clung to each other, desperately, silently, as the waves of pleasure poured over them, and eventually Coral was able to open her eyes.

The room was just as dark, and Edward was just as present, just as masculine, just as strong. He slowly lowered her to the floor but he held onto her, for which Coral was grateful. She was not entirely sure her legs would carry her.

"That…that was…"

"I know," said Edward in a jagged voice, his eyes meeting hers. "I have never before…that was…"

Coral's heart leapt. She was his first. Despite all his bravado, despite his handsome looks and winsome charm, they had shared something together that was unique.

"I…I thought lovemaking always had to occur in a bed," she whispered a little shyly, hardly sure what to do with herself now she had shared something so intimate.

Edward grinned wickedly, and Coral's heart contracted—and something lower between her legs started to warm again. "Oh, Coral. We are just getting started."

CHAPTER FOURTEEN

January 3, 1810

T RY AS HE might, it was rather difficult for Edward to silently close the front door of his London townhouse.

In the early hours of the morning, even the small click of the door handle returning to its natural position made Edward wince. Surely the entirely of his household—goodness knows how many servants, for he was starting to find it difficult to keep track— would hear him.

But nothing happened. As he stood there, in the great cavernous entrance hall his father had decorated in the latest style not five years ago, the only sound Edward could hear was the frantic beating of his own heart and tension creaking in his lungs.

He leaned against the door.

Well, he had done it. He had done what he had believed impossible. He had bedded Coral de Petras.

A small smile crept across Edward's face. And not just once, oh no, though that was marvelously incredible and far more hedonistic than he had imagined.

No, they had spent...well, the entire night at it. Teasing pleasure from one another, exploring each other's bodies, using all the French letters he had kept in his waistcoat until he was left with no alternative but to kiss Coral's secret spot until she cried out his name softly under her breath, desperate not to be discovered....

His smile broadened. As though that was a hardship.

He had not attended Lady Romeril's card party—without an invitation—with such an idea in mind, but the moment Coral had said those fateful words, Edward had known his self-control had finally reached the end of its tether.

"If you were bold enough, I would say yes."

Edward shivered at the intensity of that memory. Coral de Petras was a woman unlike any he had ever known, and the worst of it was, she knew it.

She knew how spectacular she was. She knew how gentlemen of his acquaintance were starting to talk about her. The beauty who had managed to enter her third Season without being snapped up. Not for lack of the *ton's* trying.

Edward sighed, trying to let out his breath in a gentle, slow stream, but it was difficult. His body seemed to be shocked into an entirely different rhythm, as though he had been struck by lightning.

Perhaps he had been.

Nothing had prepared him for the rush of intoxication that had seared his mind the moment Coral had carefully, with just a gentle hint of shyness, removed her gown.

Edward clenched his jaw. He was spent, nothing left in him to make love with, and yet still the mere memory of Coral's body was enough to start hardening him again.

The trouble was, his seemingly clever plan had failed.

What had he told himself, that once he bedded Coral de Petras, she would be out of his system? That he would be free of her once he had taken her, once he had tasted her—and could then set her aside?

He had been a fool—and not for the first time when it came to Coral de Petras. No, every interaction with her was another opportunity to make him look a complete fool.

Edward staggered forward and pulled off his boots, leaving

them at the front door. They had agreed to their story, of course, before they had crept out of Lady Romeril's house as morning approached. It had still been dark. The last thing he needed was to see Coral's name torn apart in the scandal sheets.

He would say he had been to his club. That was easy, many of the gentlemen there were so inebriated, they would be unable to say whether they themselves had been there.

"And I?" Coral had whispered as she had slowly buttoned up his shirt—most regrettably, in Edward's opinion.

And he had smiled and said, "You have your own bedchamber at home, do you not?"

The mere mention of the word bedchamber appeared enough to make Coral flush—astonishing, considering what they had shared. "I do."

And he had flushed at those words, spoken so innocently in the darkness of night after they had shared what newlyweds would share.

"Just tell your family you left Lady Romeril's card party early," Edward had said hastily, pushing past the awkward moment, certain it was only he who saw it. "And you went to bed early. If you are able to creep into your bedchamber, no one will be any the wiser. It will probably be best if we do not see each other for a few days. A week, perhaps. Just to ensure there is no gossip…"

Edward scratched his jaw thoughtfully as he crept up the staircase. It was foolish really. He had no need to be sneaking about. He was master of his own home.

But there was something about this sensation, this secrecy. It excited him, yes, but Edward knew now, beyond a shadow of a doubt, that he was not in a small amount of trouble but a great heap of it.

He loved Coral de Petras.

There, he could think it, even if it was in the privacy of his own mind. Wild horses would not drag it from him, Edward thought wearily as he opened his bedchamber door and collapsed onto the bed fully clothed.

Yes, he had bedded Coral, and he loved her, and he was almost certain that she considered him with a fair amount of affection.

It was not just anyone that a lady let do that to her...

Edward knew it was Mrs. Opal de Petras he would have to speak to.

Because he was still no longer on this mythical list, was he? As Edward looked up at the canopy of his four-poster bed, he knew his own foolish eagerness to show off and tease the woman he had just met was now finally about to become his downfall.

Why, oh why, had he thought this was a good idea? He had been so certain he would be able to make her care for him, prove that her list was nothing but nonsense, and she did not need a list to fall in love...

That he had fallen in love himself. Without, more's the point, eliciting a declaration of affection from her.

Edward had thought, for a while, that she had been just teasing him. He was a duke, after all. He had wealth, status, a title, and a magnificent house she had now seen. Surely that would compensate for the deficiencies in sisters, dark hair, and love of Mozart.

But apparently not. Otherwise, why would she have whispered what she said just as they had parted not half an hour ago in the shadow of Lady Romeril's home?

"Such a shame you are not on the list, Edward," Coral had said, with just a hint of mischief. "What a shame."

And then she had gone before he could say anything.

Edward sighed heavily, tiredness tugging at his eyes. Now here he was, in love with the damned woman, utterly besotted with her and determined to make her happy for the rest of her life...and even a night of scandalous lovemaking had not managed to make her include him as a potential suitor. What else did the woman want?

Sleep, that was what he needed. It was not often he stayed up all night in the arms of a beautiful woman...

Edward sighed, tiredness forcing his eyes to close. If he could just sleep, then everything would be easier. If he could just rest…

When he awoke, it was dark still, which did not make any sense. Only when Edward forced himself to sit up and caught a glimpse of his grandfather clock did he groan.

A quarter past five—in the afternoon. He had slept the entire day away.

Forcing himself to get up, Edward trotted downstairs to find his butler raising a curious eyebrow.

"Your Grace."

Edward tried not to think about how he was dressed in the same clothes as yesterday. "Any post for me, Jacques?"

His butler shook his head. "Regrettably no, Your Grace, although Lady Romeril did visit and left her card."

The servant handed over the pink card, and Edward tried hard not to shiver. That was the trouble with turning up unannounced to a card party—one's hostess then thought she had the opportunity to befriend one.

"Right…" Edward said thoughtfully. It was not too late. Almost outside of visiting hours, but not quite. If he could be quick, he could be at the de Petras house within ten minutes.

It was agony, being this far from Coral, for this long. How did she stand it? How was she able to—

"The papers have been put in your study, Your Grace."

Edward started. "Papers?"

He had not been expecting any papers, had he? Not that he could think straight at the moment, lust and desire and longing playing an intoxicating medley in his heart, drowning out any thought. Any coherent thought.

"The financial accounts from the last quarter, from your steward, Your Grace," said Jacques politely, as though his master did not need to be reminded of his own business.

Recollection seared Edward's mind. "Yes. Yes! Yes, I will deal with them directly."

"I am given to understand that there are some complications,

Your Grace," the butler said with some delicacy. "Needing your immediate review. Apparently. It appears *he* cannot do without you."

Edward tried not to smile. Was it always the way in households this size, the butler and the steward finding chances to disparage each other at every opportunity?

"Right," he said heavily. "I shall go to the study for a few hours before dinner…"

In fact, it took almost a week to untangle the mess of papers that had been delivered to Edward's study. He was not one to criticize—he certainly did not have the most mathematical mind—but even he could see the discrepancies here.

Only after a barrage of letters that went back and forth between himself and his steward, and some rather hard questions, did Edward reach the bottom of it—each day constrained by his growing desperation to be free of this paperwork.

To find Coral.

Was she wondering why he had not been in touch with her? Why he had not appeared at once at her parents' house? Did she worry he had forgotten her? The thought consumed Edward at night, as wild schemes of proposals skimmed through his mind— all preposterous, of course.

He had even written a letter. Several letters, all more foolish than the last. How did one even write a love letter to a woman whom you had bedded but had ended the evening firmly putting you back in your place?

My darling Coral…

Coral, you must allow me to express…
Your damned list is the only thing keeping us apart…

All had been torn up, thrown in the fire, and gone unsent. How was he supposed to explain his feelings, his anger at her stupid list? He could barely think of the words, let alone write them down with any coherence.

But one afternoon, after his business was all cleared up and his steward suitably chastised, Edward came downstairs with a smile on his face. Today he was free. He would go to the de Petras house, and he would…precisely what he would say, he did not know.

"If I may be so bold, Your Grace."

Edward blinked. His butler was frowning as only a butler could. "Yes?"

"If His Grace was considering going out to visit…oh, I do not know, a certain young lady," said Jacques delicately, "not that I would wish to cast any aspersions, of course…"

"Get to the point, man," said Edward testily.

"I would merely wish to remind His Grace that he would benefit perhaps from a rest. And a shave," said his butler blandly. "And a bath."

Edward opened his mouth to argue, then looked at himself. He was wearing yesterday's clothes, and he had been rather…well. Lax in his bathing of late. Perhaps seeing Coral in this state would do little for his efforts.

There had been no mention of bathing routines on her list, but every woman had a standard.

"Fine, fine," he snapped. "Tell Wright to have everything ready."

Jacques bowed. "I will inform your valet immediately, Your Grace."

Edward had to admit, when he awoke the next morning, bathed, shaved, and with a decent amount of food and sleep in him, he did feel much better. But it had been forever now since he had seen Coral, and he was certain she just waiting about at home, desperate for him to call.

Well, far be it for him to disoblige a young lady.

He took care about his dress that morning, so much so that his valet was astonished.

"You wish to try the *a la Byron* knot?" he repeated in amazement.

Edward had the good grace to look a little bashful. "You are the one who has been singing its praises all last year!" he pointed out.

"Yes, but...well. Marvelous," said Wright with a smile. "Thank you, Your Grace."

And so, when Edward arrived on foot—the air was so crisp today, it would be a crying shame not to breathe it in—outside the de Petras house, it was difficult not to feel a certain amount of pride.

He had done it. He had bedded Coral de Petras, and neither of her parents were any the wiser either, or he would have received a rather stern visit from both Mr. and Mrs. de Petras, if he was any judge. And now he could make good.

When he rang the bell, the maid looked astonished to see him. "Your G-Grace!"

"Hullo," said Edward with a smile. Nothing could dim his spirits today. "Miss de Petras."

He had already taken a step into the house in his eagerness but was forced to halt when the maid put out a hand. "But Coral is not here, Y'Grace."

Edward halted, his spirits falling immediately. "Not—not here?"

The maid shook her head, obviously rattled to be putting a duke in his place. "No, Y'Grace."

Edward stared. It had not even occurred to him that Coral would not be at home—but then she was a lady in Society. She probably had invitations pouring out of her ears. A card party, elevenses, a walk in the park with her sisters...she could be anywhere.

Edward's shoulders sagged. "Oh."

"Who is that at the—Your Grace, what a pleasant surprise!"

Edward straightened hurriedly as the maid stepped aside and Mrs. Opal de Petras strode toward him. "Mrs. de Petras."

"Oh, what a shame we did not have sufficient time to speak at Lady Romeril's card party. I saw you were there but missed you—awfully hot it was," Opal said with a beaming smile so like her daughter's. "I suppose you left early, as my Coral did, because of the heat?"

Edward tried his best not to smile. *Well, the poor woman could not possibly guess.* "Yes—yes, that is quite right. The heat."

Opal shook her head with a knowing look. "Lady Romeril does keep the place warm, and I own it is her house and she can do what she likes, but to frighten away two of the most handsome people in the room, such a shame."

Edward nodded, desperately hoping to escape. If only he could discover the whereabouts of a certain young woman—

"You are here to see her, I take it? Coral?"

Edward nodded again, feeling the fool he was.

Opal beamed. "Of course, you are—and what a shame you missed her! She mentioned meeting a gentleman at...now where was it... Don Someone's Coffee House?"

It was all Edward could do to keep his smile intact as the horrendous words slipped into his mind. *Coral—meeting another gentleman, at the place they had shared such exquisite moments?*

"Don Saltero's Chelsea Coffee House."

"That's it," said Opal, smiling indulgently. "So popular, my Coral, as is to be expected. And just what are your intentions towards her, may I ask?"

The genteel warmth left the matriarch's voice in that instant, replaced with a steely focus that almost made Edward step back in surprise.

Opal was examining him openly, calmly, with the clear intention to know just what he expected to do with her daughter. And she was quite within her right to, Edward had to admit. Even if it did make him a little queasy to think about it.

"Intentions?" he repeated, buying himself time.

Opal arched an eyebrow. "That is what I said."

He could lie, Edward knew—but in that instant, he knew there was little point. Opal de Petras appeared to be the sort of woman who could see through that sort of thing with very little difficulty. No, the truth was what was called for...if only he knew it himself...

"My intentions toward your daughter, Coral," said Edward, his face serious, "are everything honorable, Mrs. de Petras."

For a heart-stopping moment, she continued to examine him—then she smiled. "I knew they were. Now, off you go—I suppose you are the gentleman she intended to meet, and she quite forgot whether it was here or there. Go on!"

And so, chivvied away from the house like a schoolboy, Edward walked down the street toward the coffee house, heart pounding, as though he had just received Mrs. de Petras's blessing.

And had he not? If she was against his suit, would not Opal de Petras have warned him to stay away from her daughter? In fact, was it not a resounding encouragement?

Edward found his heart was filled not just with joy but with expectation. He was going to do it. He was going to propose marriage to Miss Coral de Petras. Why not? It was clear to him, and surely to her, that they were well suited. They did not need a list of qualities to know that they were perfect for each other.

She was surely just waiting for his proposal. In fact, Edward's heart leapt at the thought, perhaps there was no gentleman she was supposed to be meeting at the coffee house, but she had frequented it in the hope of seeing him?

His footsteps increased in speed, desperate to reach her, to tell Coral just what he thought, what he felt—what he wanted. What he was sure she would also want.

As he reached the coffee house, spirits high and determined to visit a jeweler the moment he had secured Coral's hand, Edward glanced into the window of Don Saltero's Chelsea Coffee House, where his favorite table sat.

His feet halted as his gaze caught sight of a woman with fiery red hair.

Edward smiled. *Coral.* The morning light illuminated her, likely hiding him from her view, the glass playing tricks on the eyes. She was smiling, laughing, in fact, her hand resting delicately on the table—but it was not alone.

With a painful sinking feeling, Edward's gaze followed her arm to her hand, to her fingers…fingers entwined with those of another.

There was a gentleman seated opposite her—almost beside her, his chair pulled so close around the table it was almost scandalous. He was laughing, too, a handsome man with dark hair and a teasing expression. He was holding Coral's hand, and she was laughing.

Edward took a step back, almost falling into the street, mind utterly overwhelmed.

Coral, with another gentleman. Sitting there, at the table he thought of as their own. A gentleman who was holding her hand with such familiarity, there was no possibility she had only just encountered him today—nor could this be their second or third meeting.

No, though it pained him to accept, Edward knew now Coral had been courted by this gentleman for some time—perhaps weeks. Months.

"Out husband hunting?"

He had spoken those words flippantly with Coral and her sister in the park—and she had laughed, her cheeks flushed, as though ashamed merely at the suggestion.

But she was not ashamed. Edward stared, unable to believe it, as Coral said something to the man, something he could not hear, and the man threw back his head and laughed.

It was such a strange, bitter betrayal that Edward did not know what to do with himself. Wretched and heartbroken at the very sight of the woman he loved, clearly unfaithful to him, Edward straightened and took a deep breath.

Well, he had been a fool long enough. He should have known, the moment he read her list in the newspaper, that this was all a joke to her. There was no reason to interrupt her nonsense, no reason to enter the coffee house and confront her.

Coral had had her way with him for long enough. Why, for all he knew, she had merely bedded him as something to while away the time. Was he the first? Perhaps not the last.

Edward walked away, every step hurting as the agony of separation increased.

He had been a fool indeed.

CHAPTER FIFTEEN

CORAL GLARED OVER her steaming cup of coffee at the gentleman just to her left in the coffee house. She had never met a more irritating man in all her life. The blaggard—yes, she would think of him as a blaggard, even if she would never be able to bring herself to call him that to his face—the *damned blaggard* was an absolute disaster.

The trouble was, he did make her laugh. Oh, he was funny, but the situation could not be less so. He was a devil of a man.

Worse, he was a miscreant! He was a disgrace to his family, to Society in general, and she was starting to run out of justification for sitting here, in the coffee house, listening to him prattle on with his excuses.

For a moment, the briefest of moments, Coral thought she had seen Edward out of the corner of her eye. She had turned her head briefly, hoping it was him, heart surging…but it must have been a trick of the light. When she looked out of the window, there was no Edward.

Forcibly pushing the thought of the handsome and debonair man from her mind, Coral turned to look once more at the dark-haired fool beside her.

Coral frowned. "You are a disgrace, I hope you know that."

Micah grinned, pushing his hair back lazily from his eyes before loosening his cravat slightly. "You do not mean that."

"I most certainly do," said Coral firmly. *Really, her brother was truly the most irritating man.* Why was it ladies had to behave themselves, but a gentleman could make mistake after mistake! "You know it is true, Micah, do not pretend you do not feel the disgrace."

She watched his eyes closely, hoping to spot some sign of contrition. It was rather scandalous, what he had been caught doing this time—and though Coral finally knew the pleasures one could experience, it was not right that Micah had been caught…well…kissing a young lady in a place a lady certainly should not be kissed.

She shivered. At least, not when one was caught.

"Miss Howarth is a young lady who is by no means unprotected," said Coral, lowering her voice even though the raucous chatter around them covered her words. "Her father—"

"Her father will do nothing," said Micah dismissively, picking a pastry and taking a large bite. "I promise."

The last two words sprayed pastry across the table. Coral brushed them off irritably and tried to calm herself as she looked at her brother. It was a wonder sometimes they had come from the same parents. They could not be more different.

Well, perhaps that was not entirely fair. *Sapphire appeared to have been cut from the same cloth*, Coral thought wryly, which did not bode well for when the youngest de Petras came out into Society. She was going to be a handful, too.

But the matter at hand was Micah—Micah and his inability to see there were consequences to his actions, no matter how wild and radical.

"You were found," said Coral in a low voice, feeling her cheeks flush but unable to prevent it, *"kissing* Miss Howarth…kissing her on—"

"On the stairs," interrupted Micah, a slight flush tinging his own face. "Damnit, Coral, you think I want to discuss such a thing with my own sister?"

"You were the one doing it!" Coral shot back, trying her best to keep her voice low. Her hands cradled her coffee cup, something to hold onto in the medley of nonsense Micah was throwing her. "Oh, Micah, why could you not keep to your mistresses? Women who had no reputation worth losing?"

She could not help but permit the anxiety of their situation to percolate into her voice. *Well, really.* The family of Miss Howarth was demanding that Micah marry her, and Coral could see their point. Miss Howarth would never wed anyone if the truth got out, and it had happened at Viscount Braedon's dinner just a few days ago.

There was a man with little substance and no intention of holding his own tongue...

Coral took a deep breath. There was only one thing for it. "You must marry her."

"Like hell I will!"

"Micah!"

Her brother had the grace to look bashful. "Well, hell, Coral. You know I have no intention of marrying, at least not yet. I am so young!"

"Old enough to get half of Society's debutantes into scandalous positions," Coral said dryly with a shake of her head.

At least his mistresses knew Micah de Petras could never offer them anything so stable as a marriage proposal. Miss Howarth, on the other hand...

"You do not like her then?"

Her brother gave a shrug that seemed to mean that he liked her plenty enough to ruin her, Coral thought darkly, but not enough to do anything about it.

"She is all very well," Micah said quietly. "I would say nothing against her, truly, but that does not mean I wish to wake up every morning beside her."

*Wake up every morning...*Coral pushed aside the thought. She would not think of Edward, not now. She had far more pressing matters to attend to.

"I am not entirely sure you have much of a choice," Coral

pointed out. "You were found, Micah. Discovered, there is no way you can pretend—"

"One day, you will kiss a gentleman," said Micah sullenly, "and you will find it not so easy to act all innocent, as though butter wouldn't melt."

Coral was forced to look away, taking a hasty gulp of her scalding coffee, as though that would explain the flush on her cheeks. *If her brother only knew...*

Well, it was probably for the best that Micah had no idea what Coral had shared with Edward. She was certainly ready to force Micah to marry Miss Howarth for what they had shared on that candlelit staircase when they had believed everyone else at dinner...the thought of Micah attempting to force her to marry Edward...

A flicker of joy, unexpected and pronounced, soared through Coral's heart. *Marrying Edward.*

It was a heady thought, and she had certainly considered it far more often these last few days. Days empty of Edward, most frustratingly. She had considered going to see him, considered whether she should once again arrive at his townhouse, unannounced, but it had been impossible.

After risking so much at Lady Romeril's, Coral was not sure her luck would hold.

But being away from him was hard, despite her resolution to wait for him to return to her. Harder than she had thought. His touch on her skin, the way he made her whole body shiver...

When one had experienced such things, it was difficult to return to normality.

"Coral?"

Coral blinked. Micah was staring with concern. Drawing herself up, she affixed her brother with a stern expression.

"The point is, Micah," she said as though she had not just permitted her mind to wander, "that you have been found in compromising positions far too many times."

"Mistresses do not count."

"Mistresses *do* count," said Coral with a dry laugh. *Really, he was useless.* "Micah, do you not see what a devastating impact this is having on your reputation?"

Micah brushed aside her words with the wave of his hand. "Oh, reputation—that's only the sort of thing you girls have to worry about."

A curl of anger tightened around her chest. "Perhaps," Coral said tautly. "But I can make it something you have to worry about."

It was the first time Coral had thought about it, but she was right—and Micah knew it.

All the color drained from his face. "Oh, Coral, don't be like Mama."

"She and I understand the importance of keeping this family respectable, something you know little about," said Coral, a little bite in her voice. *Really, the boy was unmanageable.* "We will have to bear the burden of heading this family, and—"

"And don't I know it," said Micah bitterly.

Coral hesitated. She could not imagine what it was like for Micah, seeing all his friends take positions of responsibility and power within their families as they came of age. But not Micah. No, that was reserved for her—much good it was doing her.

She tried again, a slightly different tack. Perhaps guilt would work.

"You know Mama and Papa are starting to despair of you," she said conversationally.

There. There it was—just before Micah was able to put up a façade of disinterest, she saw hurt crease his face. He did care what their parents thought of him, after all.

"What does that concern me?" he said with a lazy shrug Coral now knew she could disbelieve. "It has been so long since they were young, they have no memory of—"

"Do not give me that, it is tired and trite, even for you," she snapped.

She had hoped to see Edward today. Every minute seemed to

eke out painfully the longer she was away from him, but her duty was to her family, and in this moment, it was Micah who was threatening to ruin them all.

Perhaps if she could just get him to understand in the next…oh, ten minutes? She would still have time to visit Edward before luncheon. She had waited long enough.

"It's money I need, not a wife," said Micah, a light appearing in his eyes. "Do you think if I did propose matrimony to Miss Howarth, Mama would give me my dowry?"

But Coral was wise to that. She was not about to permit her brother to attempt to rob her parents—for rob it would be, considering how delicately he had phrased that particular question.

"I think you would actually have to be married to Miss Howarth to receive the dowry," Coral said warily. "You cannot expect it beforehand."

All the excitement departed from Micah's eyes, and he slumped back against his chair.

Coral shook her head. So predictable—did he think her such a fool she would hand over such a sum, only to see it disappear into gambling dens and the pockets of his mistresses, Miss Howarth left at the sidelines to be utterly ruined by the scandal of being jilted?

"All I am saying is that you should consider settling down—marry Miss Howarth, if she is agreeable to you," said Coral gently. "At the very least, stop putting Society's debutantes in scandalizing positions!"

"You are the one scandalizing Society," shot back Micah in an undertone. "Not me."

It was such an unexpected response that Coral hardly knew what to say.

"M-Me?" she stammered, hating her forceful voice abandoned her just when she needed it. "What on earth do you mean?"

But she knew precisely what her brother meant—at least, that was the only thing she could think of.

Kissing Edward in the Axwick garden…kissing him in his library…creeping up the stairs of Lady Romeril's home, sneaking into a bedchamber, experiencing all the pleasurable delights a body could offer…

Coral swallowed. No. Surely her brother did not know about that—any of that!

"That list of yours!" Micah said with a laugh. "You cannot honestly think that publishing such a thing in all the newspapers of London would not get you noticed?"

"Oh, that, I do not mind—"

"And not necessarily for the right reasons either, Coral, so do not pretend that you did so in an attempt to be noble," said her brother, cutting across her. "Some of the things I have had to bear at my club, you have no idea!"

She had no idea. Coral blinked, trying to take in his words. She had certainly noticed a few more glances shot her way when they attended parties, dinners, balls, and the like, but she had assumed it was nothing but curiosity.

Had gentlemen really been…well. Put off by the list?

It had seemed like such a good idea, a way to filter out those who would have been most unsuitable.

"Spending all that time with that duke of yours, even though you constantly say that he does not meet the requirements of your foolish list," said Micah, a hint of anger in his voice. "Why you allow yourself to be seen with him so often—"

"Edward—the duke is helping me find the perfect suitor," said Coral quickly, hating she had accidentally said his name, but her brother did not appear to have noticed. "That is all."

That is all?

Oh, it had ceased to be that simple a long time ago, Coral thought ruefully, even if she would not admit it to Micah.

"Well, I think you're being unfair to him," said Micah darkly. "Prancing about with him at balls, going on walks with him, I have not seen you spend more than five minutes talking to another gentleman and yet you keep saying you will not marry him—"

"This is not about Edward," Coral snapped.

"Not about *Edward*?" Micah repeated incredulously. "You honestly call him by—"

"I said this was not about him," said Coral irritably. "Come on, Micah, you think I have come here to have *you* tell *me* how to behave? You are the one causing gossip wherever you go, you are the one disappearing after stealing money from Mama, you—"

"Yes, yes, I am the black sheep, I do not need to be told!" Micah said, and Coral saw at once that the jovial tone she had attempted to maintain had been lost. "Damnit, Coral, do you not ever tire of being right all the time?"

Coral opened her mouth but had nothing to say.

"I am sick and tired of always being the one whose behavior is scrutinized," said Micah bitterly, throwing the remains of his pastry onto the plate before him. "Sick and tired of always being criticized, of never being enough—never being you!"

Coral stared. "M-Me?"

"The future head of this family."

Throwing back his chair, Micah stormed out of the coffee house without a second glance at his sister.

Coral sat stunned, hardly able to believe it had all happened so quickly.

Her siblings…the people in the world she was closest to, that she had thought she knew well. If she could be so mistaken about them, what did that mean for someone like Edward?

What did she know about him, really?

Coral swallowed, tension building in her neck. She had spent much time in his presence, far more than most couples did before they were wed. Not that they were going to wed, of course.

But the hours of conversation, the meandering walks, their lovemaking…what did she actually know of him?

Coral knew he was bold and witty and charming. But she did not know his family. His story. What he had done in the years since becoming a man.

"Well, I think you're being unfair to him. Prancing about with him at balls, going on walks with him, I have not seen you spend more than five minutes talking to another gentleman and yet you keep saying you will not marry him—"

The memory of Micah's words flickered painfully in her mind. She had discounted him, presumed that any man who could not complete her list was not worth speaking to.

But what if she had been hasty? What if the list had not elucidated her path, but had instead blinded her? Blinded her to the possibility of a man who, on paper, was most unsuitable, but made her heart…

It was a disconcerting thought, and for a moment, Coral allowed it space in her heart, causing her knuckles to whiten against the cup she still held.

But then it passed. *No, Micah was merely attempting to distract her,* Coral thought firmly. After all, the list was designed to make her happy. Why shouldn't she have certain expectations of a future husband?

Glancing at the grandfather clock in one corner, Coral sighed heavily. Too late, too close to luncheon to justify a visit to see Edward. She would be expected home in the next fifteen minutes.

What a shame.

She would simply have to wait for Edward to call on her.

A smile crept across Coral's face as she left two shillings on the table and rose to take her leave. She may be a de Petras, but she could not be expected to do all the chasing…

CHAPTER SIXTEEN

January 5, 1810

"**A**ND I WOULD rather the silver dinner service was taken with us, too," said Edward, his gaze falling down the long list in his hands. *Damn, so much to do…* "I do not like the idea of it being left here with the place shut up, not knowing if the place is safe…"

"Old Mr. Rogers will be staying on, Your Grace, to keep an eye on Glaenarm House," said the footman, Frost, politely. "I am sure he is trustworthy, and more than capable of—"

"'Tis no reflection on Mr. Rogers, who has been a dedicated servant to this family, to this house for the last fifty years," said Edward with a wry smile. *As though he would be so foolish as to discredit in public a man who had given so much in service to the Glaenarm name.* "But he is getting a little on in years, and if the place was burgled, I am not sure what he would do. No, pack it up please."

Frost bowed and turned from his master as he returned to the dining room to share the order with the footmen who were currently putting the room to bed.

Edward sighed heavily as he turned on his heels in the large hall.

Putting the room to bed. It was a phrase he had never understood until he had seen it done—the large flowing white sheets, expertly tailored to perfectly fit the furniture, the way carpets and rugs were beaten, rolled up, and put on the side, and the chimneys put out, cleaned, then covered in a sheet.

Usually, he was gone before the process began, which was how he liked it. He preferred to leave one place alive and full of people, then arrive at another one of his properties just as alive, just as thriving. But this time he had to stay, had to make sure it was done properly. Had to oversee the complete closure of Glaenarm House.

"You're not selling?" Jacques, his butler, had said in horror only last night as Edward had revealed he would not be returning to London for the foreseeable future.

"Selling? This old place?" Edward had laughed. "I think my ancestors would turn in their graves to think Glaenarm House could leave the family. No, not selling. Just closing it for good. I will not be back."

There had been a certain amount of defiance in his voice, and Edward had almost been certain Jacques would challenge him, ask why he was running from London, why he had not bothered to fight for Coral, why he had so assiduously avoided all invitations and opportunities to mingle with Society.

Perhaps Jacques did not need to ask because he already knew.

Edward stood in the hall as maids rushed from one to the other, fetching and carrying for the footmen issuing orders at a rapid pace.

"—dinnerware to be packed also, ensure to let Mr. Jacques know that—"

"—blue saloon ready for its cotton, can someone tell Jemima to bring it over with—"

"Mr. Rogers has been informed, and there'll be a tab at the butcher's, he's to send all receipts to—"

It was amazing, even Edward had to admit. Why, he had lived the life of a gentleman all his days, always knowing he would be a duke, and it was marvelously astonishing how little he knew about the mechanics behind the houses in which he inhabited.

"Excuse us, Y'Grace."

Edward stepped to the left as a grandfather clock was carefully carried by what appeared to be all his footmen. "Where are you taking—"

"All clocks are going in the drawing room," called back one of his footmen. Edward could not quite see which one. "Orders of Mr. Jacques."

Edward nodded as though that explained everything. Well, if his butler had asked for it, there must be a reason for it.

None of his servants had asked why the Duke of Glaenarm was deciding to leave London right at the height of the Season. None of them, evidently, had believed it their place to inquire, though Edward had overheard some astonished questions in the kitchens when he had gone downstairs to hunt for a morsel a few nights ago.

The hustle and bustle of the house continued around him. He hated to go away really. He had seen so little of Society, all his time spent with a certain Miss de Petras. Time he had believed well spent.

But there was nothing for it now. Not after seeing Coral with that gentleman. He had to return to the countryside. It was too painful to stay, too many opportunities to go to places where he and Coral had been, too many chances to accidentally run into her on the street.

And worse. Edward's stomach clenched painfully as he watched a maid cover the looking glasses in the hall and he thought about all the potential places where he could see Coral.

Anywhere. Any drawing room, any card table, any ball. To think he could be innocently dancing with another woman and as the line moved down, could find Coral once more in his arms…

Worst of all, he could not be in London when her engagement was announced.

"That is almost all of it, Your Grace."

Edward blinked. Frost was standing before him. "All of it?"

The footman nodded. "Save your last few personal effects, which Wright will bring. The coaches are ready."

"Ready?" Edward repeated. The man wasn't making any sense. *Why, only a moment ago he had been watching the maids…*

Edward looked around the hall. So lost in his thoughts, he had barely noticed the maids and footmen had finished their work. It was done. The house was put to bed. The only thing left was to leave himself.

His shoulders tightened, his body rebelling at leaving Coral. But what choice did he have? She had made it abundantly clear she had no interest in receiving his addresses. Why else would she have chosen that particular seat at Don Saltero's Chelsea Coffee House, if she did not care who knew that she was meeting with that man?

"Your Grace?"

Edward cleared his throat loudly as Frost still waited. "Yes. Yes, the coaches! Yes, please organize the servants to take three of them, leaving one for myself. I will follow. Soon."

The footman looked a little concerned but evidently thought better of contradicting his master. "Of course, Your Grace."

Edward stood in the hall as the sound of carriages pulling away from the front of the house echoed around him.

One, two, three. There. They were all gone—all save Mr. Rogers, of course. Edward smiled wanly. There was something about the finality of leaving a place like this. He knew he would not be back. Not while Coral de Petras still lived in London, anyway, and that seemed unlikely to change.

Perhaps he would go to the Continent. Perhaps he would risk it all and take a berth to America. Perhaps he would find himself a new life, a new way of enduring the days, one after another. Or perhaps he would not. Perhaps the specter of his love for Coral would hang over his life forever. Perhaps—

A jangle. A heavy, loud, metallic noise, one that Edward had not been expecting.

Someone had just rung the doorbell.

In any other scenario, of course, Edward would merely have waited for someone else to open the door. His butler, a footman, anyone. But they were all gone. Only he and Mr. Rogers remained.

Edward sighed. *Well, it has come to this. Now he was answering his own door.* He stepped forward.

It was a good thing he had the door handle to hold onto. Edward's jaw dropped.

Maltravers raised an eyebrow. "My my, you have fallen on hard times indeed if you are opening your own door, Your Grace."

Edward closed his mouth hurriedly. *Christ, he must look a complete fool!* He needed to say something—anything.

"Are you going to invite me in?" asked Maltravers sharply, proving him wrong.

Edward glanced behind him. The house was shut up, there was no furniture not covered with a white cotton cloth. The place was certainly not presentable for a guest.

Presentable for a guest? What was he thinking?

"Glaenarm?"

"Yes," Edward said hastily. "Yes, yes, come in."

Maltravers looked around him curiously as he stepped into the hall. "Redecorating?"

"Retreating," said Edward thoughtlessly as he closed the door. "I mean, leaving."

"Leaving?"

Edward swallowed. He could not have this conversation here.

"Come, let's speak in the breakfast room," he said weakly.

The breakfast room was just as covered, but it was at least easier to remove the cotton sheets from a few chairs. Edward indicated one of them. Maltravers remained standing.

"Leaving," he repeated again, staring most curiously. "Going somewhere?"

Edward cleared his throat, but no words appeared willing to leave his mouth. All he could think about was the sight of the woman he loved—despite all his intentions to merely tease her—sitting with that man.

"Y-Yes," he stammered, hating the weakness in his voice but unable to remain calm. "Yes, I am leaving. Leaving London."

Maltravers's brow furrowed. "Why?"

He could lie. He could tell his friend he had been called away, a problem with the estate. He could say he was hosting a house party and needed to away to prepare. He could say anything, anything, and he would not be able to refute him.

But as Edward stood there, in his white-covered breakfast room, with Maltravers before him, he realized there was only one thing that he could do now. Speak with brutal honesty.

All chance to be Coral's husband was gone. Edward was not so much of a fool to think that situation could be salvaged…even if she had not been meeting with that fellow, he was no closer to meeting the requirements on her damned list than when they had first met.

"Maltravers, I am heartbroken," Edward said helplessly, looking into his bright eyes. "The idea of seeing her in town, in finding Coral at the same invitations, the same card parties…to run the risk of being seated next to her at dinner…"

Edward could not finish the sentence. All he could do was be honest, debase himself in his friend's eyes by speaking so openly of his heartache, then try to let Coral go. He had to let her go.

"It would be too painful," Edward said finally, forcing himself to continue. "I cannot do it. I cannot live here so close to the de Petras family, all of them…so I am leaving."

There. The words were said. There was still pain roaring through his body, and he had hoped that by speaking the words aloud, he would feel relief—but if anything, it was worse.

"I see," said Maltravers, nodding thoughtfully as the door behind him opened.

Edward glared at the footman who had appeared in the

doorway. *Of all the bad timing for a man to suffer!*

But his rage disappeared quickly, transforming into confusion as Frost stepped into the room, seemingly uncaring that he had just interrupted his master in a private conversation with a gentleman, and started to remove the cotton coverings from the breakfast table.

"Wh-What are you doing?"

The footman did not look immediately at him, but at Maltravers. Then he turned to Edward. "Orders, Your Grace."

Orders? It was not now merely confusion, but anger that rushed through his veins. He was still the Duke of Glaenarm, was he not? Surely, he should expect his orders to be followed!

If only Maltravers were not here, it was remarkably difficult to concentrate on stringing words together, Edward was finding when his friend was standing before him with a growing smile on his face. A smile that made no sense.

"Orders?" he repeated as two maids came into the room and started removing the fireplace covers. "My orders were to pack up, for the house to—what are you doing?"

One of the maids looked up, confused. "Lighting the fire, Your Grace."

"Lighting the…" Edward stared, utterly at a loss.

Perhaps he had fallen asleep and this was some sort of strange fever dream.

"Your orders were to unpack, y'see, Your Grace," said the footman nervously as he folded the breakfast table's cotton covering. "You changed your mind."

Edward stared. *Now he knew he was dreaming. Changed his mind?*

"That will be all, Frost," said Maltravers lightly. "Thank you, girls."

Maltravers was smiling, a smile far too knowing for his liking, and as the servants trooped out of the room, shutting the door quietly behind them, he continued to smile. A little knowing, a little pleased with himself, but full of genuine joy.

"Since when," said Edward quietly, "do you order my servants about?"

Maltravers's smile widened. "You cannot just give up, you know."

"Give up?" repeated Edward. Did the man not understand? "I saw her at Don Saltero's Chelsea Coffee House with a gentleman, and they seemed rather comfortable with each other!"

"You never had coffee with a woman you had no intention of marrying?" his friend asked delicately.

Edward opened his mouth, considered, then closed it. "That is completely different."

"And why, precisely, is that?"

"You know full well why!" Edward spluttered. Was his friend being purposefully obtuse? Did he revel in the idea of pushing the man too hard? "Ladies have to take much greater care with their reputations, you know that better than anyone. Gentlemen—"

"Gentlemen typically do not publish letters in the papers listing out their requirements for a spouse," Maltravers remarked dryly. "There is only one Coral de Petras, Glaenarm, and you are going to lose her if you do not go to her."

"Go to her? Make myself look a complete fool?" Edward hung his head; it was almost too much to bear. "Do you think I have a wish to debase myself before her so entirely that I end up on my knees, begging?"

There was a strange look on Maltravers's face. "Better to end up on your knees asking a very important question, if you ask me."

Edward swallowed. A very important question. Yes, very clever; he should have expected his friend to pick up on that turn of phrase.

The trouble was, the thought had rushed through his mind at times—late or early in the middle of the night. Thoughts of long speeches that seemed to roll off his tongue, of Coral beaming with delight that he had finally come to his senses, of her ripping up that damned list and throwing it away as she threw herself into his arms.

But they were just thoughts, just hopes, just dreams. They were just hopes.

Hopes that would immediately be dashed if he was fool enough to attempt it in person.

What would Coral say if he was to ask for her hand—when they both knew full well that he did not meet her list, and that she was already being courted by so many others?

A heavy hand on his shoulder. Edward blinked to see that Maltravers had a serious look on his face.

"If you never ask," his friend said seriously, "you'll never know."

CHAPTER SEVENTEEN

January 12, 1810

CORAL LISTLESSLY PICKED up the book and put it down again. She really must do something. She could not merely sit here in the parlor whiling away the hours in the hope that Edward would come to call.

Because he would, would he not? After what they had shared, what they so clearly were to each other…

"I…I thought lovemaking always had to occur in a bed."

"Oh, Coral. We are just getting started."

Coral swallowed. They had hardly enjoyed a traditional courtship; in many ways, she could not have imagined a more unusual one.

The list she had created, the advertisement she had placed in the newspaper—her absolute certainty that she had no wish to marry a gentleman who did not match the list, and Edward's bold declaration that he would help her hunt for the perfect husband…

Was it possible, after all her foolishness, because she was starting to see it as foolishness now, that the most perfect husband could have been right there before her?

"I said it before, and I will say it again," said a quiet voice. "You are moping."

Coral looked up. Her mother had arched her eyebrow over

her sewing, the embroidered pattern slowly taking shape during the slow afternoon into a diamond pattern of pansies.

There was an altogether-too-knowing look on her mother's face, and Coral did not like it.

"I am not moping," she said aloud, though with very little feeling. "I am just—"

"Moping," said Opal succinctly.

Coral scowled. Well, if she wanted to sit here in the quiet all day, why should she not? Sapphire was out somewhere, with Maltravers if she had to guess, and Emerald was likely as not hiding upstairs in the hope that visiting hours would disappear before she was subjected to the presence of anyone beyond the family.

Jasper was, as far as Coral could tell, visiting her brother. Not that she knew that. Micah's whereabouts were a consistent question for the family, and she had to hope they would manage to wrangle his address out of him soon.

"It's that list of yours, isn't it?"

Coral looked up. That was the trouble with mothers; they always seemed to be able to root around in one's heart and know precisely what you were thinking.

Most irritating.

"I was thinking nothing of the sort," she said haughtily.

It was a lie, but her mother did not need to know that, did she?

"You're lying," said Opal calmly, gently forcing her needle through the embroidery hoop and pulling it back through again. "I would not bother, Coral, I am your mother."

Coral sighed. "I thought he would be here."

"He?"

Too late, she realized what she had said. If only she could keep her mouth closed!

But it was difficult to do so when one's mind ran so deeply on Edward. Edward, laughing at one of her jests. Edward, dancing opposite her, her body tingling with every connection they made.

Edward, kissing her, murmuring words of affection she could not stop hearing...

"Coral."

"What?" Coral said, starting almost out of her seat.

Her mother shook her head, just ever so slightly, as though wishing to inform her daughter in no uncertain terms that she was not convinced for a moment. "You set too much store by that list, you know. I wish to goodness you had showed it to me before you had sent it to—"

"You would only have tried to encourage me to tear it up completely," Coral pointed out, the slow crackle of the fire the only other noise in the room. "You would take Lady Romeril's side, I think."

"She has a point," Opal said quietly. "This obsession, Coral, with your list...all these requirements that you believe will make you happy—"

"And should I not be happy?" Coral shot back. "Should I not be looking for a gentleman who I believe will suit? I have already missed my opportunity for a love match."

She saw the sadness in her mother's eyes at her words and bit her lip.

She should not have said that. What did pointing it out help, after all? But Coral knew she had to force her point home if only a little. She had wished to marry for money when a child, and her parents had managed to convince her out of that...but that only worked when there was sufficient money in the family to marry for love.

Her dowry impoverished, there was no other choice now. She had to make a good match, without a dowry, and she knew what would make her happy.

Didn't she?

"If only your father's ships..." Opal hesitated before continuing. "Money. It is always such a trouble."

Coral snorted. "That is easy for you to say, you have always had so much of it!"

She expected her mother to roll her eyes, perhaps tell her stiffly that having money did not mean one could not value it. She expected Opal to be dry, to laugh, to jest about the fact that it was her inheritance now that was keeping the family afloat.

But she did not.

To Coral's amazement, Opal hesitated, a slight flush tinging her cheeks. Her eyes darted over to the other side of the room, where her correspondence was piled up.

Now that was most odd. what was going on?

"I...I need to tell you something," Opal said quietly.

Coral leaned forward. Her mother was not one to keep secrets, at least, not secrets that really mattered. The whole story of Jasper's...misplacement, to use the term her mother preferred, had never been discussed fully with the de Petras children. In a way, Coral was glad.

There were some things about one's parents one never wished to know.

But that letter, the one Opal had refused to let anyone read. How long ago had it come—and yet still there had been no explanation.

Was Coral finally to understand what it was?

"My family is complicated," said Opal quietly.

Coral had to laugh at that. "Don't you worry, Mama, Micah will settle down eventually—and as long as we can get Emerald talking and Sapphire to stop talking for more than five—"

"I did not mean you four," interrupted her mother. "I meant my family. My parents, my...my brother."

Coral stared. Her brother? There had never been any mention of a brother. No uncle had ever visited from Italy. No uncle had ever been hinted at.

"But...you are an only child, aren't you?" she said quietly. "You always said—"

"I lied," Opal smiled weakly. "Did you never think I may have once or twice told a falsehood?"

Coral sat, stunned. Her mother, lied? An uncle?

There was so much she did not know about her mother, did not know about her father, either. And why was her mother raising this now? Why was it so important that she tell her something?

Something about her past?

"I received a letter a little while ago. I am sure you noticed, for you are intelligent, Coral, and curious," Opal said quietly. Her embroidery had been completely laid aside, and her gaze flickered once more to the pile of letters on the console table. "I thought long and hard about how to respond to it—whether or not responding to it was, in fact, the right choice. But a week ago I did, and I need to tell you now because…because…"

Someone knocked on the door. "Your guest, m'lady."

Coral looked up as Mrs. Clarkson curtseyed, their housekeeper disappearing and leaving behind…

A girl.

A woman, really. Coral could not precisely guess her age, but she was probably only a few years younger than herself. Young, with a similar complexion to Emerald and that startling wide gaze that all her siblings shared.

Her mother's gaze.

Coral's mouth fell open. "What the—"

"This," Opal said, interrupting her, "is Amethyst. Amethyst de Petras."

Coral turned her gaze frantically back to her mother. When her father was absent, when he was missing, when the family had no idea where he was—surely her father would never have—

"Your cousin," said Opal quietly.

Coral closed her mouth, conscious that she probably looked a complete fool, and turned back to the woman, who flushed at the focused attention.

"Amethyst," breathed Coral.

It did not seem real. Why would a cousin of hers be suddenly here? The mere fact that she had a cousin at all, in truth, was rather disorientating.

"My brother was cut off from my parents' will, which dictated that all money go down the female line," her mother was saying as though from a long way off. "Amethyst's mother died recently, and my brother not long after. She has nowhere to go, except…except here."

"Here?" repeated Coral.

"Here," confirmed Opal.

"I—I thank you for the warm welcome you have given me," said Amethyst in a prickly tone. "I suppose I can look forward to just as hearty a welcome from the rest of my cousins."

A little irritation seared Coral's heart. Well, what did the woman expect! She had never heard of her before, never known she'd had an uncle, let alone a cousin. And she was going to live here! Here, with them?

"I…" Coral swallowed. What did one say to a cousin one had no idea existed until five minutes ago. "I am sure you will receive much the same welcome."

Her mother snorted, and Coral flushed. Well, she had not intended it to sound like—

"I see," said her cousin coolly. "Well, in that case, Aunt Opal, I will retire to my bedchamber. Your servant can show me the way."

Coral stared, wishing she could say something but having absolutely no idea what. Amethyst closed the door behind her, leaving the two ladies alone.

She rounded on her mother. "Mama, why would you—"

"What choice did I have, Coral?" Opal said with a heavy shrug. "You think I would have been better served leaving her on the streets?"

Coral frowned. Of course, she would not wish that on anyone, but in the situation they were in—three dowries were just about manageable, but did Amethyst's presence here mean that her mother intended to—

"Ah, there you are, Jasper," Opal said with great relief as the door opened once more but revealed a far more welcome face. "I have just introduced Coral to her cousin."

Coral looked at her father as he fell into an armchair. How long had he known? Had he realized just how swiftly their lives would change again with the intrusion of a stranger into their midst?

Oh, Emerald was not going to like this…

"Any news from that duke of yours?" Jasper asked, face morose.

Scarlet heat seared Coral's face. "He is not my duke."

If only he were. She had been so certain, so sure that he would propose. That he would know her well enough to look past the list, the list she had been so careful to draw up and ask for her hand.

Of course, there was the possibility that he had decided against it precisely because of the list.

Coral's stomach did not appear to wish to settle, which was most provoking. How was she supposed to think with all these thoughts whirling around her mind? Edward, the gentleman she wished to marry; Amethyst, a new cousin now living in their home; Micah, always here, there, and every—

"I just can't stop thinking about them."

Coral blinked. Thinking about them? Her father's words did not make much sense, at least, they did not match the rest of the conversation. Who was *them*?

Opal placed a hand on her husband's arm. "It is not as though you could have done anything, not from here."

"I know, I know," said Jasper wretchedly. "It's just…it was payday today, and their widows and mothers…a long line of women at the door, waiting to collect their dues…"

It was all Coral could do not to shiver. Such a terrible thing for their family, yes, to lose her father's three ships—but how much worse for those who had lost their lives on such an endeavor?

"Sometimes I think I should just pack in the whole lot and sell what's left of the business," her father was saying as Mrs.

Clarkson brought in a note and silently offered it to her master. "The best thing I could hope for…"

Coral bit her lip as the housekeeper left the room and her father opened the letter. That was when everything had changed. The loss of her father's ships had been the spark that made her write the list in the first place.

What would the last few months have been like if there had been no list?

Would she have met Edward? Would he have asked to be introduced to her, would Maltravers have made the connection?

Would she have fallen in love with a man she now was unsure would make her his wife?

"Jasper? Jasper!"

Coral looked up. Her mother's face was full of concern, her father's eyes wide as he read the letter.

"Jasper, what is it?" asked Opal urgently.

A slow yet steady smile crept across his face. "They…they've been found."

Coral's heart leapt. "Found?"

"Who's been found?"

"The ships! The ships, all three of them, all cargo and all hands safe," said Jasper triumphantly, beaming at his wife and daughter, hands clutching the letter.

"Found!" Coral could hardly believe it. "How on earth is that possible?"

"They found a cove, a bay where they could shelter from the storm, and it has been too difficult to return—they sent word a week ago, they are on their way home," said Jasper frantically, waving the paper in his hands as though it were a pardon from the gods. "They're safe!"

"Oh, that's wonderful, Jasper!"

Coral watched with a grin as Opal launched herself into Jasper's arms, embracing him closely as they both breathed heavy sighs of relief.

They were found. All those widows and mothers, they would

welcome home their loved ones.

And perhaps more importantly for her…

Stomach lurching, Coral attempted to focus on her father's joy, but it was impossible not to think about what this meant—what it meant for all of them.

Her father's shipping business, his fortune, was saved. Retrieved. Though they had not known it, it had never truly been lost. And that meant—

"Oh, Coral, you must be delighted!" Opal said, turning to her daughter.

Coral tried to smile as naturally as she could manage. "Yes, it is wonderful news, Papa."

"And for you, too," pointed out her mother. "You can tear up your list now!"

Coral blinked.

"Well, you only created that thing when you decided you could no longer marry for love, remember," Opal said. "And now you can."

She could marry for love.

The thought was heady, giving Coral the sensation she had drunk a little too much wine without eating enough at dinner.

Yes, she could marry for love. She could seek out a gentleman who spoke to her heart just as much as the list of requirements she had carefully constructed.

But what was the point when…when she had fallen so completely in love already?

Edward. She would never be able to be rid of him now, not just because he had bedded her but because there would be no one else for her.

Well, it was difficult not to feel a little humbled.

Coral swallowed. She was in love. And though she was almost certain Edward loved her in return, what difference did that make…if he did not propose?

CHAPTER EIGHTEEN

January 13, 1810

EDWARD TOOK A deep breath, raised his hand, hand clenched...then dropped it again.

He hung his head. This was ridiculous. Two previous attempts to walk down this street, reach this door, and raise his hand—only to leave again, certain he would be making a complete ass of himself...

He was being ridiculous, and worse of all, he knew it.

Strangers passed by, walking around him and shooting him curious glances.

As well they might. *It was a rather strange sight, after all,* Edward thought darkly. A gentleman standing outside a house, about to knock, yet never making contact with the door.

He had thought about this, considered it carefully. Back and forth he had gone with his decision, hardly knowing whether he was making it for the right reasons or perhaps more frighteningly, not making it for the wrong reasons.

But Edward had returned, time and time again in his mind, to this spot. To the words he must say, an unknown gentleman in the coffee shop be damned.

Because he loved Coral. He knew it, felt it in the very core of his being. Attempting to deny that would only bring him harm, hurt him in the most agonizing way.

In the darkness of late last night—or it could have been the early hours of this morning, Edward was not entirely sure—he had even considered calling around to Maltravers to ask his opinion on the matter.

He knew the family, after all, Edward had thought wretchedly, lying in bed unable to sleep. Perhaps he would know the gentleman in question, the man who had made Coral laugh.

But even if she had been continuing to court others, Edward had discovered that when he truly thought about it, he could not hold it against her. He, after all, was not considered a potential match in her eyes—merely because of that list that plagued him as it had undoubtedly plagued others.

If she could relinquish the damned thing…

Well, Edward told himself firmly on the de Petras doorstep, there was no knowing whether she would consider his suit seriously, even if he did propose, but he could not help himself. He had to ask.

Taking another deep breath, as though this would make any material difference, Edward raised his fist again. Before he knew quite what was happening, he had knocked.

Eyes wide at his own audacity, Edward let out his breath slowly and watched it billow on the air. It was a little early, to be sure, but once he had made up his mind, he could not wait in that large house for the hours to tick by.

No, he had to see her. Had to tell her how he felt—although Edward would be very much surprised if Coral did not already know. He needed to tell her he wanted to marry her. To make her his wife.

The door opened, and Edward took a hesitant step back.

A frown was creasing the forehead of the woman standing before him. "Yes?"

Edward smiled weakly. This was no maid—a housekeeper, if he was any judge. Guarding the front door like a dragon.

Well, he would have several obstacles to overcome to gain

Coral's hand, he knew that—his own mistruths were just one of them. He could surely overpower a housekeeper.

"Good morning," he said brightly.

The frown deepened. "It is indeed—very early morning, though I say so myself."

Edward's smile slackened slightly. This was not going at all well. "I am the Duke of Glaenarm," he said rather foolishly.

That at least changed things. An expression of shock covered the housekeeper's face, and she spluttered inconsequential nonsense to him.

"B-But you cannot—a duke? Here? M-My ladies are not—too early for—"

"Thank you, Mrs. Clarkson," said a smooth, calm voice. "I will take it from here."

Edward's shoulders relaxed as the stupefied housekeeper was gently removed from the doorway, her place taken by the mistress of the house.

"Mrs. de Petras," he said smoothly. "I was just saying to your housekeeper—"

"Yes, I heard," said Opal de Petras with a wide smile. "How nice to have the pleasure of your company so early, Your Grace."

Edward blinked. *Why did people keep mentioning the early hour?* True, it was before visiting time, and in all honor, he probably should have waited, but to mention it so often…

He pulled his pocket watch out and examined it. *Ah. Just gone a quarter past seven. It was indeed, early.*

"Oh," said Edward helplessly, putting away his pocket watch and looking back at Opal, who was grinning. "I appear to have mistaken the…oh dear."

"Come, let us not stand upon ceremony, we are friends here I think," said Opal generously. "I take it you have come to be honorable?"

Edward swallowed. There was a particularly discomforting and knowing look on the matriarch's face, as though she was under no illusion whatsoever as to the nature of the duke's visit to her home at such an ungodly hour.

Well, there was little one could get past these women, Edward thought helplessly. Mrs. de Petras, Lady Romeril…there was a certain type of woman whose penetrating stare was able to precisely understand one's meaning. Even if one did not wish it to.

"You appear to be a little pink, Your Grace," said Opal cheerfully. "Despite the cold weather, it is much to your valet's credit that he is able to bundle you up so warmly."

Edward glanced at his greatcoat, then smiled sheepishly. "Yes. Yes, my valet…yes, Mrs. de Petras. I have come to be honorable. At least, I suppose I have."

There it was—that arch of the eyebrow so like Coral.

"Goodness, what a resounding beginning," Opal said with a gentle laugh. "You had better come in."

It was not the start Edward had been hoping for, certainly. As he stepped into the hall and allowed Opal—against his wishes—to personally remove his greatcoat and hang it on a coat hook, he tried to slow his frantically beating heart.

This was it—though he had no reason, in truth, to be afeared. It was not as though he was expecting anything other than a resounding yes to the question he would soon be putting to Coral de Petras. How could she say no?

Edward straightened a little as his confidence grew. He was a duke. He was not unattractive. He was wealthy…even if he had no singing voice.

Because he knew her. He loved her. Coral was the woman he wanted to spend the rest of his life with, and the moment he was able to explain that to her, show her just how much he cared for her—

"I will speak with you in a moment, Amethyst," Opal was saying just under her breath. "Now is not the time to—"

"But you promised me my inheritance!" the woman hissed. "You promised!"

Edward could not help but stare. The woman was pretty and

strangely familiar. As though young Sapphire's features had been blurred slightly, changed in small ways that made this woman disconcertingly well-known.

"Go upstairs," Opal said sharply, "and we will talk about this later."

The woman shot Edward a glance, a glare that he could feel the heat from, but did not speak back to the matriarch of the house. Turning on her heels, she strode away.

Opal sighed heavily, and Edward made sure to rearrange his features into a vague smile as she turned to him.

"I do apologize, Your Grace, a small matter," she said smoothly. "I hope you are not—I said not now, Amethyst! Oh."

Edward followed her gaze to the stairs, where clearly she had expected the strange woman to be returning.

But it was not her.

A gentleman was walking down the staircase. A gentleman he knew. A man whose face had been indelibly marked in his memory as being the man he hated more than anyone else in the world.

The dark-haired gentleman that Coral had been laughing with at the coffee house, their coffee house, was walking down the stairs with his cravat untied and his hair unruly, without a care in the world. As though he had nothing to be ashamed of.

As if he belonged there.

Edward stiffened. This was not what he had expected, to find the cad here—far earlier than he was, and coming downstairs!

A terrible thought struck him, one which he would never have countenanced if he had not seen the gentleman emerging from upstairs with his own eyes.

Was it possible…had he been a fool all along?

Was Coral playing him for an idiot, giving her favors to more than one gentleman? Was the innocence all a pretense, a trick for getting him to consider her more kindly?

Opal turned to see where he was staring and beamed at the gentleman.

Damn, Edward thought darkly. More favored by the mother. That was not a good sign for his suit.

"Ah, do you know—"

"I do not," said Edward stiffly, glaring at the man as he reached the bottom step and stood, rather bemused, in the hall.

Well, he should probably have been more polite, but it was not as though the brigand deserved any of his respect.

The gentleman raised his eyebrow at Edward's sudden and unexplained rudeness. "Well, I know you, sir, and I must say I am astonished to find you here this time of the morning."

Edward bristled. *The rudeness—the cheek!* "Sir" instead of "Your Grace," but worst of all, questioning his place here when the rake was coming down the stairs as if—as if he had bedded one of the de Petras daughters!

It was unheard of—it was scandalous! It was strange indeed that Opal appeared to be entirely unaffected by the whole thing.

"Now then, I do not think we mind that His Grace is here," she said with a smile at the gentleman. *A smile!*

Edward drew himself up. If this was how the de Petras family managed things, permitting strangers in their daughters' bedchambers, no wonder there was a whiff of scandal about the place.

"I think I would prefer it if you were not here," said the gentleman slowly, examining Edward carefully.

"If I were not—how dare you, sir!" Edward spluttered, hardly able to believe what he was hearing. "Why, I should call you out for such blatant disregard for the etiquette of Society—the devil are you doing here?"

"Your Grace!" said Opal, astonishment across her face. "You—"

"What the devil am I doing here?" the gentleman said, clearly dumbfounded. "By God, man, I live here!"

Edward hesitated, blood boiling in his veins but the last few words were incongruous to everything he had expected. The gentleman lived here? Was he perhaps a tenant, someone paying for a room here at the de Petras family?

"By Jove, I never thought I would see the day when one of my sister's suitors would be so damned rude," the gentleman was saying, shaking his head.

I never thought I would see the day when one of my sister's *suitors would be so damned rude…"*

Understanding, awkward and rather unpleasant, started to dawn in Edward's mind as his heart started to slow and he stared at the gentleman before him.

A gentleman whose raised eyebrow in sardonic examination was painfully familiar.

"Ah," said Edward helplessly.

Opal and the gentleman, who could only be the mysterious and previously unseen Micah de Petras, stared at him as though he had entirely lost his wits. Perhaps he had. *Perhaps this was what happened when one was in love,* thought Edward wildly. One lost all sense of proportion.

"Your Grace, may I introduce my son, Micah de Petras?" said Opal quietly, still staring as though there was a great deal of concern for his sanity. "I do not believe you have met."

Her son…Coral's brother…

And the reality of what Edward had seen in the coffee house unfolded, and he felt such a fool. Coral, laughing with a gentleman…no, with *her brother!*

Suddenly Edward realized what a fool he had made of himself—not only when staring at Coral through the window of the coffee house, but now. Before her mother.

Oh, blast.

"I must apologize," he said frankly. Well, he had many faults, but his ability to recognize when he needed to say sorry was not one of them. "I have entirely mistaken you for someone else."

"Someone who has done you a great injury, I'll be bound," said Micah with just a hint of sarcasm. "Dear Lord, man, you were about to call me out for coming down my own stairs!"

Edward smiled weakly. "I…uh…"

"His Grace has come to see Coral," said Opal quickly, giving a significant look to her son. "To *speak* with her."

Micah sighed heavily, which was not in Edward's view the most promising opinion from Coral's only brother. "Well, I tried to warn her. I'll be out, Mama, just going to see—"

"Where do you think you are going?" asked Opal, alarm in her voice. "No, Micah, I thought we could discuss—"

"There is nothing to discuss, Mama, as I have said before."

Micah had stridden to the front door and was pulling on what Edward was almost certain was his own greatcoat, but he had not the presence of mind to say anything.

Opal turned hastily to him. "The drawing room, Your Grace. I will send Coral in the moment she is—Micah, wait!"

The entire situation was awkward enough without Edward standing there, gawking. Quite happy to escape the argument between mother and son, he slipped into the drawing room where he and Coral had escaped from Opal's luncheon a few months ago and waited.

Coral. His heart started to thump again, though partly from embarrassment at getting it so wrong with her brother. He would have to apologize again, most likely, and explain things to Coral.

The door opened, and the vision of beauty who appeared before him was so much more startlingly stunning than his memory of Coral, he was quite taken aback.

Her hair was unbound, pouring down her shoulders in curls and waves. It was such an intimate view of her that Edward's breath caught in his throat. He was early, that was true, but he was glad of it now. Glad to see this side of Coral before she became his wife.

"My mother said there was someone in here who needed to speak to me urgently," said Coral rather breathlessly, as though she had been forced from her bedchamber before she was quite ready for the day. "But it is only you."

If Edward had been a lesser man, he would perhaps have been a little discomforted by the way she had spoken so dismissively.

"But it is only you."

If he had not encountered Micah de Petras in the hall, Edward would certainly have been concerned Coral was hoping it would be the dark-haired gentleman and not himself.

But now that misunderstanding—his own foolish assumption, one he would never have made if he had just walked into the coffee house and asked to be introduced—was cleared from his mind, Edward could think only of the happiness they were about to share.

When she agreed to be his wife.

"Only me, indeed," he said softly, stepping toward her and taking her hands in his. "But I hope not unwelcome?"

"Unwelcome?" Coral shook her head, a wry smile creeping across her face. "You know me well enough, I think, to know your presence here would never be unwelcome. I have to tell you—"

It was too much. Edward had promised himself that he would not kiss her, would not permit himself that pleasure until he had gained her consent to be her husband.

But the proximity of such a beautiful woman as Coral, knowing how fiery she was, how much passion lay under that cool demeanor, was too much. Pulling her into his arms, Edward passionately claimed her lips, pouring onto them all the fears and frustrations that the misunderstanding had caused in his heart.

Coral sank into his kiss, welcoming him immediately, and Edward could have cried out for joy. This was where he belonged, where they both belonged. In each other's arms.

How long they stood there in the quiet empty room, passionately kissing, Edward did not know. It was only when his hands dipped to her buttocks and they knocked into a chair, such was the depths of their passion, that Coral pulled away from him.

"We cannot!" she hissed under her breath, eyes bright and lips curling into a smile that belied her words.

Edward tried to pull her closer, desperate for her touch. "Of course we can—"

"My family might come in here at any moment!" Coral slipped from his embrace, standing tantalizingly out of reach. "No, I will not kiss you, Edward! Not here. Not now."

There was teasing laughter in her voice that told Edward she would rather like to be kissed if she felt she could get away with it—but she stepped just out of his reach once again as he moved toward her.

"They will not come in here," he attempted to reassure her.

A slight frown puckered between Coral's eyes. "How do you know that?"

Edward swallowed. He had not precisely planned this; at least, he had thought much about the consequences of such splendid news, both for her family and for themselves, but the exact wording...

Well, he had assumed it would come to him. Rather disobligingly, it was not.

"Because...because they know I have something very important to ask you."

Coral stared. "But I need to tell you something! I—what on earth do you—Edward!"

She gasped his name, breath caught in her throat, as Edward did not attempt to pull her once more into his arms—but this time lowered himself onto one knee.

Edward looked up at her, the woman he had given his heart to, and gloried in the happiness he was about to give her. Everything she wanted, even the things she perhaps had not known herself...she would be gaining them all.

"What...what are you doing?" Coral whispered, eyes wide. "Edward, what are you—"

"Coral de Petras," said Edward quietly, interrupting her and not looking away from her face. "I knew the moment I saw you in Almack's that you were special."

"I...I..." spluttered Coral.

"Please, let me speak," Edward said with a warm smile. "I

think you will like what you are about to hear."

Coral looked as though she would rather argue but managed to hold her tongue. That was one of the many reasons he loved her so much. Always something to say. Always an opinion.

"When I offered to help you find the perfect husband, I never expected to fall in love with you myself," said Edward simply. "And I did. I love you, Coral, and I want to make you happy—I know I can make you happy, list be damned. The question is, will you make me happy…by agreeing to become my wife?"

He could see it in an instant, the war in her eyes. Coral stared as though unbelieving what she had just heard, as though she was perhaps dreaming and would at any moment wake from this stupor.

The war in her expression continued, and Edward could almost hear her thoughts. She cared for him, but she had the list, had been determined to find a gentleman who could complete it. What would win out? Her heart, or her head?

"Oh…oh Edward," Coral said softly.

Joy rose in Edward's heart as he straightened up. "I knew you—"

"You don't fit my list."

Edward hesitated, heart thumping as he saw the distress on her face. "I know that."

"I made that list—"

"Pox on your list," Edward said warmly. "No, listen to me, I'm going to say something I should have said a long time ago."

She was staring at him as though she had never seen him before.

He hesitated for a moment, but the words poured from him before he could mediate them. "I've had enough of your list, Coral, not because it is too detailed, but because it is not detailed enough!"

"Not…not detailed enough?" breathed Coral.

Edward shook his head. "No. there are so many things that should be on there that should be—the perfect man for you should make you laugh, should hold you when you cry. He should defend you to the hilt, even when you're wrong—"

"Especially then," cut in Coral with a wry smile.

He laughed at that. "Especially then," he said, warming to his theme. "He should consider you just as beautiful in your sixties as in your twenties, long for the moments when he can hold you in his arms—"

"It sounds to me as though you are writing a new list," she said with a raised eyebrow.

"Perhaps I am," Edward said with a wry grin. "And I meet it, Coral, every single one. And I don't have siblings, though I think you have more than enough for the two of us—"

"Too true."

"And I don't sing—or at least I do, but badly—and I hate Mozart, but those things don't matter, don't you see?" he said urgently. Oh, if only he could make her see. "I love you, Coral. Loving you should supersede any list, and it does. I don't know if I can ever match up to your standards, and God knows you deserve the best but…oh Coral. Could you love me?"

Edward reached out, his hands shaking slightly, unsure what his reception would be—and Coral allowed him to take her hands. Her hands were warm, and she stepped closer to him, a small smile creeping across those kissable lips.

"I suppose your new list," she said with a teasing grin, "is enough to marry you."

She was in his arms. "I don't want you to marry me for pity!"

"Oh, it would be a pity indeed if I did not marry you," Coral quipped. "I was trying to tell you, but you would insist on kissing me—"

"I did not hear any complaints," Edward said wryly, heart singing.

She grinned. "We have had news—the best possible news! The ships have been found!"

Edward blinked, his mind entirely focused on Coral, not ships. Ships? Whose ships?

"The ships that were lost—my father's ships!" Coral said, tapping him on the chest. "Honestly, you never pay attention. My father's ships that were lost, impoverishing my dowry—they were found."

"Found?"

"They had slipped into a small cove to wait out the storm, all hands saved, all cargo safe!" Coral said, eyes bright. "I tore up my list this morning. I can marry for love once again."

A strange sense of growing joy was growing in Edward's stomach, warm and hot, spreading through all his limbs. "Tore it up?"

She kissed him, hard and briefly, on the lips. "Marry for love, Edward. You do know what that means, don't you?"

Edward knew a broad smile was tugging his lips, and he did not attempt to hide it. This was how it was supposed to be after all. This was the perfect time to finally reveal the truth.

"I cannot hide that I am relieved the list is gone."

"Oh, I am sure there will be other requirements that crop up," Coral said with a laugh. "Over time."

"Well, let us hope," he said easily, "that my charms make up any deficiencies."

CHAPTER NINETEEN

February 13, 1810

CORAL TIGHTENED HER grip around the man she loved and sighed happily. Well, they should not really be here, of course. They had promised themselves they would wait, that it would not be long before the wedding, a special license guaranteed by Edward's close familial connections with the Archbishop of Canterbury…but still…

Edward shifted underneath Coral's embrace, and she snuggled in, the warmth of her chest nothing to the heat within him.

That was always the trouble with making love in her bedchamber when the rest of her family were in the house. They had to be so quiet. Coral fairly flushed to think of it, but the proximity of her family had not managed to cool their ardor.

Having Edward in her arms, in her bed, within her…it was all she wanted. Any evening in which she could not have him felt like an evening wasted. But nights like this…they made all the difficulty sneaking him up the servants' staircase worth it.

"You know, it's tomorrow."

Edward grunted. "Surely it's today."

"You know what I mean," said Coral with a quiet laugh. Thank goodness the walls in their home were nice and thick. "Tomorrow. Today tomorrow. I heard chiming downstairs."

Edward placed his arm around her, and Coral luxuriated in the sensation of his skin against hers. There was nothing like it.

"Well, it is my pleasure to see another day in with my beautiful bride in my arms," said Edward, his voice sleepy.

Coral poked him with a finger. "Not your bride yet."

It had been an age since they had revealed their mutual affection—at least, it was to Coral's mind. Whenever she thought ahead to their wedding day, it appeared about a thousand years away.

"I still think it a miracle I managed to convince you to marry me at all."

"I think it more a miracle you decided to pursue me in the first place, after my rather radical introduction," said Coral with a gentle laugh, splaying her fingers over Edward's chest. "What was it I said?"

"'What is your income, Your Grace?'" Edward said promptly.

Coral's eyebrows rose. "You memorized my words!"

"Well, close enough," said Edward with a low chuckle. "You have to remember just what an impact they made on me. Words etched onto my mind. You and that ridiculous list."

Still, the list had done something, at the very least. It had brought her to him.

"I do not think you could have made more of an impression if you tried."

"Who said I was not trying?" teased Coral. "Though I admit, I perhaps should not have been quite so direct with gentlemen about my desire for specific traits."

"I admit, I do not like the idea of you being so direct with other gentlemen," came the rueful soft voice of Edward beneath her. "But who knows. Perhaps without your directness, I would never have been so attracted to you at the beginning! That, or that stupid newspaper advertisement…"

Coral smiled as she settled into Edward's arms. Yes, she had certainly got his attention—and in hindsight, she should have known her request for him to help her find a rich husband would have attracted more than a little attention.

Whatever had made her do it?

But that was all in the past now, and she would never have to worry about how it had started. He loved her, and she loved him, and they would be together—for the rest of their lives.

Still, there were a few questions bubbling in her heart, questions Coral saw no reason not to ask.

"What made you want to marry me?" she asked quietly, almost afraid of the answer. "In the end, I mean. After you realized you…you cared for me."

It was strange, they had shared almost everything a gentleman and lady could—although Edward had made mention of a few ways of making love that could only be performed in a four-poster bed, a hint that had made Coral shiver with anticipation.

Yet there were still topics they had not spoken on, still questions about their courtship from both sides as yet unresolved. Coral did not feel shy, precisely…but still. There was a hesitancy there, nonetheless.

Would that fade, in time? Would it be different as they grew older? Perhaps with each passing year of wedded bliss, one more layer of protection around their hearts would come down? And what happened when there were none left, when they knew each other better than themselves?

Coral smiled. It was a heady thought, one to dream of. One to delight in.

"What made me want to marry you?" Edward replied in a soft voice. "Why, the realization I could not live without you, of course."

Happiness, pure and simple, radiated through her heart at those words. Oh, he was a better man than she could imagine.

Only now was she starting to understand the depths of agony her mother had suffered when Papa had been misplaced all those years.

"I am sorry, you know," said Coral quietly. "About my family."

Edward chuckled softly. "Oh, I would not worry about that."

"No, really," Coral insisted, a flicker of shame in her stomach. "They are intolerable."

"They are happy," Edward countered gently. "And you cannot blame them—or at least, I do not, which I suppose amounts to the same thing. 'Tis natural for a family, any family, to be glad a daughter of theirs is getting married."

Coral tried not to think about the moment when they had announced their engagement. Emerald, she had expected to be quiet, and Micah was not even there—but their mother…

"I think your mother would have us run away to Gretna Green if we could manage it."

Coral buried her face in Edward's chest. "I know, she is awful!"

"She is certainly eager," came Edward's quiet teasing, "far more eager for this marriage than you are, some days."

"And Sapphire!"

"Oh, you cannot blame her," came the gentle words from her husband-to-be. "She speaks her mind. I like that in a woman. In a sister, I should say."

Coral sighed heavily. The outpouring of excitement from her younger sister when the proposed marriage was announced in the newspapers was absolutely ridiculous, and worst of all, she had not been able to stop Sapphy from speaking to Edward when he had dined with the de Petras family that evening.

It had been…excruciating.

"She has been desperate to enter Society for some time," Coral said by way of explanation. "That is all—and in some ways, she is still a child. She does not precisely know the ways and etiquette of Society."

Edward shifted underneath her, bringing her closer into his warm embrace. "Coral, you do not need to explain her to me. She is your sister, and she is young. I am sure I will grow to understand her…her exuberance, for want of a better word."

Coral would have snorted with laughter if she was not so

eager to keep quiet. "Exuberance! Yes, I suppose that is one word for it. Please do not make any promises to her, even if she demands them—no matter how many gentlemen she asks to be introduced to."

"Never fear, I would not dare unleash Sapphire onto any of my acquaintances."

Coral grinned. She had hoped, when she had thought about it at all, that her future husband would wish to know her family, to love them as she did. The de Petras family may be a little...unusual, but they were still family. Her family. The only family she had ever known.

"I might buy your sisters a puppy, you know."

Coral rolled her eyes. "You cannot be serious."

"It always amazed me that your family doesn't have a dog," Edward's voice said softly. "You spoke so fondly of—Admiral, wasn't it? If I found you a puppy, would Sapphire look after it?"

"Probably not," said Coral honestly with a wry smile. "I think Emerald would be a safer bet on that front."

"The question is, I suppose," came his quiet voice, "whether your brother will ever congratulate me."

She stiffened, suddenly mute. There was no critique in Edward's words, no harshness, no criticism. But curiosity, certainly. He wanted to know about her brother, and she could hardly blame him. He and Micah had not shared two words since that strange misunderstanding.

In fact, Micah had not been seen by the de Petras sisters since he had left that day. Her papa had mentioned him once or twice but had ceased to do so after spotting the pained expression on his wife's face.

But it was foolish, really. Unlike his father, Micah was not missing. They knew precisely where he was. Or at least, whom he was with. Unless he had changed mistresses again, which was more than likely.

"Oh, I am sure he will, at the wedding," Coral said awkwardly. "You know how it is with brothers."

"Not in the slightest," said Edward sleepily. "Only child, remember. No sister, as per your list..."

She saw his eyelids drooping, heavy with tiredness. It would not be long before her future husband would succumb to sleep—and though that would not matter usually, it was imperative he was able to slip out of the de Petras house successfully tonight.

If tomorrow was to be as they had hoped, anyway.

"You saw him anyway, once," said Coral quietly. "That's something."

It was important, even if she could not explain it to him, that Edward liked her siblings. The de Petras family stood together, no matter what, and one day...one day it would be hers to manage.

"Twice."

"Once," corrected Coral, feeling tiredness tug at her own eyes. "Here, the day you proposed."

"And at Don Saltero's Chelsea Coffee House."

Coral frowned. She had not met with Micah and Edward at the coffee house... "Well, I do meet with him there most weeks, if he can make it, but when would you..."

She felt Edward swallow beneath her.

"I saw him there. The two of you. Before I proposed."

Coral pushed herself up on her elbows. "You did?"

It was unfathomable. What was Edward doing there—and if he had seen her, why had he not said anything? It would have been a nice opportunity to introduce him to her brother.

"I thought...dash it all, I thought he was a gentleman you were trying to marry," came the sleepy words of her future husband. "Someone who finally met the criteria on your damned list. I was jealous. Foolish, really, in hindsight, but there you go."

Coral stared at the handsome blonde duke who had entirely stolen her heart, then put a hand over her mouth to prevent herself from laughing.

"You are laughing at me." Edward had not opened his eyes.

Coral tried to swallow her laughter. "Maybe."

"Outrageous," said Edward sleepily, eyes still shut. "Laughing at your husband will not be permitted."

"You are not my husband yet," Coral pointed out. "Trying to marry Micah, honestly! Why did you not say something? Anyone who marries Micah will have a great deal of work on their hands."

"Well, I wouldn't know anything about that," came Edward's sleepy reply.

Coral nudged him playfully on the shoulder. "The cheek of it all—Edward? Edward!"

Edward's eyes opened blearily, unfocused and clearly exhausted. "Say what?"

The words she was about to say were not ones she wanted to speak, but she could not leave it any longer. A clock had just chimed one o'clock, and Edward needed to leave.

Even if the parting was painful, it would not be forever.

"You need to go, Edward."

Edward groaned, turning his face away and closing his eyes. "Five more minutes."

"If I fall asleep, too, we'll both be awoken by the screams of my mother's lady's maid," said Coral wryly, pulling herself with great difficulty from Edward's arms. "Go on."

With a none-too-gentle shove, she pushed Edward right to the edge of her bed. It was fortunate really that he opened his eyes in time to see just how close to danger he was, for Edward stumbled to his feet.

"Fine," he said quietly, sighing heavily and pulling his breeches toward him. "I will see you later today?"

Coral smiled, joy rushing through her whole body as she looked at the man she loved more than anything. "I'll be the one at the altar."

EPILOGUE

February 14, 1810

IT WAS ALL Emerald could do not to shrink into the pew, but there was no getting around it. She was right at the front. On the front pew. Where everyone could see. *Everyone was watching.*

The tightness in her lungs was overwhelming, preventing thoughts, preventing reason, and Emerald clutched at the flowers in her hand as though they could protect her from the hordes of eyes.

Eyes, staring at her. Right when she wanted to become invisible—which, now she thought about it, was most of the time.

Emerald took a jagged breath and wished it did not echo so in the church. That was the trouble with this particular moment—it was so silent. Everyone waiting. Waiting for the bride.

"There she is!" Opal de Petras nudged her hard in the ribs. "Oh, does she not look the picture of a beautiful bride?"

Emerald would have admitted that her older sister did—if she had had any breath in which to speak. Thankfully, however, as the countless faces in the church turned to watch the bride in a delicate light orange gown step slowly up the aisle with their father, the tightness in her chest was starting to dissipate.

"I still think I should have been the one to give her away," muttered her mother under her breath. "I am the head of the family, after all."

If it had been possible for Emerald to melt into the stone floor of the church, she would. Was it not enough that their family was entirely unlike any others—did her mother really have to declare it so loudly at Coral's wedding? "I am glad the duke and Coral have reached their understanding that both of them will keep their respective names and if Coral gives birth to sons, they shall have their father's name, and if daughters, our last name. A fair arrangement."

Opal sighed as she shook her head at Emerald.

"Don't worry yourself, Mama," murmured Micah under his breath. Emerald glanced at him gratefully before he continued, "There is enough scandal in this marriage that we're covering up, we don't need more."

Emerald stared at her brother, a dissatisfied and rather irritable expression on his face. *What on earth did he mean by that?* Surely he could not suspect the Duke of Glaenarm, a very respectable gentleman, of anything…well. Untoward?

Perhaps it was because Micah had been forced to shave and wear a relatively stiff jacket and waistcoat, Emerald mused with a small smile. Her brother never was one for formality, especially not with his family.

But a wedding required a certain expectation of civility, and a wedding to a duke…

Emerald could hardly believe it, in truth, even as Coral stepped up the aisle past her family and joined the beaming Duke of Glaenarm right at the front of the nave.

Her sister, a duchess. Well, it was a welcome relief, Emerald thought as the congregation was invited to be seated. Now Coral would always be the one everyone looked at, wanted to speak to, and invited to their parties.

And she could stay at home. In the quiet. Where she liked it.

"Oh, such a beautiful bride," whispered her mama happily, pulling a lace handkerchief out of her reticule and sniffing into it. "And such a handsome groom!"

Emerald glanced at the gentleman who would, within the hour, become her brother-in-law. Yes, she supposed he was handsome, in that rather obvious sort of way. Thankfully her sister had never asked her opinion on the man who was to be her husband, or Emerald could have been forced to say something rather trite and forced.

"I never thought I would live to see this day," murmured Jasper de Petras, and Emerald looked at her father. "My Coral, marrying a duke!"

"He is lucky to have her," retorted a voice behind them.

Emerald turned, cheeks scarlet, to see Lady Romeril sniff most heartily.

"If you don't mind," came the icy tones of the bride. "We are actually in the middle of something here."

Ripples of laughter flowed through the church, and Emerald wished she could simply disappear. *Being a part of this family, it was a nightmare!* There was always something going on, always someone ready with a quip or a jest.

If only they could allow her to go through the world in peace and quiet…

The wedding itself was over rather quickly. It was a relief to escape the church, to watch the people pour out of it and hopefully go along their way—but of course, she had forgotten about the reception.

Edward's townhouse was large but did not feel so with the entire wedding party there.

"I could just go home," said Emerald hopefully. "Take care of Captain."

The dog her now brother-in-law had turned up with that morning, taking care not to see his bride, was nothing more than a scrap of a puppy, but Emerald had been rather taken with it. Captain, they had named her, despite Micah pointing out that ladies couldn't be captains. Mothers couldn't be heads of houses, their mama had said pointedly, and the discussion was swiftly closed.

Leaving the puppy behind that day to attend the wedding had been difficult, but now provided the perfect excuse.

"She will need someone to take care of her and—"

"And there's Lady Romeril!" Opal winked at her daughter. "Oh, I bet she is absolutely heartbroken my daughter has married a duke."

"Serves her right," opined the youngest de Petras, Sapphire, holding a glass of champagne she probably should not have. At least, in Emerald's opinion. "I always thought Lady Romeril—"

"That's enough of that, Sapphy," said their father hastily, removing the glass from his youngest child's hand. "No more, you hear me?"

Sapphire grinned at Jasper—with confidence Emerald, though years older, had never possessed. "You know it is true, Papa. She really is a—"

"If you cannot behave," murmured their mother quietly, "you will go home."

"And where is Micah?" added Opal.

Emerald's stomach twisted. *Not again, surely…*

"He appears to have left the church but not yet made his way here," said Jasper quietly. "Do not make a scene, Opal."

"Make a scene? Me, make a scene?" Opal looked outraged. "I have never made a scene in my whole—"

Emerald slipped away. The more noise her family made, the more eyes would turn to examine them, and she had absolutely no desire to be the center of attention—unlike Sapphire.

But it was Coral, the eldest of the de Petras siblings, who was the true center of the party. Emerald smiled wistfully as she left the hall where Opal and Jasper were now having a good-natured argument in public, to what appeared to be a splendid saloon.

There, at the other end of the room, was her sister, arm in arm with her new husband. They were standing alone, though the room was starting to fill up with a few excited chattering groups.

Taking her opportunity to congratulate the happy couple while few others were close by, Emerald slipped past the unknown strangers and smiled nervously at her new brother-in-law.

"Thank you," she said quietly, "for taking Coral off our hands."

"I'm coming out next month!" piped up a voice from behind her.

Emerald caught Coral's eye and smiled as Sapphire pushed her way forward. "Are you indeed?"

Sapphire nodded, eyes bright and eager. "Mama promised that one month after one of you were married, I could come out. Isn't it exciting?"

Emerald could not understand what she was so thrilled about. She had dreaded her first entrance into Society, and inexplicably, it had only become more and more difficult at each juncture. Every invitation was an opportunity to embarrass herself, every conversation one in which her opinion was demanded.

Why could she not just stay home in peace?

"I think you will need to stay on your best behavior for Mama to keep that promise," Coral said gently, a knowing smile on her lips as she glanced at the duke. "We cannot have you disgracing us now, can we?"

Sapphire replied by sticking out her tongue, making a rude noise Emerald could not believe she was doing in public, and scampered off.

Heat seared Emerald's face. *To think her youngest sister had done that in company—before a duke!*

"I-I am so sorry, Your Grace," she stammered, looking at the Duke of Glaenarm. "I cannot believe she—"

"Please, call me Edward, none of this 'Your Grace' nonsense," he said.

Emerald smiled weakly. Her sister had chosen well, after all. Anyone not shocked by Sapphire was someone worth keeping around.

"Not me," said Coral with a teasing smile. "I demand to be addressed as Your Grace."

Of course, she did. If there was one thing Emerald was certain of, it was that Coral was going to rather like being a duchess.

"And th-thank you for the puppy," said Emerald quietly, finding it far easier to focus on her new brother-in-law's cravat than his face. "She is beautiful."

"Long walks," he said cheerfully. "Give you a chance to meet more people."

Emerald's cheeks flushed. What had her sister been saying to him? Did he already know just what a disappointment she was to them all? How all the de Petras family wished for her to marry, to be comfortable in Society—in short, to be her sister?

"It will be your turn next."

"No," Emerald said quietly. "No, I will never marry."

"Never marry?" Coral had spoken far too loudly for Emerald's taste, and she jerked around to look to see if anyone was staring—but her sister continued before she could ascertain just how much of a ruckus she was making. "Emerald, you must marry—but marry wisely! That's what I did."

Yes, Coral had always been rather direct about the gentleman she wished to marry. The whole of the *ton* had known, truth be told, something Emerald had hated. All those eyes looking over at them whenever they entered a room, whispering about her sister…

"No, I mean it," said Emerald quietly.

Marriage…yes, it was all very well, but the attention! The talking to people, their gazes focused on her, the complicated conversations one could not have directly, trying to understand whether one person liked the other without actually saying anything…

Emerald shivered. *No. No, it was not for her.*

"You cannot be in earnest," said her sister Coral slowly, her face falling.

Emerald nodded. "I have no desire whatsoever to be married."

Discover if Emerald will ever meet a gentleman to change her mind in…The Contrary Debutante…Book 3 of THE DE PETRAS SAGA.

About Emily E K Murdoch

If you love falling in love, then you've come to the right place.

I am a historian and writer and have a varied career to date: from examining medieval manuscripts to designing museum exhibitions, to working as a researcher for the BBC to working for the National Trust.

My books range from England 1050 to Texas 1848, and I can't wait for you to fall in love with my heroes and heroines!

Follow me on twitter and instagram @emilyekmurdoch, find me on facebook at facebook.com/theemilyekmurdoch, and read my blog at www.emilyekmurdoch.com.